THE
Dragon
WARRIOR

(Lochguard Highland Dragons #4)

Jessie Donovan

This book is a work of fiction. Names, characters, places, and incidents are either the product of the writer's imagination or are used fictitiously, and any resemblance to actual persons, living or dead, business establishments, events, or locales is entirely coincidental.

The Dragon Warrior
Copyright © 2017 Laura Hoak-Kagey
Mythical Lake Press, LLC
First Edition

Cover Art by Clarissa Yeo of Yocla Designs.

ISBN 13: 978-1942211518

Other Books by Jessie Donovan

Asylums for Magical Threats
Blaze of Secrets
Frozen Desires
Shadow of Temptation
Flare of Promise

Cascade Shifters
Convincing the Cougar
Reclaiming the Wolf
Cougar's First Christmas
Resisting the Cougar

Kelderan Runic Warriors
The Conquest
The Barren (Sept 2017)

Stonefire Dragons
Sacrificed to the Dragon
Seducing the Dragon
Revealing the Dragons
Healed by the Dragon
Reawakening the Dragon
Loved by the Dragon
Surrendering to the Dragon
Cured by the Dragon
Aiding the Dragon

CHAPTER ONE

Faye MacKenzie tapped her fingers against her thigh and the sound echoed inside her small, empty cottage.

Living alone was boring.

After years of threatening to move out because of her older twin brothers or her mother's meddling nature, Faye had finally gotten a place of her own once her mum had mated the human male named Ross Anderson. Even after a few weeks and haphazardly unpacking a few things, it still didn't feel like home. It was just too *quiet*.

Her dragon spoke up. *You'll always have me.*

I know, but it's not the same. I miss my family.

Then visit them.

She sighed. *I do every day. But everyone is newly mated, except for Finn and he's worrying about Arabella and their triplets' impending birth.*

Then find something else to do. Until then, I'm going to sleep.

So much for her dragon always being there for her.

With a sigh, she moved to the window. She missed the old days when she had been Lochguard's head Protector. Going from sixteen-hour work days to not having a steady job had been tough.

Yet as she reached behind her and touched her back, where her damaged wing bone would emerge when she shifted into a dragon, Faye wasn't delusional about her future. No amount of physical therapy would get her back into perfect shape, which was required for the head of security for any dragon clan.

Grant McFarland now possessed her old job.

Stupid Grant. While she was no longer upset at him for taking her job as head Protector, he still wouldn't enlist her as a full-time member of his team, not even for something as boring as surveillance monitoring. Aye, he'd allowed her to help with the attack on Lochguard back in January, but he'd barely paid attention to her since.

Even when she did track him down, he had been too nice to her as of late. She didn't want to think it was out of pity, but her family could meddle and might have convinced him to humor her for a time. If so, that was a million times worse.

Well, she was tired of waiting and wondering. It was time to corner Grant and force him to give her a job.

With a growl, she exited the cottage and ignored everyone she passed. Once she set her mind on something, Faye didn't like to be disturbed, especially by yet another person asking if she was okay or how was her wing doing.

If they ever looked to the sky, they'd have a bloody idea.

Her dragon raised her head. *Your temper won't convince him.*

Being nice bloody well hasn't. He didn't like it when I won against him before. I think it's time to bring up the past and use it to my advantage.

Sometimes, the past should stay in the past.

Whose side are you on?

I'm not going to answer that. Unless you start kissing him, I'm going to let you settle this yourself.

The memory of when Faye had been cleaning a wound on Grant's bare chest and he'd leaned down as if to kiss her flashed into her mind.

Faye still didn't believe she'd nearly closed the distance to press her lips against his.

No. Grant was nothing but trouble. He'd made it quite clear a few years ago what he truly thought of her. While he might be slightly more mature and had learned to be civil with her, Faye didn't think he'd changed too much.

She wasn't feminine enough for him, as he'd reminded her often enough during their time together in the British Army.

Fueled by angry memories, Faye picked up her pace. It was time to get a job, and she was going to do whatever it took to make Grant give it to her.

~ ~ ~

Grant McFarland sat across from Iris Mahajan, the best tracker out of all of Lochguard's Protectors, and frowned. "Are you sure you lost the trail? I injured him pretty badly late last year and given his age, I imagine it didn't heal clean."

Iris raised her black brows. "I understand your frustration, but questioning my abilities isn't going to help anything. We'll find your uncle eventually."

Grant sighed. "I know, but Finn wants the traitors contained or captured before the birth of his triplets."

Last year, a decent portion of Lochguard had left rather than accept Finlay Stewart as clan leader, including about half of Grant's family. Grant and the other loyal Protectors had even fought the traitors near a hospital in Elgin last autumn. Even though he'd injured his uncle during that battle, no one had seen or heard of Roderick McFarland ever since.

And given that Grant had learned many of his skills and tactics as a youth from his uncle, finding Roderick wasn't going to be easy.

Iris shrugged. "Fergus is still working his contacts, and I'll continue to sneak off when no one is looking to try to find your uncle and the others with him."

Fergus MacKenzie gathered intelligence for Clan Lochguard.

Grant stood and moved to a map of Scotland. Just as he pointed to a section to the east of Elgin, Faye MacKenzie burst into his office. "We need to talk, Grant."

"Faye, I'm busy. Come back later."

She crossed her arms over her chest. "No. This can't wait."

He took a step toward her. "Is everything okay? Is someone hurt?"

"Yes. No. In that order."

The one-word answers sent a rush of anger through his body. "Then what the bloody hell is so important?"

Faye looked to Iris. "I think you should leave."

Grant spoke before Iris could move. "Stay."

"I really think you don't want her here for this, McFarland."

His dragon chimed in. *It's never good when she uses our surname.*

Iris stood. "I was done for now, anyway. I'll check back in later, Grant."

After Iris gave Faye a quizzical look, she shut the door. The instant it clicked closed, Faye rushed up to him and poked his chest. "Why have you been avoiding me?"

"That's why you barged in here? Faye, I haven't been avoiding you."

His dragon spoke up. *Liar.*

"Oh, aye? Then why did your pupils flash just now?"

He leaned down. "Inner dragons talk, Faye. Don't be daft."

"I'm not. I want to know why one minute you were including me on top secret projects and even helping with my physical therapy and the next you disappear and I can't even schedule a meeting with you weeks in advance."

"In case you've forgotten, we're still rebuilding after the attack in January."

"Bullshit. The change is recent, and if anything, things have slowed down and you should have more free time."

"Don't pretend to know my job, Faye."

The second he said it, Grant regretted it.

Faye raised her chin. "I, more than anyone, know your job, Grant. You took it from me."

"Now, lass, you know that's not fair. Someone had to take over, and I know you're not selfish enough to wish the clan was left unprotected."

"Of course not. But even if I can never be head Protector again, I'm an asset. I need a job, Grant, or I'm going to go crazy before too much longer."

"Then why didn't you just say that instead of attacking me?"

"Because this was the only way to get your attention. Believe me, I still have an arsenal of things to use, if need be."

As they stared at one another, he admired the fire in her eyes and her pink cheeks. His dragon said, *Why do you fight kissing her?*

Because half of my family are traitors and if they get wind I took a mate, they'll go after her.

Faye can take care of herself.

Not against dozens of dragons, especially with her wing the way it is.

His beast huffed. *She is a warrior. Give her a chance to prove it.*

Faye poked his chest again. "Hello, Earth to Grant. Either share what your dragon is talking about or I will use said arsenal."

"As curious as I am about your arsenal, I'd rather not wake up with a talon against my balls. I'll find you something to do."

"When? If you put it off, I'll just keep coming back, and maybe one day you will wake up missing one of your bollocks."

He leaned back in his chair. If not for the threat hanging over his head, he'd tease her.

But Faye was safer at a distance. At least, for the time being.

Ignoring his dragon's growls, Grant replied, "How about now? I need you to lean on Fergus about the information I requested."

She put a hand on her hip and gestured with her other hand. "About what? I'm not going to do anything blind."

His beast chimed in again. *She'll find out anyway. They can't hurt her for merely helping Fergus with intelligence. You're being overprotective.*

Last year, Grant never would've hesitated. Faye was one of the people he trusted completely and she always worked hard.

But ever since she'd cleaned his wound and he'd thought of kissing her, he wanted to always protect her.

Grant didn't need any more complications in his life at the moment and kissing Faye would most definitely complicate matters.

Wooing the lass would have to wait.

His beast grunted. *If another doesn't take her first.*

Grant met Faye's eyes again. "I'm tracking down the traitors who left the clan."

Faye's posture relaxed a fraction. "Have you had any success?

"Not yet, although Iris is helping me."

She paused a second before saying, "You should ask for more help. It can't be easy for you, Grant, what with your uncle, dad, and other family members betraying Lochguard."

He narrowed his eyes. "You think I don't know that?" He stood. "One of the reasons I didn't say anything is I didn't want pity. You, out of everyone, should know how bloody awful it is to see that in someone's eyes."

Faye straightened her shoulders. "It's not pity in my eyes, Grant, just concern. Although why I'm bothered, I'll never know."

His beast grunted. *Because she wants to kiss us.*

He resisted looking at her lips. "You don't need to concern yourself about me. I'll handle the situation," Grant stated.

She studied him a second before saying, "The Grant I know would've told me to mind my own fucking business. What's wrong with you?"

He carefully kept his face expressionless. "Nothing, I just have a lot on my mind. But if you want me to insult you, I can do that quite handily, lass."

"You almost never call me 'lass.' Something is going on."

She walked up to him, and Grant resisted taking a step back. Faye's feminine scent filled his nose, and his dragon roared. *She's right there in front of you. Don't be a fool.*

He nearly reached up to tuck a stray piece of curly hair behind her ear, but instead, he took her elbow and turned the dragonwoman toward the door. "Since you're working for me now, I need you to go talk with Fergus. Unless you want me to find someone else to do it?"

After one long look, she shook her head. "No. I'll be your errand slave for now, but I might just see if I can find out information on my own as well."

"Don't even think of leaving the clan."

"The restriction on flying because of rogue drones attacking dragon-shifters was lifted last week. I can come and go as I please."

"Faye...."

"I'll report back later."

With that, Faye exited the room.

Grant ran his hands over his close-cropped hair. *She's going to go searching, isn't she?*

Why don't you trust her? She's not a teenager anymore. Faye knows how to stay hidden and also recognizes when it's time to retreat. Maybe you just don't like the thought of her finding things out before us.

You sound like her. We're too old for competitions.

His dragon sniffed. *You're becoming boring as you age.*

Rather than answer his beast, Grant sat behind his desk and looked at the printed profiles of every clan member who had permanently left Lochguard. There had to be something in them he could use. He might know his own family, but there were others he barely knew beyond saying hello or making small talk.

Regardless, he needed to find where they were hiding before Faye did. The thought of her fighting the rogue dragon-shifters on her own didn't sit well with him.

While he'd never admit it out loud, the reason was because once the threat was contained, he planned to go after Faye. Just thinking of her wild and demanding on top of him sent blood rushing to his cock. Her temper might annoy him when it came to work, but it would make her a firebrand when naked.

His dragon spoke up again. *Then stop stalling. Even without kissing her, you can court her.*

No. I don't need any distractions.

Ignoring his beast, Grant focused back on his work. He'd never have a chance with Faye MacKenzie if he failed.

Chapter Two

Faye jogged to her brother Fergus's house and tried to figure out why Grant was acting so strangely. While he'd done a good job of hiding it, she swore he'd glanced at her lips.

Maybe she was just imagining things.

Her beast sighed. *Why do you deny it? We want him and it's no longer the 18ᵗʰ century where females must wait for males to take action. Kiss him, fuck him, and then we can focus on protecting the clan.*

I know what you're getting at, but I'm going to pretend I don't know what you're talking about. That situation won't end well.

Her dragon growled. *He should be ours. Why deny it?*

And why now?

Because neither of you were ready.

I don't care if you think you know everything, it's not going to happen. Grant's mood swings would drive me crazy.

Tossing her dragon inside a mental maze, Faye picked up her pace. Exercise always helped to focus her mind and she most definitely needed to purge thoughts of Grant. Her brothers were observant and the last thing she needed was their teasing, especially if her mother got word of Grant's possible interest and nudged her to kiss the dragonman.

However, just because everyone in her family was mated but her didn't mean Faye was going to join the crowd. She might eventually want a mate and a family, but until she figured out her position within the clan and excelled at it, kissing and sex would have to wait.

She approached the old Sinclair place that was slowly becoming the MacKenzie twins' place. Two houses shared a wall, and much like her identical twin brothers, both halves might look the same on the surface, but there were minute differences. Fraser's half had random plants growing with a mixture of grass and a garden gnome riding a dragon whereas Fergus's half was well-cut and maintained with no ostentatious decorations. Each half represented her brothers well.

Faye slowed down and stopped at the stoop of the left half. She'd barely knocked before the door opened to a smiling red-haired human female with green eyes. It was her sister-in-law Gina MacDonald-MacKenzie. Faye waved. "Hi, Gina."

The human's American accent greeted her ears. "I wasn't expecting you until later, but come in."

She entered the house. "I have some clan business with Fergus. One of the Protectors said he was working from home today, aye?"

"Yeah, he's here. Jamie has a cold and Fergus is convinced it'll turn into the plague."

Jamie MacDonald-MacKenzie was Gina's son, but Fergus treated the lad as his own; after all, he'd been there since the day the bairn was born.

"Indulge him too often and he'll think he can do it all the time," Faye pointed out.

"Oh, I know. But I'm not feeling well myself, so I gave in to his demands."

Faye looked at Gina and finally noticed the circles under her eyes and flushed cheeks. "I can't believe my brother made you answer the door. You should be in bed."

Gina raised her eyebrows as she led Faye down the hall to Fergus's study. "You sound just like him. I would be in bed, but I couldn't get Jamie to settle. Fergus has the magic touch, so he's holding him and trying to get the baby to fall asleep."

Her sister-in-law put a finger to her lips and quietly opened the study door. Fergus sat inside with wee Jamie in the crook of his arm. Her serious brother had a smile on his face as he hummed a tune.

When he finished the song, he looked up and whispered, "You're early, Faye."

She rolled her eyes but kept her voice low. "I didn't realize I needed an appointment to visit."

"You don't, but it's the middle of the day," Fergus answered.

"I'm here on business. Grant sent me."

Fergus slowly stood up so as to not wake the bairn. "What about?"

Gina put out her arms. "Give Jamie to me and talk with your sister."

"But you're ill."

"You did the hard part and got him to sleep. Our little man and I can take a nap together."

Once Fergus maneuvered Jamie into Gina's arms, he kissed her cheek. "Call me on your mobile phone if you need anything."

"I plan to sleep like the dead for a few hours." Fergus raised an eyebrow and Gina sighed. "Fine, I'll keep it close."

"I love you, lass."

Gina smiled. "I love you, too." She looked to Faye. "Once I'm feeling better, we should have a girls' night with Holly and my sister. It's been too long since we all got together."

"While we can't get into too much trouble since Holly is pregnant, I'm sure I can think of something that walks the line."

Fergus growled. "Faye Cleopatra."

Faye whispered loudly, "You'd better go, Gina, or he might issue an edict he thinks you'll follow."

Gina chuckled, but headed toward the door. "See you later."

Once they were alone, Faye spoke up again. "Grant needs an update on the traitors."

"So you're working on that too now, aye?"

"Unless you want an earful, don't ask for the details."

Fergus searched her eyes. "If he does anything to hurt you, Faye, tell me. I'll straighten it out."

Knowing her brother and his overprotectiveness, Faye merely forced a smile rather than waste time arguing. "The information, Fergus?"

He went to his desk and opened his laptop. "There's not much, I'm afraid. While everyone remembers the battle near the Elgin NHS hospital, not many people have seen flying dragons in other parts of Scotland. The traitors must be hiding somewhere in their human forms."

Faye plopped down in the chair in front of Fergus's desk. "There are only so many places to hide for such a long period of time and not be noticed. Do you have a shortlist?"

"Aye, but why are you so keen? Grant didn't enlist you as a tracker, did he? You're strong, but not quite at full fighting strength"

Fergus's doubt went straight to her heart, but Faye kept her face neutral to hide it. "My job is to get as much information as possible. You're one source, but I have others." She put out a hand. "Hand over the list."

Picking up a piece of paper, Fergus searched her eyes. "Just be careful, Faye. We nearly lost you once, and you might not be as lucky next time."

She snatched the piece of paper out of his hands and stood. "The accident and resulting injury weren't my fault. No one knew the Dragon Knights would have electric blast guns that could take a dragon out of the sky. And when it comes to work, I'm always careful."

Before Fergus could say another word, Faye marched out of his office and scanned the shortlist. She desperately wanted to check out a few places on her own, but her duty to the clan was stronger.

Still, as she exited Fergus's house and headed back to the Protectors' central command building, Faye had an idea. All she needed to do was convince Grant to go along with it.

~ ~ ~

Grant left the central command building and headed toward the rear landing area. Since he was waiting for information and didn't have any appointments for an hour, he would take the time to fly and burn off some of his excess energy.

His beast was free again and asked, *And why is that?*

You bloody well know why.

Yes, but I want you to admit seeing Faye and working with her but not kissing her will be difficult. Maybe then you'll see things my way.

As he debated answering or not, he turned a corner and smacked into Faye MacKenzie.

Out of instinct, he reached out to steady her, but unlike with anyone else, he didn't release her shoulders. The rational part of his mind said it was so she didn't run away, but his dragon merely snorted and said, *It's because you don't want to let go.*

It didn't help that he wanted nothing more than to stroke the skin under his fingers and watch her eyes flash.

Clearing his throat, he asked, "Are you all right?"

"Grant McFarland, bumping into you isn't going to break any bones." She poked his chest. "You are being far too nice. Tell me what's going on." He opened his mouth to reply, but she beat him to it. "And something *is* going on. You've always told me the truth before, even if I didn't like it. Don't change that now."

He studied the sprinkling of freckles on her nose before meeting her eyes. "In certain cases, the truth can be destructive."

"Okay, now I'm more than merely curious. If you want the information I have from Fergus, then you'd better start talking."

"Withholding information from a superior? That doesn't sound like you."

She raised her chin. "When it's just you and me, there is no superior."

"Oh, aye? Since when?"

"Since always. Even when I was head Protector, it was true. I was rather generous considering what happened during our time with the British Armed Forces."

The memory of Faye pinning him to the ground after a tussle and nearly kissing him during their time with the army flashed into his mind. Being young and stupid, Grant had wanted to go after a human female for something different. To push Faye away, he'd told her she wasn't feminine enough and he'd never be interested in her that way.

His dragon grunted. *You were a fool.*

"I thought we'd put that behind us," he stated.

"So did I, but then you started acting like a stranger again. I've never called in a favor for your lack of apology, but I am now. I want to know why you're acting so strangely." She gripped his wrist and dug in her nails. "And keep in mind I'm not above a little roughhousing to get some answers. I was always better at pinning someone than you."

With Faye's body heat so close to him, it wasn't hard to imagine her soft breasts pressed against his back as she pinned him to the ground.

His eyes fell to her lips and every instinct urged him to claim her. No other female would ever keep him on his toes as much as Faye MacKenzie. More than that, she was his equal in more ways than one.

His dragon spoke up again. *Then do it. Tell her. Kiss her. Claim her.*

Faye placed a finger under his chin and raised it. "My eyes are here, Grant."

To his ears, her voice sounded husky. But given how his heart was pounding, it could be a combination of his dragon's lust and his imagination.

Don't pin your lust on me. You want her just as much as I do. Okay, almost as much as I do.

He moved a hand to cup her cheek. When Faye didn't try to move away, he replied, "You really don't want to know the reason why I'm being so nice, lass. It's something neither of us are ready for."

Stroking the soft skin of her cheek, Grant waited to see how Faye would respond. When she leaned into his touch, he nearly groaned.

Faye whispered, "You were always the annoying boy who tried to best me growing up. When did you have the change in heart?"

He leaned closer. "So you feel it too."

22

"Of course I do."

"Then you know the answer as well as I—it just did."

As they stared into one another's eyes, Grant could hear Faye's heart rate tick up. Her pupils flashed, probably much like his.

The only question was if they could both control their beasts to focus on the mission.

Thinking of the traitors and what they could do to Faye if they captured her, Grant released his hold and stepped back.

Faye blinked. "What?"

He decided to be honest, otherwise Faye would never stop badgering him. "Nothing I want is more important than finding and containing the traitors. They could take anyone or thing I value and twist it for their own gain."

Fire flashed in Faye's eyes. "You just insinuated that I can't take care of myself." When he didn't reply, Faye growled and tossed a few sheets of paper at him. "There's the information I got from Fergus. Once I have more, I'll find you. And don't worry, I won't bother you otherwise. I wouldn't want you to breathe too hard and break one of my bones."

Faye stormed off and Grant sighed. He knew how sensitive Faye was about her strength and abilities since her accident, yet he'd cut her deep to push her away. Maybe someday she would understand.

What? That you don't believe in her? You might have just lost your chance.

There's time yet to woo her.

Keep telling yourself that. She might not forgive you after this.

He watched Faye's wild, curly brown hair disappear into the distance, and he hoped his dragon was wrong.

CHAPTER THREE

Faye didn't know if she wanted to cry or to punch someone.

Of all people, she never expected Grant to dismiss her abilities. He'd been the one to help her with physical therapy after she'd been shot out of the sky by the strange electrical blast gun. She might never have learned how to fly again if not for him dragging her arse out of her mother's cottage and to the training area day after day to build up her muscles once more.

Grant was also the one who had invited her to his secret project, where they'd learned how to toss plastic containers of ground up mandrake root and periwinkle to force the dragon enemies to shift back into their human forms. She'd even been team leader for that project and had executed the right maneuvers without a problem during the most recent attack on Lochguard.

His change in attitude didn't make sense.

Her beast spoke up. *It's because he sees us as a potential mate and not a colleague.*

That shouldn't make a difference. If he wants me, he should want all of me and not try to change me.

So you admit to wanting him?

I thought so, but now I'm not so sure.

Give him time.

Why? I'm not going to wait around and pine for him. If he won't include me on plans to find and deal with the traitors, I'll do it on my own.

Before her dragon could respond, she spotted Catherine "Cat" MacAllister, the oldest of the five MacAllister siblings. Faye raised a hand in greeting and tried to change course, but Cat moved into her path and said, "Where are you hurrying off to?"

She and Cat had been close as children, but once Faye had decided to be a Protector at thirteen and Cat had set her heart on being an artist, they had drifted apart. However, as she looked at her once-friend's blue eyes and short, dark hair, Faye realized Cat had no ties to her family or the Protectors. She could say what she wanted and it probably wouldn't get back to them, so she blurted out, "Away from everything."

Cat raised an eyebrow. "Since when do you run away from your problems?"

"I'm not running away," she growled. "I'm off to solve them."

"You have the wild-eyed look my grandpa gets before he does something idiotic to his neighbor, such as drop a boulder on a shed or paint one of his cows orange. Maybe you need a breather to clear your head. That's what I try to convince my grandpa to do."

"Since your grandpa is Archie MacAllister and he's forever with Finn airing some grievance, I don't think your method works very well."

Archie and his neighbor Cal had been feuding for nearly their whole lives. Unfortunately, their antics took up a lot of Finn's time as clan leader.

Cat smiled. "It does work sometimes. Although I must admit I've wanted to tie my grandfather to a chair on more than one occasion."

The corner of Faye's mouth ticked up. "I think the whole clan has thought of tying him and Cal up at some point or another."

Chuckling, Cat motioned toward the main shopping and dining area of the clan. "I don't think I'll succeed in tying you up, but won't you have lunch with me? We can have a small cup of soup and then fill up on my mum's cake. She always keeps the best pieces for me and my siblings."

Cat's mother, Sylvia, ran the clan's restaurant. "I don't know, Cat. I have something important to do."

"Are you a Protector again?"

"No."

"Do you have a new job? I haven't heard anything around the clan."

She frowned. "I might, although I may have just gotten myself sacked."

"Right, then you're free for the time being. Come on. Consider it as a repayment for placing gum in my hair when I was asleep and having to chop it off the next morning. It was a devastating experience for a ten-year-old."

She pointed a finger. "Hey, you started it by daring your brother Connor to kiss me."

Cat shrugged. "I'm sure you did something before that to provoke me. You were always the instigator."

Faye opened her mouth, but then laughed. "I probably did start it, come to think of it."

Cat threaded her arm through Faye's. "Then come on. I'm leaving in a few days for a special exhibition that's going to tour around Scotland, and I don't know exactly when I'll be back to catch up with you."

"You're leaving?"

"Aye, for a bit. The DDA director proposed it as an outreach idea with the humans. Art can transcend cultures, and all of that. She asked for submissions a few months ago, and I was one of the ones chosen. It took a lot of work to convince Finn to let me go, and once he and Grant select a Protector to accompany me, everything will be cleared."

Faye looked askance at Cat. "So, you don't have an assigned guard yet?"

"Not yet." Cat searched her eyes. "Why?"

Faye started walking. "Maybe I can do it."

"But I thought you said you weren't a Protector anymore."

"Grant recently welcomed me back, but has yet to find a permanent place for me. Acting as your guard might be the perfect solution."

Cat picked up her pace and Faye matched it. "I like the idea. Not only do I trust you, it means you most definitely have to eat lunch with me now."

"Even after everything we did as children, you still trust me?"

"Oh, aye. You have a good heart, Faye MacKenzie. And you're loyal, too. Besides, I wasn't exactly an angel myself. We both kept each other on our toes. We also both understood about having annoying siblings that we could laugh and moan about. To be honest, I miss doing that with you."

Faye smiled. "Me, too."

"Right, then let's hurry up. I'm sure we both have stories to unload about our siblings, and there's only so much time in the day."

"You want to chat inside your mum's restaurant? If she hears us, then she'll probably serve us the moldy cake."

Cat shook her head. "We'll eat upstairs in our flat above the restaurant and lock the door. Since the walls are soundproofed to keep out the restaurant noise, no one will be the wiser. It'll also give me the chance to fill you in about my art show tour. The more you know, the greater the chance Grant will allow you to come."

Faye nodded. "You should show me some of your art, too. If I'm being honest, I haven't kept up with what you paint."

"No worries. You've had a lot going on in the last five years or so. You're quite the inspiration to the female dragon-shifters of the clan."

She turned her head. "Pardon?"

Cat smiled wider. "It's true. While the Scottish dragon clan has been more open about females playing important roles in the clan than the others in the UK, you were Lochguard's first female head Protector. Because of it, there are several teenage females who now want to one day achieve what you did."

Faye cleared her throat. "If you say so."

Cat placed a hand over her heart. "Why, is Faye MacKenzie blushing? I'm not sure I've seen that since one of our classmates pinned you to the ground during a wrestling match and tried to kiss you."

"Desmond Smith. I forgot about him."

"See? We have a lot to catch up on. I was nervous about being assigned someone like Brodie MacNeil, who rarely says two words. You are a much more entertaining choice."

As Faye looked at her childhood friend, it was as if they'd last talked a few days ago rather than many years ago. Friends like that were few and far between.

They finally reached Sylvia MacAllister's restaurant, *Dragon's Delight*. As she watched Cat order food for them and Faye exchanged pleasantries with Cat's mother, she realized how much she missed having a female friend. True, she got along with her brother's mates, but in the army and as a Protector, she'd always been surrounded by males.

She only hoped she didn't break Cat's trust if she received the assignment. Because as much as Faye wanted a female friend to talk with, she wanted to track down the traitors more. Accompanying Cat on her art show trip would be the perfect way to do it. All she needed to do was convince her cousin, Finn, it was a good idea.

~ ~ ~

Grant finished reading Fergus's report for the third time when someone knocked on the door.

His dragon perked up. *Maybe it's Faye.*

Ignoring his beast, Grant shouted, "Come in."

The door opened to reveal the blond-haired, brown-eyed form of Lochguard's clan leader, Finlay Stewart.

Grant raised an eyebrow. "I wasn't expecting you, Finn. Is something wrong?"

"Not wrong, exactly. But I have a proposition for you."

He hoped Faye hadn't gone to her cousin and asked for a favor. "What can I do for you?"

The corner of Finn's mouth ticked up. "If you're being nice to me for Faye's sake, you can stop."

"So she told you, then."

"Not everything, but enough." Finn sat down in the chair across from Grant's desk. "She mentioned not having a permanent place and made a suggestion."

"If she's wanting to go back to the front lines, I won't clear it, Finn. Not even for you."

"To be honest, I wouldn't, either. At least not yet. She still needs to fully rebuild her confidence. However, Faye has recovered enough to resume some duties. She wants to accompany Cat MacAllister on her exhibition around Scotland."

His beast huffed. *She either wants to run away from us, search for the traitors herself, or both.*

That gives me an idea.

Grant replied, "I was thinking of accompanying Cat as well." Finn raised his brows in question, and Grant continued, "I need to scout locations without the DDA getting in the way. It'll be easier to slip away for a few hours undetected if the DDA already knows I'm off our lands."

"Are you sure it's not for another reason?"

He knows, his dragon stated.

He ignored his beast. "No. Faye can handle the actual security detail, and I can be the back-up who ensures the surrounding areas are free of threats."

"The real question is whether the pair of you can work as a team or not." Finn leaned forward. "For the next minute, you are not my head Protector and I'm not your clan leader. You are the male who angered my kin and I'm her oldest living male relative who needs to look out for her."

Since Grant had worked with Finn for years, the sudden change didn't intimidate him. "Say what you need to say, as long as I get my defense."

Finn's pupils flashed. "You hurt her once before. If you do it again, I will challenge you. Understood?"

"And what would Faye say if she knew you were here speaking without her knowledge?"

"She would eventually come around."

Not likely, his dragon muttered.

Grant agreed with his beast, but from experience, he knew that arguing the point further with Finn would go nowhere when it came to his family. So, Grant merely answered, "I will treat her as I would any of my staff. If she disobeys, I won't be lenient, not even if it means pissing you off, Finn."

After one long second, Finn nodded in approval. "I respect that." He stood up. "I'll let you deliver the good news. Unless there's anything else for you to report, I need to check on Arabella. She's getting close to her due date, and I don't want anything to go wrong."

Arabella MacLeod was Finn's mate, originally from the English dragon-shifter clan called Stonefire in Northern England. She was also pregnant with triplets. "No, there's nothing really new to report about the traitors or any other threat beyond the usual caution. I hope my trip with Cat and Faye will eliminate at least part of the danger to our clan."

"Aye, I hope so, too. The rebuilding has gone well, but it'd be nice to have something to celebrate. Keep me updated whilst you're gone. I'll also try not to scare Cooper too much in your absence."

Cooper Maxwell was Grant's second-in-command. "You can try, but Iris sees him as a younger brother and is a wee bit protective. I wouldn't want to cross her."

Finn grinned. "I'll make sure to tell Cooper you only trust him to watch the clan with Iris here."

"Finn…."

Lochguard's leader waved goodbye and exited the room without another word.

His dragon spoke up again. *By spending time with Faye, you can grovel and convince her to kiss us.*

I'm not going to grovel, dragon. Besides, I plan to work. It's not often I get clearance to roam Scotland without the DDA watching my every move. I'm going to locate my uncle and the rest of the traitors before we come back to Lochguard, even if it kills me.

31

His beast fell silent, and that worried him since his dragon always wanted the last word.

Grant would just have to be extra careful around Faye. After all, she would be sharing a room with Cat, and Grant would have his own. Without her scent or tantalizing eyes beckoning him to claim her, he could focus on what was important—protecting the clan.

CHAPTER FOUR

A few days later, Faye paced the length of Cat's bedroom and back again. Her friend's voice filled the room. "If you don't calm down, Grant's going to know something's wrong."

She spun around to face Cat. "Nothing is wrong. I just can't fucking believe he's going to babysit me."

Cat tilted her head. "Didn't he say he wasn't? Something about looking for someone whilst we're touring Scotland?"

She waved a hand through the air. "That's his cover. No doubt his dragon doesn't want me out of their sight. They both probably think I'll get myself killed within hours of stepping outside of Lochguard."

Cat rolled her eyes. "You can stop with the exaggerations. My youngest brother, Jamie, is overly dramatic all the time. It never accomplishes anything with me, let alone our mum."

Faye growled. "I'm not being dramatic. I was once head Protector and now I can't do anything without a babysitter."

Zipping up her luggage, Cat moved to stand in front of her. "Then just do your bloody best and forget about what Grant thinks. You're letting him get into your head, Faye. Don't chance throwing away your future to impress a lad who hurt you not once, but twice."

"I'm not trying to impress him."

Cat raised an eyebrow. "Are you sure about that?"

Her dragon huffed. *You always are.*

Shut it, dragon.

She searched her friend's eyes. "When did you become so observant? As I recall, you only ever were that way when you were drawing or painting. Then you would spot the tiniest details."

"You may have two brothers and a nosy cousin, but I have four siblings. Four. Mum was always busy with the restaurant, and I was stuck raising the wee rascals. For better or worse, I grew up quicker than most. If I didn't notice what the devils were doing, they would've burned the house down or in the case of Ian and Emma, they would've hacked some government agency." Faye opened her mouth to apologize for being an arse, but Cat beat her to it. "Now, how about we head to the landing area and say our goodbyes? Between my family and yours, it's going to take a while."

"Just make sure Connor doesn't come talk to me or my mum will get ideas. She remembers everything."

"Well, you two did kiss once upon a time...."

"I was ten and he nine, and it was a dare."

"Maybe you should go after a younger male again and see how that goes," Cat answered, her eyes twinkling.

Faye stuck out her tongue. "Try it yourself. After all, your mum moans about never having any grandkids."

Cat shook her head. "Believe me, I know. She goes on about having two kids by my age. But finding a mate and having a child would put my art to the side. Doing that would rip my heart in two; I can't imagine not having a chance to paint every day or the option to spend an hour capturing the best shot with my camera."

Faye patted Cat's arm. "Oh, aye, I understand. That's why I'm going to do the best job I can on this assignment and prove I'm ready to protect Lochguard once more. Grant won't have a choice but to give me decent assignments again."

"Just be careful because if he kisses you, you may end up with a child even if you don't want one. You're clever enough to suspect what I do—that he's your true mate."

"True mate or not, if there's one male I can resist, it's Grant McFarland."

Cat studied her a second before saying, "Let's hope so." Faye wanted to put up a better defense, but Cat didn't let her get a word in. "We'd better go or our mums will hunt us down."

Faye snorted. "Unless your grandpa causes havoc in the interim."

"Grandpa Archie has been rather quiet as of late," Cat replied. "I hope he's not digging an underground tunnel under Cal's property. Who knows what he'd do then. Maybe he'd do like the humans in World War II and try to blast underneath his target—Cal's farm."

"With sheep flying every which way."

"And the pair of them blaming the other for the mess."

They stared at one another, and even though dead sheep flying through the air shouldn't be funny, they both burst out laughing.

Faye's beast spoke up. *It's nice being around another female our age. I thought I wouldn't like it since I'm not interested in so-called girlie things, but Cat is different.*

She and I may have different professions, but we're both fairly determined to succeed.

It will also be easier to ignore Grant with her at our side.

So now you want to ignore him?

The lust haze cleared. He was a jerk. He needs to bow down and apologize before I think of wanting to kiss him.

Faye had a feeling her dragon would lose that battle as soon as they saw Grant again, but kept that thought to herself. Unlike her brother Fraser, Faye had never spoiled her beast. She could contain her if need be.

Cat picked up her luggage and Faye did the same. As they made their way to the landing area, Faye steeled herself for what was to come. Putting her family and Cat's together should be interesting, to say the least. If nothing else, the horde of people would keep Grant away since he hated big families.

~ ~ ~

Grant tapped his hand against his thigh as he leaned against the rock enclosure surrounding the landing area. He'd already said goodbye to his mum and brother, and was ready to leave. Glancing across the wide, open space, he tried not to grimace at the sight of the MacKenzies and MacAllisters surrounding Faye and Cat.

There were so bloody many of them.

We once had that much family, too, his dragon pointed out.

Not wanting to think of the past, Grant took out his mobile phone and was about to distract himself with text messages when the crowd cleared enough for him to spot Faye MacKenzie. She wore a loose-fitting dress that hid her body, but it wasn't hard to imagine her trim waist or toned thighs.

Then the wind blew and her curly hair went every which way around her face. What he wouldn't give to gather it in one hand and lightly tug her head back to kiss her.

Blinking, he looked away before she caught him gawking. Still, he couldn't resist watching from the corner of his eye as each member of her family hugged her and said their goodbyes. He barely noticed Cat doing the same.

Seeing one happy family was bad enough, but two twisted his heart. As much as Grant tried to deny it, he missed his family. Not only his uncle, but his dad, aunt, and cousins, too.

His beast huffed. *Why mention our father? He left with the other traitors and broke our mother's heart. He's not worth anyone's time.*

He's a bastard now, but he wasn't always so. No one can just block memories forever.

I could. I'm stronger than you.

So if our dad appeared right now in dragon form, you could kill him without a thought?

I don't like to kill unless it's necessary. But I'm not above kicking his arse.

Before he could reply, Lorna MacKenzie's voice boomed across the landing area. "Grant McFarland, stop hiding in the shadows and give your old Aunt Lorna a hug."

Lorna wasn't a blood relation of his, but almost everyone on Lochguard called her Aunt Lorna.

He debated declining, but Faye met his gaze. Not wanting to appear cowardly in front of her, he walked toward the MacKenzie brood.

As he approached, Fraser and Fergus—Faye's older twin brothers—glared at him with piercing blue eyes. If not for Aunt Lorna, Grant would've given them the double-finger salute.

His beast grunted. *We can easily take them. Neither one is a soldier.*

Not now.

Later, then.

Lorna closed the distance between them and took his face into her hands. "How many times do I have to tell you not to be shy? I've known you since the day you were born, lad. You're always welcome in our family."

For a split second, Grant yearned for the warmth and peace of a family untouched by scandal and betrayal. The MacKenzies were notorious for their lively dinners and more than a few food fights. An evening with them could help him forget about his own father and how he had abandoned him.

But before he could do something stupid, such as invite himself over for dinner once they returned from the exhibition excursion, Faye spoke up. "How about you let us go, Mum? Otherwise, we'll never reach Inverness by nightfall."

Lorna tsked. "Since Cat sent her art on ahead and everyone's luggage with it, you're flying. Inverness is fifteen or twenty minutes from here by dragonwing. You have plenty of time."

Ross Anderson, Lorna's human mate, wrapped an arm around his dragonwoman's waist. "She'll be back soon enough, love. Besides, they need the daylight to keep an eye out for any hunters or Knights. Unless you're wanting them to be at a disadvantage and possibly attacked?"

Lorna smacked her mate's chest. "Ross Anderson, don't even joke about that."

Faye jumped in. "Mum, we'll be fine. I promise to call once we land and many times after that. You'll probably beg me to stop pestering you before long. After all, your mating is still new."

Fraser spoke up. "While you're ringing people, make sure to call each of us." Fraser placed a hand over his heart. "I'm just as concerned about your welfare."

"Stuff it, Fraser," Faye replied. "I haven't forgotten your recent 'gift' of a pink tutu and a note saying I could be a ballerina to fill up my time. You can just linger and wonder what happens to me."

Fraser raised his eyebrows. "And cause my pregnant mate undue stress? I'm shocked at you, sister."

Holly, Fraser's mate, sighed. "I'll handle Fraser. Have a good time around Scotland. I really hope this DDA outreach program is successful."

Faye nodded. "Me, too."

Fergus took a step forward. "Make sure to give me any intel you find straightaway via Arabella's secure network."

"I know, Fergus." Faye grabbed Grant's hand and tugged. "We're leaving now. I'll talk to you lot later."

Grant tried to ignore her warm hand in his, but he couldn't resist closing his fingers tightly. Faye shot him a glance, but he gave an imperceptible shake of his head; her family was watching and if she chewed him out now, they'd never leave until they learned everything between them.

Grant cleared his throat. "Faye can take care of herself." He looked at Cat, who was motioning them toward the center of the landing area. "Cat's already waiting for us. Cooper can handle things whilst I'm gone. We'll be in touch."

Grant walked away from the MacKenzies, never releasing his grip on Faye's hand.

Faye murmured, "Thank you. Otherwise, we'd be there another half an hour."

Since he didn't want to betray his jealousy at how much her family cared and stood by her, Grant said nothing.

Only when they reached Cat did he reluctantly release Faye's hand to tug off his shirt. Even though he and Faye had stripped and shifted a million times before, he swore he could feel her eyes on his bare chest.

His dragon growled. *I want more than her eyes on our chest. Not going to happen anytime soon.*

If not for needing his dragon to shift, Grant would've tossed the bastard into a mental maze.

His beast grunted. *But you do need me. Remember that.*

With a sigh, he tossed away his shirt and went to the fly of his trousers. He took an extra second to think of football statistics to deflate his semi-hard cock.

However, he couldn't resist sneaking a glance upward in Faye's direction. It had been longer than he liked since he'd seen the lass naked.

Cat and Faye stood nude with their backs to him. He didn't even notice Cat as he couldn't force his gaze away from Faye's toned arse. What he wouldn't give to touch her soft skin to see how her body reacted to him.

Then wings grew out of Faye's back, her limbs extended into forearms and hindquarters, and her face elongated into a snout. Within a few seconds, Faye stood in her blue dragon form and extended her wings. Because of helping her with physical therapy, he knew exactly where to find her injury and his gaze moved to the slightly crooked bone of one wing.

His dragon chimed in. *She'll be fine.*

Faye turned her dragon head around and met his eyes. She huffed at him, and he had to lean forward to keep from falling over.

That was his cue to shift.

Embracing his beast, Grant grew into his green dragon form. Being male, he stood about a foot taller than Faye and Cat. Since he knew the height difference irritated Faye, he stood taller.

She narrowed her eyes, and he shrugged before crouching down and jumping into the air. As he beat his wings and ascended into the sky, he simply enjoyed the rush of wind against his hide. With a little practice, he could treat Faye as he had for years by teasing and challenging her. Only when he was nice to her did his instinct start to take over and make him want to do things to her he couldn't. Things he couldn't do until he sorted out the traitors.

His dragon spoke up again. *But what about when we're lying in the room next door to hers? I know what I'll be thinking about.*

You should be thinking of the traitors.

Why can't we do both? Let Faye handle Cat's security detail and we can look for the traitors. That will show Faye we believe in her.

Maybe. I want to ensure there aren't any Dragon Knights or hunters in the area first.

She'll think you're coddling her.

Then so be it. After the drone attacks down on Stonefire, an enemy could be lurking anywhere.

Several of Stonefire's clan members, including its head doctor, had been targeted by small drones that had ended up drugging them. Actually, according to reports, one of the victims had been from Ireland. At any rate, Lochguard's head doctor, Innes, had gone down to help Stonefire and had ended up mating the Stonefire doctor who had been attacked.

His dragon added, *But Stonefire found a remedy to the strange drug the drone carried and we have a vial just in case. It's not a big concern.*

Do you really want to risk the drug changing and possibly killing her?

Then talk to her about it. Faye was once our equal. That's all she wants, to be an equal again. Besides, she can help keep an eye out for any threats. She can't do that if she doesn't know what threats to look out for.

Since when did you become so rational?

Ever since you became the opposite.

Grant mentally snorted. *Then we'll try it your way and try to treat her as an equal, oh wise one. But if Faye's temper gets the better of her, we'll do it my way.*

Fair enough. And now that you've listened to me about this, I'll have to pester you about kissing Faye, too.

No, dragon. Kissing the lass will have to wait, no matter how much she tempts us.

At last you've admitted that you're fighting the pull, too. That gives me ideas on how to speed up the process.

We can't endanger the mission.

We don't have to.

As his dragon fell silent, Grant studied the slightly erratic beat of Faye's wings. Simply flying had to be painful, but through sheer stubbornness, she had regained enough stamina to fly long distances. He still remembered the look of triumph in her eyes when she had stayed aloft for more than a few seconds. Of all the people in the clan, she'd trusted him and allowed him to help her.

He at least owed her a chance to prove herself.

If she could handle it, then maybe he would ask for her help with his uncle and the others. The sooner he rooted out the traitors, the sooner he could try to woo the lass. After all, Faye would never betray him.

Picking up his pace, Grant caught up to the two females again and edged out a little ahead. Since he'd made up his mind, Grant was anxious to reach Inverness. He needed to talk with Faye. Even if it meant tying her to a chair so she would hear him out, he would do it.

CHAPTER FIVE

As the river and buildings of Inverness came into view, Faye struggled to keep up with Grant's pace.

She'd tested herself and knew she could fly for hours at a leisurely pace before the pain was too great. However, Grant was flying as if they were being chased by an enemy.

Her dragon yawned. *He's probably trying to rile you up. Ignore him. Cat is having trouble, too.*

Looking to the side, Cat's red dragon form would miss a beat every few seconds. Her irritation at Grant only increased. *She's not a Protector. Grant should know this.*

Faye gave a low roar and garnered Cat's attention. She slowed down her pace and Cat nodded before doing the same. The pair of them mostly glided the last few miles to the city. By the time they reached the empty car park next to Inverness Castle and maneuvered their way down, Grant was already in human form, fully dressed and waiting.

Her beast grunted. *I was hoping to catch a glimpse of him naked. I thought you'd sworn off him?*

It doesn't mean I can't enjoy his abs or fine arse.

Leave it to her beast to make something as natural as shifting into something about sex.

Thankfully the area was fenced off and private. Faye never cared much about nudity, but humans tended to make a big deal out of it. Despite having two humans as sisters-in-law, it was still hard to trust them as a unit.

She and Cat each placed the bags clutched in their forearms, the ones holding their clothes, to the side and gently touched their hind legs to the ground. Faye imagined her form shrinking into a human. A few seconds later, she stood beside Cat as they rummaged through their packs for clothes.

She tried not to think about how Grant could be staring at her arse.

Her beast spoke up. *Forget him. He can look, but he will never have.*

Her dragon really had convinced herself she could resist Grant.

Rather than argue, Faye dressed quickly. Cat did the same. Within a few minutes, they had their packs in hand and walked up to Grant. Faye spoke first. "A DDA representative is supposed to meet us here at any minute and take us to our accommodations. Once that's done, I want to take Cat out along the river for a meal."

He raised his brows. "So you want me to scout the area first?"

"Why do you sound so surprised? It's usual practice for a security detail team to split up the work."

"Aye, but given your temper earlier, I wasn't sure what to expect," he drawled.

She frowned. "I'm not going to dignify that with an argument. Just do your job, McFarland."

He took her arm and pulled her to the side. "Speaking of that, I was thinking about the drones Stonefire had trouble with not that long ago." He handed her a vial and needle kit. "Just in case, here's one of the antidote packs. The formula may have changed by now, but it's better than nothing. The second either you or Cat is attacked, I want to know."

She raised an eyebrow. "I'm aware of protocol, Grant. If you're trying to cover your arse, there's no need."

He growled and hissed out, "Neither one of us are mind readers, Faye. I just want to be clear since I'm going to leave most of Cat's security to you."

"Truly?"

"Yes, truly. Don't sound so surprised."

Her dragon spoke up. *Let's not waste time arguing with him. I'm hungry. Let's hurry up and find somewhere to eat along the river. I'm sure some of the restaurants allow dragon-shifters. If not, I think casually showing a talon or two will convince them to change their minds.*

Faye snorted. When Grant raised his brows, she cued him in. "My dragon is hungry. Is there anything else?"

He grunted. "Just keep your mobile on." He paused, and she also heard the footsteps. Grant added, "I'll do the talking. We don't need to upset the DDA."

Rather than respond, Faye stuck out her tongue. She could keep her temper in check when it came to strangers. Grant was just trying to provoke her.

Her beast chimed in again. *Maybe the DDA human will be attractive. Now that the Stonefire dragonwoman has mated a human male, it's not so dangerous. We can widen our potential partner pool.*

No sex with the DDA person. If it's a him, you might break the male.

Her dragon huffed. *If he's weak, I wouldn't waste energy trying to nab him.*

Faye rushed to Cat's side just as a man in his thirties walked into the space. He was slightly taller than Faye with black hair that went to his chin and blue eyes. He wasn't unattractive. But from his gait and countenance, he wasn't a soldier. Faye's dragon would definitely break him.

Too bad, her dragon murmured.

The male smiled at each of them in turn, but his gaze lingered a second on Cat. He nodded. "Cat MacAllister, welcome to Inverness." He looked to Faye and then Grant. "Lochguard has been secretive about who they're sending for their security. May I have your names?"

Faye itched to answer straightaway, but bit her tongue. Grant was their security team leader in public.

Grant replied, "What's yours, first? And I need to see some identification."

The human didn't slump his shoulders or show any other signs of being intimidated. Faye gave the human credit. More than a few had cowered under Grant's dominant tone in the past.

The male finally answered, "I'm Lachlan MacKintosh, the coordinator of this event." He took out a badge and displayed it. "Here's my ID."

Grant studied the ID and nodded. "I'm Grant McFarland, in charge of surveillance and strategy. This is Faye MacKenzie. She's Cat's personal bodyguard."

Lachlan nodded to each of them as he placed his ID into one of his pockets. "Good. With introductions out of the way, we should get going. Follow me."

"Where are we going?" Faye asked.

Lachlan glanced at her. "It's confidential. There are eyes and ears everywhere. This is a known landing area, which makes it a target. I'm not about to compromise Ms. MacAllister's safety."

She wanted to push further, but Cat placed a hand on her arm and smiled. "Since the DDA director has used quite a bit of her political capital to put together this event, let's just follow him." DDA director, Rosalind Abbott, had only recently taken command after a scandal and imprisonment of the former director. Cat leaned over to whisper, "I trust you to tell me if he's leading us on or not."

Faye grunted and looked to Lachlan. "After you."

The corner of Lachlan's mouth ticked up. "And to think, dragon-shifters don't usually have a reputation for being polite."

"We can be, but it's hard to do when people are shouting or trying to kill you," Grant answered.

"Fair enough," Lachlan said. "We expect there to be some disturbances during the tour, although all of the locations have been carefully selected for a reason."

"And let me guess, the details will have to wait?" Faye drawled.

Cat jumped in. "All of the cities I saw on the list sound lovely. I'm sure we're all grateful for the chance to showcase our work."

"You'll meet the others at our destination. We have much more than just artists. I'm sure you understand our need to be secretive as to all of the details," Lachlan said.

"Let's just get to the place we're going so we can stop with all of the vague comments," Grant growled out.

Lachlan raised his brows but remained silent. The human picked up his pace, and they all followed suit.

~~~

Grant spent the rest of the walk observing the human named Lachlan.

At first, he'd worried about Faye flirting with the male. But as she questioned and talked to him, she didn't seem to show any interest in him beyond a working relationship.

His dragon spoke up. *You could stop worrying if you just pursued her openly. Then we could better focus on our mission.*

Ignoring his beast, Grant kept his mind clear of all thoughts and studied their surroundings. Since it was early evening, the streets were full of people walking home from work or heading out to shop or dine.

Everyone from Lochguard wore long-sleeved shirts against the cooler than normal temperature of early summer, which hid their tattoos. Still, a few eyed the tall Lochguard trio and moved as far away from them as possible, probably because their height and build signaled that they were most likely dragon-shifters.

Most of the humans paid them little attention, although a few did smile in passing. Inverness had been one of the friendlier cities in the past. The isolation of the Highlands had worked to Lochguard's advantage.

However, as the city continued to grow with each passing year, he wondered how much longer it would be safe, let alone welcoming to dragon-shifters. After all, there was a small Inverness dragon hunter gang. Luckily, they weren't as organized as the one run by Simon Bourne. The gang formerly of Carlyle but currently near Birmingham was tied with the Dragon Knights as their greatest enemies. Bourne's gang was more organized and had been growing in membership. Still, he would have to talk with Faye later and discuss their options in case they ran into the Inverness dragon hunter group. The last thing they needed was to draw unnecessary attention to their presence. The art show needed good press, not bad.

They soon arrived at a street that branched off into several side streets full of bed and breakfast establishments. After turning down a street and walking another minute, Lachlan entered the front garden gate of one called, "The Scottish Rose."

The building looked like a dozen others or more on the street. It was attached to another house on one side and was brick. As they entered the front door, Grant noted the B&Bs to either side posted no vacancy.

Lachlan didn't bother to check in and proceeded to the living area. Once he shut the door to the room, he turned to face them. "This B&B and the other two on either side are where all of the participants and their guards are staying."

"It seems a bit out in the open with regards to security," Grant pointed out.

"Perhaps. But the DDA owns all three of these buildings. We find it easier to come and go along the busy street full of tourists, especially since we book rooms to anyone who wants it most of the year. Even the locals think this is just another bed and breakfast." Lachlan pointed toward the ground. "However, there is also a tunnel underneath that serves as an escape route, in case we need it. The DDA has taken every precaution to ensure this event goes forward."

Grant grunted. "We'll need to see the tunnel and study its exit point."

"In time," Lachlan answered. "First, I need to brief Cat and the others on the event. You're the last to arrive. Wait here while I fetch the remaining participants."

The human left, and Grant looked to Faye. She nodded in understanding—she would locate all of the available escape routes as soon as possible as well as find the nearest place they could shift and fly away, if need be.

In that second, Grant forgot about the traitors in his family as well as him trying to resist Faye. It was nice to be doing more than paperwork behind a desk. Being the head Protector wasn't always as glamorous as some might think.

Grant's thoughts were cut short as another human entered the room. His worn-leather jacket and the battered fedora in one hand made him blink.

However, before Grant could say a word, the human grinned and took Faye's hand. "Nice to meet you." He moved to Cat. "I've been itching to talk with some more dragon-shifters." He moved to Grant, but at his glare, resisted taking his hand. "Although, maybe you can stand to the side if all you're going to do is stare at me."

Grant growled out, "Who are you?"

The man put his hat over his heart and stood tall. "I'm Maximilian Holbrook, the premier dragon-shifter archaeologist in the UK. You can call me Max."

Grant vaguely recalled the name from a report. "You're the one who bothered one of my clan members on Skye and we had to relocate you."

"I wasn't bothering anyone," Max answered. "That dragon intruded on my dig site. I was a bit friendly, but it was one of the first times I'd seen a dragon-shifter in the flesh. An older female, correct? I liked her. Although the other dragon female who took me back to Suffolk handled me a little rough."

"Iris took you back. And from all accounts, she was trying to shut you up," Grant stated.

Max raised his eyebrows. "Is that so? I thought she was telling me she couldn't hear, so I only shouted louder."

It was a miracle Iris had delivered the human in one piece. Grant would've been tempted to drop him into a loch.

Cat stepped in between them. "Hello, Max. I'm Cat, one of the artists. I thought this event was dragon-shifters showing off their creative talents? Pardon me asking, but what is an archaeologist doing here?"

Max's gaze moved to Cat's. "Ah, but the event is called, 'Unmasking Dragon-shifters' and that's what I do. I bring a historical perspective. It's hard to understand the present without knowing the past."

Grant crossed his arms over his chest. "I would think that a dragon-shifter archaeologist would be a better fit."

"There aren't many of them, sadly. Besides, I have a knack for digging in places most can't access since I'm human. No one knows more about dragon-shifters in the Roman period in Britain than me."

Grant didn't care if Max had more artifacts than the bloody queen, he could make Faye's task difficult if he followed Cat around and made a spectacle of himself. According to his report from Iris, the human didn't understand self-control or how to keep under the radar.

Cat spoke up again. "Well, then, you'll just have to share some of your stories with us over a meal at some point. I don't know much about dragon-shifter history, apart from what we're taught in school. But I'm sure there's plenty of little-known, interesting stories to hear."

Max opened his mouth, but thankfully Lachlan returned with a few other dragon-shifters. Grant didn't recognize any of them.

Lachlan pointed to each in turn as he introduced them. He gestured toward a male in his forties, with slightly graying hair. "This is Dylan Turner from Stonefire, who is a silversmith." Then Lachlan motioned toward a female in her fifties. "This is Nia Merrick, from Snowridge, who will be displaying her sewing and craft skills." He indicated the last male, who was about Grant's age. "And this is Caelen Corr, from Northcastle. He's a woodcarver. And everyone, this is Cat MacAllister from Lochguard, and she's an accomplished painter and photographer.

The only human participant is Max Holbrook. He's an archaeologist who specializes in dragon-shifters."

As everyone murmured their greetings, Grant noted that each of the dragon-shifter clans in the UK had a representative, except for the one in southern England—Skyhunter.

Considering that clan's leader had recently been convicted of giving the order to murder a number of his clan mates, all to help the former DDA director Jonathan Christie, Skyhunter had more important things to worry about than sending someone to an art show.

The absence reminded Grant that he needed to talk with Finn once they returned home. If Lochguard wanted to try an alliance with Skyhunter, then reaching out as soon as they finally selected their new leader would be the perfect time to do it.

Grant paid attention once more as soon as Lachlan spoke again. "Everyone will have a chance to introduce their security staff at a later date. I'm going to go over the schedule and rundown of events. We can also get your questions out of the way." He looked to Grant and Faye. "You two can go to your rooms and settle in. This building is secure."

Faye looked to Cat and her friend said, "I'll be fine here. I promise not to wander off or dare anyone to kiss each other."

Grant didn't get the reference, but Faye grinned. "You'd better not. I want to be there when you do." Lachlan cleared his throat and Faye moved to Grant's side. "Fine, we'll leave. Just make sure one of your staff shows us the security plans for the event."

As soon as Lachlan nodded, Grant and Faye exited the room. A human female stood waiting and guided them to their rooms upstairs. Once she handed over the keys, Grant opened his door. "Come in for a moment. I have a few things to discuss with you."

"I'm not sure why you're so formal about it, but okay." Faye shut the door behind her and crossed her arms over her chest. "So, what's so urgent? You already know I'm going to scout out escape routes, unless you were just making eyes at me earlier for no reason."

He ignored her prodding. "I need you to keep a close eye on that human, Max. If Cat does dine with him, you need to force him to be more inconspicuous."

She shrugged. "I'll try, but I kind of like him. He wasn't intimidated by you, and that's a rare thing."

Taking a step toward Faye, he put every bit of dominance in his voice he could muster. "That's not a thing to be admired. You need to watch him. If he gets Cat killed, it'll be your fault."

Fire flashed in her eyes. "Of course I'll protect Cat. But if you think I have mind control abilities and can make him do my bidding, then maybe you need to take a holiday and have your brain checked."

He took another step. "Maybe you should just follow orders and control your temper."

Faye uncrossed her arms and closed the distance between them. "I would control my temper if you stopped treating me like a newly minted Protector. Unless you have something useful to say, I'm going to check out our surroundings from my room, as any seasoned warrior would do."

His beast spoke up. *Yes, provoke her some more. I like it when her cheeks turn pink.*

Stop it, dragon.

Why? We want the same thing. You just waste time by putting it off until later.

Faye's hot breath caressed his chin, and his eyes darted to her pink cheeks. He wondered if the color was solely because of her temper. Maybe his nearness affected her as much as hers did him. It was hard not to reach out and pull her close.

His dragon hummed. *I wonder where else she's turned pink.*

"Grant? Are you going to answer me?"

He met her gaze again. Between her scent filling his nose and her standing close enough he could feel her heat, Grant wanted to kiss Faye and strip her naked. Surely if he kissed her, he could focus back on his assignment. After all, she'd be his and other males would stay away. If not, he could finally growl and chase them away.

His beast chimed in. *Yes, yes, kiss her. That one kiss will give us what we really want.*

At his dragon's reference to the mate-claim frenzy that would result in a child, it was as if a tub of ice-cold water splashed over his body. He couldn't sacrifice a week or more for his own desires, no matter how much he wanted to.

Grant took a step back and cleared his throat. "Update me before you take Cat to dinner."

Faye remained silent a second before asking, "Are you sure you don't want to come with us? If you growled and glared at Max all night, he might restrain himself a bit."

Watching Faye as she laughed and enjoyed the evening with Cat would only tempt him. He shook his head. "I'm going to do my first scouting session of the surrounding countryside this evening."

"Okay. But remember, you need to eat, too."

His beast said, *See? She cares about our wellbeing.*

Only because she wants me to find the traitors and protect the clan.

You can tell yourself that if you wish.

He answered, "I'm not a lad in nappies. I can look after myself."

Rolling her eyes, Faye moved to the door. "Always Mr. Invincible." She paused a second before she whispered, "Don't be afraid to ask for help if you need it, Grant. Regardless of what you may think, I can keep a secret if need be. You don't have to go after your uncle or family alone."

It was on the tip of his tongue to dismiss her offer, but as Faye scrutinized him, he replied, "Thank you."

"Of course."

With one last long look, Faye left and Grant was alone. Yet as he turned toward his bed, all he could think about was Faye standing close and her breath on his skin.

Running his hands across close-cut hair, he turned toward his luggage, which had arrived ahead of them. Taking out a map of the surrounding area, Grant planned his excursion for the night. While he'd check out the art show venue first, he planned to travel at least ten miles in every direction from Inverness to survey the countryside. Maybe if he flew long and hard he would avoid dreaming. Because if he did dream, he had a feeling Faye would tempt him yet again.

Staying in close quarters with the female who was his true mate was going to test his limits.

Chapter Six

Faye finished surveying the nearby buildings from her window and plopped down on her bed.

Even though she was on assignment, she was back to doing nothing.

Her dragon chimed in. *There are other Protectors in the building. Maybe one of them is a single, attractive male.*

She sighed. *Not this again.*

Why not? Unless you're waiting and pining for Grant? He doesn't believe in us or our skills. He lost his chance.

Faye wanted to agree with her beast, but a small part of her wondered if her temper had gotten the better of her earlier. Yes, Grant had been an arse, but searching for family traitors had a way of taking a toll on someone. No doubt, most of Grant's actions were because of stress and bottled up hurt feelings.

Her beast huffed. *We all have our own pain. That's no excuse to ignore who we are and what we're truly capable of doing. It's not bluster—we have shown strength since the accident.*

True. Faye sat up and checked her mobile, but there wasn't a message from Cat. *Let's scout out the other Protectors.*

Since her dragon didn't argue, Faye took that as a yes to the idea.

She was most anxious to meet the dragons from Northcastle, the Northern Irish clan. Finn and Bram had wanted to reach out to the only dragon-shifters in Northern Ireland, but the ongoing feud with the clans of the southern Irish Republic had kept everyone away. Faye wasn't one to dig too deep into politics, but even she knew that Northcastle blamed Glenlough and the others in Ireland for stealing their land centuries ago and cutting their two clans down to one. The human dispute between Ireland and Northern Ireland had only exacerbated the situation over the years.

However, if Northcastle had sent a representative to the event, they might be open to talking with the other British dragon clans. According to her history lessons as a child, the Northern Irish clan had once been close with all the dragon-shifters on the isle of Great Britain.

Faye changed her clothes and filled her bag with items she might need before exiting her room. She had no idea who was staying where. She'd start on her floor by knocking and see where it led her.

She moved past Grant's room to the one at the end of the hall. She rapped on the wood and did her best not to tap her fingers against her leg.

A tall male with dark hair and brown eyes opened the door and she blinked. It was Aaron Caruso from Clan Stonefire. "Aaron?"

He grunted. "I wondered who Lochguard would send."

"Who else is here from Stonefire?"

"Quinn Summers."

She vaguely remembered the male from an earlier meeting. "Maybe you can help me. I'm trying to figure out where the Protectors from the other clans are."

"Did you try asking the lady downstairs, who runs the place?"

"No. I thought it'd be more fun to knock and find out for myself."

Aaron shook his head. "Don't expect me to join you. I need to save up my charm for the humans at the exhibition."

She eyed the Stonefire dragonman. "What happened to the teasing Aaron Caruso I met before? He was always charming and didn't have limits on it."

"He has a lot on his mind." Aaron moved the door closed a fraction. "If that's all, then I'm going to go back to taking a nap."

She studied him. "You are grumpier than I've ever seen before."

He shrugged. "It's justified."

She wanted to probe further, but Aaron had the door halfway shut, signaling that he wanted her to leave. Since she already had a grumpy Grant to deal with, she didn't need another grumpy male. If something was wrong with Aaron, she trusted his fellow Protector, Quinn, to sort it out.

Waving goodbye, she headed down the stairs.

Faye found the woman at the front desk and smiled at her. "I'm looking for the dragon-shifters from Northcastle. Can you tell me where they are staying?"

"I'm sorry, lass. I'm not allowed to give out that information."

Before Faye could say anything else, a deep male voice in a Northern Irish accent boomed behind her. "If a pretty female like you is looking for me, then here I am."

Faye resisted rolling her eyes. Focusing on the importance of the meeting, she pasted a smile on her face and turned around.

The male was quite possibly the tallest dragon-shifter she'd ever seen and had to be closer to seven feet than six. Broad shoulders, close-cropped blond hair, and blue eyes only made the package more attractive. He had to have some Viking heritage in his family tree.

Her dragon growled. *Yes, he'll do.*

Ignoring her beast, Faye walked up to him and put out a hand. "I'm Faye MacKenzie, one of Lochguard's Protectors."

"A female Protector? That's rare."

She kept the smile on her face. "Perhaps in Northern Ireland, but that's not important. Who are you?"

The male flashed a grin and Faye's heart skipped a beat. "I'm Adrian Conroy, the second-in-command of Clan Northcastle. Care to tell me why you're looking for us?" He lowered his voice. "I'm more than happy to show you where my room is located. After all, you seemed keen to find it a few minutes ago."

It seemed Adrian Conroy was a flirt.

Torn between finding out as much as she could and being true to herself, Faye compromised. "How about we get a coffee? I saw a self-serve stand near the entrance. Then we can talk some more."

Despite Adrian's handsome exterior, his eyes were intelligent. Trained as she was, she could tell when someone was sizing her up and assessing a threat.

Adrian finally turned and motioned toward the entrance. "After you."

Faye walked past him. "For a clan who's isolated, you seem friendly."

He shrugged. "You're Scottish. It's the English dragon-shifters we don't care for."

Interesting. As she fixed her coffee, she glanced at him. "Care to embellish on that statement?"

"They helped the Irish bastards. That's enough."

She wanted to point out it was a long time ago, but held her tongue. Grant might provoke her to say the wrong thing, but with any other male unrelated to her, Faye knew how to keep her temper in check.

Once they each had a coffee, they moved into the smaller living area. Thankfully, it was empty.

Faye sat down in a chair and Adrian took the sofa. After taking a sip, she broke the silence. "If you don't mind the Scots, then why not reach out to Lochguard? I'm sure my clan leader would be honored to meet yours."

He waved a hand in dismissal. "Let's not talk about what our clan leaders are doing. This is my first time in Scotland. You should tell me what to see in the area. Your clan isn't far from here, right?"

She took another gulp of coffee. "No, it's not far, but I'm not sure we'll have much time for sightseeing. The schedule is somewhat aggressive."

Adrian laid an arm on the back of the sofa. "Maybe for you, but not us. This will be like a holiday to me and my compatriot."

She leaned forward. "What do you mean?"

Just as Adrian opened his mouth to answer, Grant's voice drifted from the entrance. "Who's your friend, Faye?"

~ ~ ~

Grant had hoped to leave the building without incident, but as soon as he saw Faye chatting with the tall, handsome dragonman, both man and beast had stopped in their tracks.

Changing course, he reached the entrance to the smaller living area and asked, "Who's your friend, Faye?"

Even though he directed his question to Faye, Grant never took his eyes off the male.

His dragon grunted. *I don't like how he was smiling at Faye. We need to watch him closely.*

The stranger answered before Faye could. "I'm Adrian Conroy of Northcastle. You're Scottish, too, so you must be from Lochguard." Adrian looked to Faye. "I now see why you resisted my offer."

"What offer?" Grant bit out.

Faye narrowed her eyes a second before returning them to normal, conveying that she wanted him to calm down.

Adrian spoke again. "Why, the one where I invited her to my room."

Grant clenched his fist and counted to five. He couldn't afford to punch the Northern Irish bastard and possibly start a feud between the clans.

Faye stood between them. "I don't know what you think you know, Adrian, but Grant is merely my boss." She met his eyes again. "Nothing more."

Her words stung, but given how he'd treated her, Grant couldn't blame her.

He finally tore his gaze away from Faye and moved until he could look into Adrian's eyes again. "Our personal relations shouldn't matter. As long as you stay out of our way and don't endanger our clan member, we should get along fine."

Adrian raised his brows. "I'm not sure I need your reassurance or permission."

"Maybe not, but I heard about the growing number of dragon hunters gathering near Belfast. You may need our help sooner than you think."

"We can handle them. Dragon hunters are nothing more than minor pests," Adrian answered.

"Not accepting help will lead to your downfall, Conroy," Grant stated.

Adrian took a step toward Grant, but Faye moved a little closer to stand between them and said, "How about we tone it down, lads. You're both strong, capable Protectors or you wouldn't be here. If whipping out your penises and comparing them is what it takes to end the bickering, I'll avert my eyes to allow you the pleasure."

Adrian winked. "Looking away isn't what I want, though."

Grant growled, but before he could move closer to Adrian, Faye raised a hand to signal him to stop. Looking him dead in the eye, she murmured, "Enough. I need you to scout the area. Go."

His dragon snarled. *We shouldn't leave her with him.*

We have no claim on her yet.

So you're just going to hand her over on a silver platter?

No, I'm going to do my job and trust Faye. It's time for me to be the rational one again, or you're going to fuck up any chance we have with her.

Before his dragon could reply, Grant constructed a mental maze and tossed his beast inside.

He nodded at Faye. "I'll go and send you a text when I'm done."

The irritation faded from her eyes. "I'll be waiting."

He wished she meant waiting for him, but it was a good start. Grant needed to show Faye he believed in her. Seeing her interact with another strong male made him realize that if he kept pushing her away, he might do so for good.

Forcing his gaze away from Faye, he looked to Adrian. "I hope to chat with you again later. There's much we can learn from each other."

Adrian raised a hand in parting. "I'll keep her safe."

"Faye can take care of herself," Grant stated.

From the corner of his eye, he saw her eyes widen; however, Faye quickly recovered and stood tall. "Of course I can. Maybe I should invite Iris and even Nikki Gray from Stonefire to show Adrian what his clan is missing out on by not having female Protectors."

The corner of Grant's mouth ticked up. Putting those three females together would be a wake-up call for Adrian Conroy. "Aye, we can propose it to Finn once we finish this assignment." He turned toward the door. "You'll hear from me within the hour, Faye."

As Grant exited the bed and breakfast, his dragon banged against the walls of his mental maze. His beast clearly didn't agree with Grant's new tactic.

However, he'd make his dragon accept his choice. Grant wasn't about to ruin his mission by constantly being jealous of males who looked at Faye with desire or interest in their eyes. Only those who believed in her would stand a chance to win her heart. Grant may have to delay the wooing aspect for a bit, but he was patient. Laying the groundwork in the present would help him later on.

~ ~ ~

Cat MacAllister tried to focus on what Lachlan MacKintosh was saying about schedules and events, but as she watched her fellow participants, she itched to take out her phone and snap a few shots. Each of their profiles told a different story. Even if she hadn't met any of them before, a picture could frame the story she wanted to tell; each photograph was its own reality.

Her dragon spoke up. *Then stop thinking about it and do it. Being cautious is boring.*

Says the dragon who wanted to land en route to Inverness to watch the rays of sunlight dancing on a loch, without thinking of the possible danger.

Her beast grunted. *I like pretty things. It gives you ideas for painting.*

However, before she could reply, Lachlan's face filled her visage. With his chin-length black hair framing his jaw and his blue eyes flecked with gold staring straight into hers, all thoughts of the others fled her head. The human male would make an interesting subject. Not just because he was handsome, because he was, but also because he straddled the world between humans and dragon-shifters. That opened a lot of possibilities for what she could shoot or even paint.

His voice cut through her thoughts. "Have you heard a word I said, Ms. MacAllister?"

"Call me Cat. And yes, you were rambling about punctuality and avoiding confrontation."

He raised an eyebrow. "Impressive."

"Why? Can't you do two things at once?"

The second the words left her mouth, she wanted to take them back. Being selected for the exhibition was an honor. The last thing she needed to do was insult the head coordinator.

Lachlan straightened up again. "I can do three, if I concentrate, and maybe even five if I've had a few pints. The more I drink, the more invincible I become."

She resisted breathing a sigh of relief and decided to play along. "So, are you drunk now?"

Dylan chuckled at her side, but Cat never took her eyes away from Lachlan. Yet as he continued to stare without saying a word, Max's voice filled the room. "I'd much rather see a pissed dragon-shifter. Maybe we should all go out for drinks."

Lachlan never took his gaze from Cat. "No drinking to excess." He finally looked to each person in the room. "Remember, you are the public face of all dragon-shifters in the UK. We need this event to go well in Scotland if we're also to go to England, Wales, and Northern Ireland in the future. The director of the DDA is counting on you. Do you understand the importance of being on your best behavior?"

She didn't like being treated like a child, but as the others murmured their assent, she followed suit. It was hard for her not to be the one in charge, like she'd been with her siblings growing up.

Yet as Lachlan glanced at her for a few seconds longer than the others, her dragon took notice. *He's definitely not our sibling.*

And he's most definitely off limits. Besides, what about Dexter?

Her dragon huffed. *He's boring. I don't know why you keep dating him.*

To keep Mum off our backs. Humoring her means more time in our studio without her interference.

But Dexter won't make you happy long term. Have a little fun, like we used to do with Faye when we were younger.

Maybe later. Now, hush unless you want the human to lecture us again.

Her dragon fell silent and Cat went back to studying Lachlan. She wouldn't dare ask him to model for her, so she would just have to memorize his features and sketch them back in her room. Hopefully Faye didn't plan on going to supper straight away because Cat would never be able to concentrate until she unloaded her latest subject onto paper.

And she couldn't wait to sketch Lachlan's cheekbones, his broad shoulders, or trim form. He wasn't as muscled as a dragon-shifter, but he still carried an aura of power and confidence.

That intrigued her.

Half-listening to Lachlan's speech, she proceeded to memorize his body. The trick would be not to get caught gawking.

CHAPTER SEVEN

As Grant soared over the darkening landscape, he studied the ground for anything unusual. Since dragon-shifters could see well in the dark, he didn't worry about the fading light and took his time. He needed to be thorough.

The last place he'd seen his uncle had been near Elgin, which was to the east of Inverness. But that meant little considering his previous sighting had been months ago.

While scrutinizing the landscape, he noted the shape of the trees, hills, and lochs. Despite living his whole life in the Scottish Highlands except during his two years with the British Armed Forces, the beauty of his home country never failed to amaze him.

Since he'd had to free his dragon to shift, his beast grunted and said, *I'd much rather see a different kind of scenery.*

If we weren't one and the same, I'd love to see you ask to admire Faye's scenery. However, I have no desire to be kicked in the bollocks.

She wouldn't do that. At most, she'd sweep our legs out from under us and straddle our chest. Would that be so bad?

The image of Faye's warm body on top of his chest flashed into his mind. He'd try to roll her over and she'd find a way to be on top again.

Things would never be easy with Faye MacKenzie, but Grant looked forward to it. Any other female he'd tried to pursue in the past had lacked Faye's spark. He easily tired of tame and well-behaved. He didn't want someone who tried to please him. His mother had done that with his father and they'd never formed a strong connection. Even when dragon-shifters weren't true mates, they could still have passion.

And Grant wanted plenty of it, but only with a certain female.

If only he hadn't been such a bloody idiot as a young man when he'd said Faye wasn't feminine enough for him.

He beat his wings harder. Being the head Protector of a clan was both easy and challenging. Apart from Finn and the MacKenzies, everyone looked to him for guidance. He wasn't one to dispense advice, so he merely led by example.

Of course, the females only saw the image he projected. Faye was one of the few who had seen him at his worst and still forgiven him in the long run. He was determined to also show her his best.

Finishing his final sweep, he glided around and headed back toward Inverness. He hadn't expected to find any signs of his uncle on the first night, but a part of him was still disappointed.

His beast huffed. *I'm disappointed, too. I was hoping to root out the threat and woo Faye tonight.*

It's going to take more bloody work than one flight over the countryside.

Not everything has to be difficult. Of course, if you merely snogged her a little to show her a preview of what's to come, then I might stop doing this.

His dragon sent a stream of images that all involved Faye naked. Some with her under him, some with her on top, and more than a few with him taking her from behind.

Stop it, dragon. That won't be happening anytime soon.

It will if you kiss her.

And start the frenzy?

So you finally acknowledge she's our true mate.

I'm not stupid. But I also can't risk the frenzy overtaking either of us.

I think she's strong enough to contain it. Aren't you?

Probably, but it's not up for discussion.

His dragon continued to send naked pictures of Faye into his head the whole flight back.

They finally landed in the cordoned section of Inverness Castle's car park, which was the site of the Inverness Sheriff Court and a concealed DDA holding cell. The DDA had determined it to be one of the safest places for them to land and take off from in the city.

Grant imagined his snout shrinking into his nose, his wings melding into his back, and his limbs morphing back into human arms and legs. Once he was human again, he barely noted the red sandstone castle as he walked to the secure lockers at the edge of the protected area. After donning his clothes again, he checked his mobile. There was a text message from Faye: *Cat is dining with the other participants and the DDA's security team. I'm going to the curry place near the river with some of the other dragons. It's the same restaurant as Cat and the others.*

His dragon spoke up again. *We should go and make sure no one tries to take her away from us. Only Stonefire will leave her alone.*

He wanted to dismiss his dragon's thoughts as silly, but couldn't. *I think we should check out the other Protectors. Faye may be strong, but if several of them gang up against her, she won't stand a chance. As much as I'd like to believe Snowridge and Northcastle are allies, I don't have enough information to make that determination.*

I would say that it's unlikely they would attack her, especially if Stonefire is there, but I won't discourage you because I want to see Faye. Although I would be careful not to anger her again.

That will be harder than it sounds.

You like interesting. Faye is a puzzle that we need to solve. I still say we should kiss her.

He ignored his dragon or they would argue about kissing and fucking the entire way to the restaurant.

Since Inverness Castle was situated just above the river walk, Grant jogged down until he wove around the humans going about their business. Restaurants and shops lined the walkway next to the river. If he weren't anxious to find Faye, he'd take a moment to enjoy the lights reflecting off the water.

He went into the first curry place he found, which was up one flight of stairs, on the first floor. Once he reached the top of the stairs, he scanned the room. A hostess walked up to him. "May I help you?"

Grant looked at the human and did his best to keep his face free of his anxiety about finding Faye. "Is your establishment welcoming to dragon-shifters?"

"Aye. Most restaurants in Inverness are. After all, you helped protect the city many years ago during the War."

He nodded, not wanting to get into World War II dragon-shifter battles and victories. "Then I'm looking for a group of dragon-shifters that might be dining here. In particular, I'm looking for a female with curly, brown hair past her shoulders and a tendency to raise her voice."

The woman smiled. "Aye, she's here. We had to move the whole dragon-shifter party to a private room because she was singing a bit loud for the other patrons."

He frowned and spoke to his dragon. *Since when does Faye sing in public?*

There is much we need to learn about her. Hurry up and find her. I want to see her in action.

He focused back on the human. "Could you show me where they are? They should be expecting me."

"Right this way."

They walked past the other tables. He spotted Cat and the other participants toward the back with the DDA male and a few other humans who had to be the DDA's security team. Cat raised a hand at him in greeting and he returned the gesture.

The hostess guided them down a hall to a closed door. While it wasn't that far from Cat's table, he didn't like the distance. He was going to extract Faye from the rest of the group and they could dine at a smaller table in the main dining area.

His beast spoke up again. *I like that plan. We'll have Faye to ourselves.*

More importantly, we can do our jobs.

Before his dragon could speak, the hostess opened the door and Faye's singing voice greeted his ears.

However, he barely noticed that she was singing off key. All he saw was her arms wrapped around a male to either side of her. One of them was the Northern Irish bastard Conroy and the other male was unknown to him.

He was tempted to take her hand and pull her into the hallway. But his dragon chimed in. *I want to listen and watch. She looks so happy.*

Faye smiled as she sang and joy shone in her eyes. In this room, she wasn't Faye MacKenzie, the former head Protector with a bum wing. No, she was merely Faye, the carefree lass having a good time without the usual censure from her family.

He answered his dragon, *Fine. But once she's done with this song, I'm taking her out of here.*

With a growl, Grant stood at the edge of the room and waited for her to finish the song.

Faye hadn't socialized outside the clan since the accident that had damaged her wing. Without her protective brothers, cousin, or mother around, Faye had been able to do as she pleased. So on a whim, she suggested playing a tune on her mobile and doing their own ad hoc karaoke.

She wasn't sure if it was because the others wanted to have a good time or if they simply wanted to embarrass her, but the lads from Northcastle had joined right in.

And since they had been moved to a private room, all three of them were belting out the latest pop tune as loud as they could manage. The two males from Stonefire were more concerned about their food, but the male and female from Wales would occasionally mumble the chorus.

With Adrian and his clan mate, Kaine Ferris, on either side of her, Faye swayed in time to the music. For a brief moment in time, she wasn't a dragonwoman struggling to find her new place in the clan. No, she was just Faye MacKenzie, female Protector and young woman out on the town to have a good time. Maybe next time, she could have a little fun with Cat. They might even be able to set up a weekly date to meet and escape their families for a little while. After all, Faye had learned every which way to sneak out of Lochguard by following her older brothers as a teenager.

As she and the others sang the final notes to the song, Faye gave Adrian and Kaine a pat each on the back. It was then she noticed Grant hovering near the door. "Grant. Good to see you found us. I ordered an extra big portion of tikka masala, in case you're hungry."

Grant didn't so much as smile. "Can I speak with you privately, Faye?"

Adrian chimed in. "Can't it wait, McFarland? We have another song queued up to go and Faye was really looking forward to it."

Faye put up a hand. "It's okay, Adrian. Grant is my boss, after all." Faye skirted round the table. "But let's make it quick. I don't want my naan to get cold."

Grant remained silent as they exited the private room and into the hall. Once the door was shut, he asked, "Why aren't you sitting closer to where Cat is?"

She frowned. "The six-person DDA security team is having supper with the exhibition participants. If there was a problem, they'd sound the alarm and we'd have plenty of time to act."

"I bet Adrian Conroy convinced you to move rooms."

She searched his gaze. "So, now I'm nothing but a starry-eyed adolescent who can't think with anything but my lady parts?" She turned away from him. "I don't have time for this."

Grant took her wrist. She tugged, but his grip was like steel. "You and I have unfinished business."

She glanced over her shoulder. "What? Did you find anything during your flight?"

"Not yet."

"Then I don't understand what the hell you're talking about. Stop being so bloody cryptic."

He tugged her further down the hall and turned her until her back was against the wall. He caged her body with his arms to either side of her torso. Grant's face was close enough she could feel the heat of his breath on her lips. Each whisper of air against her skin sent a tendril of heat straight between her legs.

If only it were as simple as kissing him once to get the male out of her system and going back to work with a clear head.

73

She nearly missed Grant's husky question as he asked, "Are you trying to wind me up on purpose, Faye MacKenzie?"

The gravelly sound of his voice combined with his nearness and heat made Faye's heart thump faster. Her beast growled. *Don't give in to him so easily. He needs to grovel.*

I have no intention of kissing him.

Are you sure?

Her gaze dropped to Grant's firm lips. A small part of her wondered what his serious mouth could do to her. Maybe Grant would let loose when they were alone and naked.

Blinking at that thought, Faye looked back to Grant's deep brown eyes. His pupils flashed between slits and round. Faye had never been good at keeping her mouth shut around Grant, so she asked, "What's your dragon saying?"

Grant leaned an inch closer. "He's talking about you, lass."

As Grant stared, her heart rate increased. She should push him away and go back to the room with the others, but she couldn't find the strength to do it. "Tell me what he's saying, Grant. There shouldn't be secrets between Protectors."

He moved to her ear and she shivered at his hot breath against her skin. "So we're merely clan mates, aye?"

When Grant didn't say anything else, all she could think about was how close his mouth was to her ear. If he nibbled her earlobe, Faye wasn't sure she could walk away without doing something she shouldn't.

Her dragon grunted. *That's right, we shouldn't kiss him. He's an arse.*

At the word "kiss," Faye reached out a finger and traced a figure eight on Grant's chest. She would prefer his lips, but his pec would have to do.

Despite the fabric between them, he sucked in a breath, and she smiled. *But you can't be against teasing him a little.*

Her dragon sighed. *Teasing is fine, but I don't think you can resist him.*

Before she could reply, Grant placed his hands on her ribcage and slowly caressed down to her hips. The action left a trail of fire down her body. Maybe he'd pull her close and drive her mad without so much as a kiss. There were many things he could do without starting the frenzy.

She nearly frowned at that thought and focused back on the situation at hand. However, Grant merely stared at her and kept his hands in place.

Grant moved to meet her eyes again and finally murmured, "Tell me the truth, Faye. What do you think of me?"

"You don't want to know."

"That bad?" The corner of his mouth ticked up and she wanted to trace the curve of his lips. Grant rarely smiled and certainly not in such a sexy manner at her.

She bet every female in the clan noticed when he smiled.

Her dragon huffed. *Why should we care?*

Ignoring her beast, she answered, "Right now, 'bad' isn't the word I'd use."

He raised an eyebrow. "Then what would you choose? Strong? Reliable? Handsome?"

She frowned. "You're not one to fish for a compliment."

He squeezed her hip and she wished his hand would move further down. Of course the blasted male kept it in place as he replied, "No, but the longer I keep you here, the better chance I have of convincing you that I'm the only male you should look at."

"Grant, we—" He ran a hand up her side, her neck, and finally to her jaw. As he stroked her skin, she whispered, "We shouldn't, Grant. It's a bad idea."

Grant continued to brush his fingers against her skin, and each pass sent a rush of warmth between her thighs. He chuckled, and the sound reverberated through her entire body. She couldn't resist him when he laughed.

Grant's husky voice filled her ear. "It's a bad idea, why, exactly?"

He kissed her ear and Faye was grateful for the wall supporting her. Somehow she forced her brain to work. "I'm not ready for a baby, Grant. And I'm not sure I could resist the mate-claim frenzy."

He brushed his lips against her skin once more, and Faye clutched Grant's shirt in her hands to help keep her steady. "You're the strongest female I know. If anyone could contain their beast and keep the frenzy at bay, it's you."

As he nibbled down the length of her neck, Faye debated whether she was strong enough or not. Her beast spoke up again. *It's not a matter of strength. He still needs to grovel.*

Faye wavered on what to do. Grant's lips on her skin set her on fire, and she was close to pulling him against her and kissing the living daylights out of him.

However, before she could make a decision, Lachlan MacKintosh's voice boomed down the hall. "There's a problem. You two need to come with me."

In the next second, Grant stepped away from her and looked at Lachlan. "What happened?"

The human shook his head. "Not here."

Without another word, Lachlan turned around and banged on the door to the private room. Faye barely had time to smooth her hair before Grant said, "Let's go," and entered the room after the human.

Her dragon spoke up. *That was close. You need to stay away from Grant.*

And if I can get him to grovel for you?

That's not important right now. I'm curious to see what's happened.

Pushing aside her memories of Grant kissing her neck, Faye took a deep breath and went into the private room. She could corner Grant later and discuss the possibilities for their future. Faye wasn't completely dead set on pushing the male away, provided they established some ground rules.

Not that she had the faintest idea why she wanted to deal with the grumpy male on a possibly long-term basis.

But figuring out what the hell was going on between her and Grant would have to wait. For the time being, she looked to the human, Lachlan, and waited to see what all the bother was about.

CHAPTER EIGHT

Grant was grateful for Lachlan's interruption. Another minute and he might've allowed his dragon and cock to ruin their assignment.

His beast huffed. *I wasn't trying to ruin it. Taking Faye would allow us to perform better.*

Even though he shouldn't, Grant thought back to how Faye softened under his fingers. Or how she leaned her ear toward his lips, as if asking him to take her lobe between his teeth.

Aye, Lachlan's interruption had prevented him from acting without thinking. He would need to be more vigilant in the future. As much as he wanted Faye in his bed, the clan came first. If he failed his mission, who knew what could happen.

His dragon chimed in. *They haven't acted in months. A week or two more wouldn't matter.*

He couldn't allow his dragon to sway his decision, so Grant ignored him. A week or even a few days could make all the difference in the world when a threat was concerned.

As Faye entered the room, he avoided looking at her. Thankfully Lachlan spoke up as soon as Faye closed the door. "Max Holbrook went to the toilet twenty minutes ago and never came back. He left a brief note in the toilet saying he had an errand to run, but no one saw him leave the restaurant."

He shot a look at Faye and raised his brows slightly. If they had been alone, she would've stuck her tongue out at him. Grant had been right about needing to be closer to the DDA party in the restaurant.

Aaron Caruso from Stonefire asked, "I'm not sure why you're talking to us about it. He's not any of our charges."

Lachlan's voice remained calm as he replied, "I'm aware of this fact, Mr. Caruso. However, the exhibition is set to debut tomorrow evening. If we can't find Max Holbrook, we can't hold the event."

Faye spoke up. "Why? All of his artifacts should already be in the DDA's custody, aye?"

"Yes, but this event can't be tinged with scandal. I will postpone it indefinitely unless we find him."

"And by 'we' you mean 'us,'" Grant stated.

Lachlan met his gaze. "Dragon-shifters see better at night than humans. It's only logical that I ask for your help."

Adrian chimed in. "You're not asking, you're telling us. You should still ask first."

"We're all working as a team for the time being," Lachlan answered. "I'm not about to waste time when I know you want this event to be a success, just as I do."

Grant grunted in agreement. If the exhibition were canceled, Grant and Faye would have to return to Lochguard and he wouldn't be able to look for his uncle or the others. For Lochguard's sake, Grant needed to ensure the event opened on time.

"Was the note in his handwriting?" Faye asked. "Given how important the exhibition is, it could be one of our enemies that took him."

Lachlan stood a little taller. "Max has a tendency to do this. Before we selected him, we vetted him thoroughly and looked

79

into his past. He's gone to the toilet and left a note before disappearing on digs before. And before you ask, my security team kept an eye on the hallway where the toilets are located. Since we're on the first floor, we didn't worry about any windows."

Aaron spoke up. "And that was probably your mistake."

Lachlan ignored the Stonefire dragonman. "My security team will look into nefarious possibilities and sweep the area nearby. I need your help in looking further afield in case he did disappear to do some digging."

Grant could tell some of the dragon-shifters were on the fence about helping because of their dubious expressions. As much as he wished Lachlan would plan with them, he wasn't about to let the whole event fall to pieces at this stage. He looked to Aaron. "What do you say, Caruso? Shall we stretch our wings? Unless you're getting too old and need to take a nap."

Aaron was a few years older than Grant and he ribbed the English dragon-shifter whenever he could about it.

Aaron took one last bite of his curry and stood. "Quinn and I will fly circles around you. I only hope you can catch up."

"We'll see, old man." Grant looked to Adrian of Northcastle. "And you lot?"

The Northern Irish dragonman shrugged. "I suppose we could help otherwise Faye and I will never get the chance to sing that song together."

His dragon chimed in. *Ignore him. Faye was about to kiss us in the hall, not him.*

The Welsh dragonman, Wren, joined in. "We'll help as well, although we don't know the Scottish countryside as well as you."

"No worries. We'll form a grid pattern and divide up the work." He looked to Lachlan. "Can we entrust our clan members to your security team? I doubt Max is part of some nefarious scheme to capture everyone, but I want to play it safe."

"Are they going to pay attention this time?" Adrian drawled.

Lachlan moved his hands to behind his back and gripped them. "Once everyone is inside our accommodations, it would take an army to break our defenses. They will be well protected."

Grant's dragon spoke up. *I believe his words.*

So do I. Maybe we should suggest that all meals are taken inside the B&B from now on.

Grant focused back on the human. "In case Max did go off digging, do you know of another archaeologist you could call? If there's a special dig site nearby, even a fabled one, we need to know."

"Of course. I know someone in Wiltshire. Let me call her whilst you organize the search," Lachlan answered.

Before Grant could do more than nod, Lachlan took out his mobile and went into the hall.

Adrian's voice filled the room. "It looks as if you've taken charge, mate, but why do you trust him so much?"

Grant shrugged. "He has the most to lose if the exhibition fails. That should motivate him to do whatever it takes, which includes keeping our clan members safe."

Aaron jumped in. "I agree with Grant. Arguing will only take away precious time that could be used finding the annoying human." He motioned toward Grant. "What's your plan?"

Grant would have to keep an eye on Adrian. He didn't need dissent among the dragon-shifters. "Since there are four pairs of us, we'll each cover one compass direction. Since Faye and I know the landscape better, we'll take the direction with the most potential dig sites. We'll check in every fifteen minutes until we find him."

81

The Welsh dragonman spoke up again. "We might not find him, McFarland."

Grant looked the male dead in the eye. "We need to. Otherwise, you can explain to all of our clan leaders why we failed with this assignment."

Since Grant didn't know Wren all that well, he wasn't sure if the male would challenge him or fall in line. After a few beats, the Welsh dragonman bobbed his head. "Fine, we'll look until we find him. But if I do spot him, I'm not going to be gentle bringing him back. He's not part of my clan."

"Fair enough," Grant replied.

Lachlan walked back inside. "My contact provided me with a list of possible sites, all related to dragon-shifter history. I have them here."

The human turned his mobile around and Grant scanned the list. One stuck out to him. "Craig Phadrig is the easiest to access of the lot. It's to the west."

Adrian asked, "How do you know that?"

"I visited the place as a boy. It's an old fort and there are trails that take you to the top. While's it's famous for the Pictish occupation, there's been a lot of speculation that dragon-shifters once helped protect the area during its heyday. But none of that matters. I have a feeling Max would love nothing more than to do a little digging at night, without any prying eyes. Of course, he'll have to take a taxi or a car, so we might be able to head him off. Faye and I will take the west of the city where the fort is. Northcastle can take the east, Stonefire the north, and Snowridge the south. Any questions?" When no one said anything, he continued. "Then let me give you my mobile phone number as well as Faye's. We'll coordinate the information."

Not giving anyone a chance to protest, Grant rattled off the numbers. He then looked to Lachlan. "Just make sure the DDA knows what we're doing. I don't want to be shot down by mistake."

"I'll tell them as long as you promise to tell me directly when you find Max. The DDA will want to find a way to contain him. If he indeed ran off to do some illegal digging, then he'll be assigned a team to watch over him."

Or, rather, babysit him. "That's fine. Humans aren't my jurisdiction. You can do what you like with him," Grant replied. "But I do expect you to watch over our clan members whilst we're away. And try not to lose any more of the participants."

Lachlan clenched his jaw, but it was the only outward sign that Grant had struck a nerve. The human replied a beat later. "As I mentioned, we'll be going back to the B&B, where it's more secure. No one will be allowed in or out until you all return."

"Good. Then let's not waste any more time. Faye, come with me."

As Grant made his way out of the room, he didn't bother to check that Faye followed. He knew she would.

His dragon spoke up. *Adrian looked less than pleased.*

Someone needed to step up, and I did. The Northern Irish dragonman can glare at me later, after we find the troublesome human.

I'll make sure to flash my teeth at Max. Maybe it'll scare him into cooperating.

I doubt it, but we can still try.

His dragon fell silent and Grant picked up his pace. The sooner he found the human, the sooner he could corner Faye again and pick up where they'd left off. Even if he wasn't going to claim her until the mission was complete, there was a lot he could do without initiating the mate-claim frenzy. Once Faye had a taste, he was sure she'd come around to the idea, especially if he could contain his jealousy and some of his alpha tendencies. If he wanted Faye, he needed to work on giving her room to thrive.

His dragon chimed in. *Now you're trying to take credit for my ideas.*

Since we are one and the same, they've always been our ideas.

That's not quite true, and you know it. Next time, I'll keep my ideas to myself until I can wrestle away control from you.

Grant resisted sighing. *How about we just focus on retrieving the human? We work best together when it comes to tracking. It's also something you like to do.*

His beast paused a second before replying, *Okay. But only because of what awaits us when we return.*

As his dragon fell silent, Grant hoped his beast wasn't coming up with a plan of his own to win over Faye. His beast could be persistent and liked to take control. Grant wasn't sure how Faye would respond to that approach.

~ ~ ~

Faye had known Grant was a leader, but since her accident, she'd had little chance to witness him in action. He was far more commanding than she remembered from their time in the army.

She was a big enough person to admit he was a good choice for head Protector.

Her beast chimed in. *I never doubted his ability to lead, only his ability to notice other people's feelings.*

We've known Grant our whole lives. He's never really been someone who displayed his own feelings, let alone was able to gauge others' easily. His family wasn't as open as ours.

He's lived on Lochguard most of his life. There's no excuse for his behavior.

84

THE DRAGON WARRIOR

Then let me ask you this: Would you want him to act like our family? I don't know about you, but living with someone like one of our brothers or cousin, Finn, would be...tiring.

Her dragon paused a beat before answering, *Maybe.*

Good, then we're on the same page.

I still think he needs to grovel.

She tried not to laugh at her dragon's petulant tone. *I didn't say I was going to sleep with him or have his babies. But it was nice to have his attention for a while. Just imagine what all of his intensity could do if focused on us.*

Speaking of the devil, Grant looked over his shoulder at her. Faye quickly pushed aside thoughts of Grant's attentions and tilted her head. "So, great leader, care to tell me when you went to Craig Phadrig and how you know so much about it?"

Grant grunted. "Now's not the time."

"We're on the way to the castle to shift. There's not much else we can do before that. You have a minute or two. I know silence is your default setting, but how about humoring me?"

He checked his mobile before answering, "Dad liked to watch that human archaeology show, *Time Team*, when it used to air on the telly. It was the only time the entire family sat down together to watch anything. Most of the time he was busy fixing or building houses, but on the rare occasion, he would take me and my brother to archaeological sites to look for old dragon-shifter artifacts. Craig Phadrig was one of them."

She couldn't remember ever seeing the McFarlands out together as a family. Truth be told, she didn't know much about them. She hoped to rectify that shortly.

Her dragon spoke up. *And why is that? I knew it. You do want to have his babies. Just know that I won't let you give in to him too easily.*

Ignoring her beast, she caught up to Grant so that they walked side by side. "You've never talked much about your family, even before some of them left the clan. Not even to me. Why?"

He glanced at her. "No one wants to hear about difficult times."

She touched his bicep. "I want you to be able to tell me anything, Grant. I mean it. Everyone should have someone they can confide in."

For a few beats, he remained silent, and she wondered if she'd pushed too far.

His voice filled the evening's air again. "Only if you do the same, lass. You might be outgoing and laughing on the outside, but I'm not the only one with demons in my past."

She frowned. "I'm not sure what you mean."

"You never met your dad, Faye. He died the night you were born. I'm sure it haunts you from time to time."

When Faye's mother had been in labor, her dad, Jamie MacKenzie, had raced home during a storm to be with his pregnant mate. Since he had been killed by lightning en route, he'd never seen his only daughter.

Faye tried not to think about her father much. Doing so almost seemed like a betrayal to her mum, who had worked doubly hard to be enough for her children. Still, she wished he'd survived the storm. While all of the stories said her dad had been a little more serious, like Fergus, he had treasured his children and mate.

Her mum had recently found a second chance at love, but for too many years Lorna MacKenzie had been lonely. Faye had always wondered if her mum thought Faye was partly to blame.

Her dragon growled. *She doesn't. She's said it before.*

Maybe. At least she has Ross.

Then why do you worry about things you can't change?

Not wanting to answer, she looked back to the dragonman who knew so much about her.

Damn Grant and his knowledge. Sometimes knowing a male your whole life made things difficult. "I think about him sometimes, but I had my mum. Everyone on Lochguard knows your mother's heart broke when your dad left. There's a big difference between someone leaving by choice and someone being ripped from your side because of reasons beyond your control." Grant merely grunted and Faye continued, "I think that once we go back home, you need to invite her over to a MacKenzie family dinner. Your brother, too. All three of you could do with a night of mayhem."

He shook his head. "I'm not sure being hit by a flying bread roll would lift my mum's spirits."

She grinned. "Maybe not. But if I can convince her to do some throwing of her own, it just might. I'm sure Fraser would sacrifice himself to the cause."

The corner of Grant's mouth ticked up. "He did release some rabbits into my mother's garden as a lad. Mum has a long memory."

Faye laughed. "Then it's settled. You all are coming to dinner."

Looking at Grant, smiling faintly in the moonlight, she decided she liked him better like this, when he was honest and somewhat open. She had a feeling he hadn't laughed enough over the course of his life. In that instant, Faye made a vow to ensure he laughed a lot more in the future.

It didn't matter that a lot of her plans involved offering Fraser up as a sacrifice to her nefarious plots. After their childhood, her brother had a lot of payback coming his way.

They reached the edge of the fenced off area near the castle. The smile faded from Grant's face and his expression morphed into a more serious one.

It was back to work. Maybe someday they would have a respite from trouble and pain and she could show Grant a good time.

Grant picked up his pace. "We can discuss dinner plans later. For now, we need to find the irritating human. I'm not about to let Cat's hard work be taken lightly."

As Grant stripped and stowed his clothes, Faye barely noticed his nakedness. All she could think about was Grant's childhood and how he cared about Cat's success.

There was more to Grant McFarland than what she'd thought.

Her dragon sighed. *You're not going weak in the knees for him, are you?*

I'm not saying one way or the other, but why are you so dead set against him? Usually when it comes to true mates, dragons can't keep quiet about sex and babies.

Because we've worked too hard to give it all up. Grant may be sexy and clever, but he's overprotective. A bairn someday would be nice, but both of us would go crazy staying home and doing nothing else. Grant would try to force us to stay home.

Her dragon was most likely correct.

Yet as Grant turned toward her and motioned for her to undress, she knew she wanted to know more about the male fate had chosen for her. Maybe, deep down, he was more understanding about gender roles. Faye may no longer be a soldier, but her heart was still that of a warrior. All she had to do was convince Grant of that, too.

Stripping off her clothes, Faye stored them inside a locker and imagined her body morphing into her blue dragon form. She would start convincing him straight away. If Max Holbrook was anywhere near Craig Phadrig, Faye would find him.

CHAPTER NINE

For the first time in months, Lachlan MacKintosh was tempted to have a drink.

He'd been sober for ten years, in large part to implementing structure into every aspect of his life to prevent a relapse. Planning events had been his calling and he'd worked his arse off to secure the first official outreach program by the British DDA.

And yet, all of his planning had been foiled by one rogue archaeologist.

A soft, feminine Scottish voice filled his ear. "Don't worry, everything will be fine. Grant and Faye are some of the best Protectors in the world."

He looked over to see the dark blue eyes of Cat MacAllister. "Have you met every Protector in the world?"

"No."

"Then don't say you know for certain."

She raised an eyebrow. "Someone's crotchety this evening."

"Crotchety is something my gran would say. How old are you again?"

Cat rolled her eyes. "You sound like my brother Connor."

While he'd perused all of the participants' files closely, he'd looked over Cat's again right before supper. She had tried to hide it, but he'd caught her staring at him. He wondered why. "Then

Connor sounds like a fine lad. Embellishments can often hide the truth."

He'd done it often enough when all he could think about was his next drink.

She searched his eyes. "Aye, but sometimes we want to hide the truth. Only then can you help someone forget the present and make them laugh."

"And again, you sound like a grandmother, but this time, as if imparting wisdom to a younger generation. Odd, considering I'm older than you."

"Some of us grow up faster than others." Before he could ask her to clarify, the corner of her mouth ticked up. "If you think that was bad as far as advice, you should meet my granddad. He wouldn't be above dropping boulders on someone's barn to get their attention."

"What are you talking about?"

However, before she could reply, one of the DDA security team motioned for him to meet them in the hall.

Lachlan looked back to Cat. "Thank you for your reassurances, but I have matters that require my attention. If you'll excuse me."

As he turned to leave, he heard Cat whisper, "It would take less time to say, 'I have shit to do.'"

He chanced a glance over his shoulder, and Cat's face was one of pure innocence. She even raised her brows in question.

Shaking his head, Lachlan went into the hall. He knew working with artists was going to be different than the bureaucracy and campaign events he was used to, but he was quite certain no one had ever suggested he swear as a matter of efficiency. In his experience, most enjoyed the formality and praise.

He wondered if all dragon-shifters acted like Cat MacAllister. In all his time working with the DDA, he'd only focused on the human public relations side. For the most part, women were inspectors since human sacrifices tended to open up to other women. There were few chances for men to visit the dragon clans, let alone interact with them unless they were in the armed forces.

However, with Rosalind Abbott in charge of the Department of Dragon Affairs, he had a feeling a lot more changes would be coming and he'd be seeing plenty of dragon-shifters in the near future.

But first things first, he needed to ensure his inaugural dragon-related event went smoothly. Otherwise, he'd never be given another.

Stopping in the hall, he looked to Arjun, the head of the DDA's security team. "Is there any new information?"

The man's Birmingham accent filled the hall. "It's too soon to hear back from the dragons on patrol, but one of my contacts spotted a man wearing a worn leather jacket to the west of here. I think the Lochguard bloke was right about where Holbrook went."

"Good. Then we'll wait for their call. In the meantime, have you found someone to watch over him?"

"I was talking with my team and we think he should be assigned a dragon-shifter."

"Explain."

"Well, if he tries to run off, the dragon can easily scoop him up. Besides, Holbrook seems fascinated with them. Maybe that will tame his wanderlust for a bit."

Lachlan nodded. "It's a good idea. I'll talk to the Protectors once they return. For now, do another perimeter check. We can't risk anyone else trying to leave or come in."

"Yes, sir."

With that, Arjun disappeared down the hall.

Lachlan debated going back into the main living room, but decided against it. He couldn't afford to be distracted by Cat MacAllister and tales of her strange family. His assistant could look after them.

Besides, he would need to report to his superior at the DDA as soon as Holbrook was found. He needed to prepare and smooth things over. He'd done it many times before, but when things tended to stray from the plan with dragon-shifters, his superiors would sometimes overreact.

However, before heading upstairs, he did take one last peek into the living room through the window on the door. He saw Cat laughing at something Dylan from Stonefire said. He wondered what his life would be like if he could afford to be carefree and take things as they came.

Focus on your work. Lachlan knew what lay ahead if he deviated from his routine and organized lifestyle. He'd relapse and end up drinking.

And that was something he vowed to never do again.

Turning away from the laughter, he went back to work.

~~~

Grant hovered above the clearing on the hill where the fort had once stood long ago. There weren't any lights glowing and to human eyes, the pitch darkness would be almost impossible to navigate without a torch. He wondered if Holbrook had the skill to climb the place and rummage in the blackness.

There was just enough room at the top of the hill for Grant to touch his feet to the ground and fold his wings to his back. Faye was keeping an eye on the surrounding area from the air. If she found anything, she would give a specific series of low roars to tell him and vice versa if he needed assistance.

After laying down the small satchel he'd clutched in his front limb, he imagined his body shrinking, and Grant stood in his human form a few seconds later. Thanks to it being early summer, he could wander the hilltop naked and not end up with hypothermia. He picked up the small pack that contained his phone and took off toward the fort's boundary wall.

Grant watched where he walked and avoided stepping on anything that could give away his location. Max had no military training that Grant was aware of, but just in case he was working with a partner, Grant wasn't taking any chances. While the human seemed sincere in his interest of unlocking history, there were many humans in the world who may want his skills and force him to do their bidding.

As he made his way silently around the edge of where the fort once stood, he kept an eye out for anything unusual. But as he went, no one jumped out of the trees or tried to shoot him. Tracking Max was more time consuming than usual since the area was frequented by hikers and he couldn't simply look for broken branches or footprints. Instead, every fifteen or twenty seconds, he paused and listened for the slightest sign of another person.

The faint breeze blew the branches of the trees, but he pushed past that and listened for the minutest details. If Max Holbrook was stealthier than him, Grant would eat his own shoe.

His beast huffed. *Hurry up and find him.*

Ignoring his dragon, Grant continued around the perimeter of where the fort's walls once stood. When he reached the area assumed to be the rear, there was a male grunt. Sweeping the area with his eyes, Grant finally spotted movement a few feet beyond the tree line.

Careful to keep a wide berth, Grant finally saw the crouched form of Max Holbrook. He looked to be using his trowel to uncover something in the dirt.

As soon as Grant was close enough he could tackle the human to the ground if need be, he said, "What the bloody hell are you doing?"

Max didn't stop his actions. "Looking for proof of a dragon-shifter settlement in the post-Pictish era."

The human continued to dig with his trowel in the dark. He was fairly certain the male was working alone since no one else had made their presence known. Grant stated, "You can't possibly see anything."

Max glanced up, and Grant finally noticed the strange goggles. "A friend of mine invented these. Even if they're not as clear, they're less bulky than standard night vision goggles and work well enough for what I need." He looked back toward the ground. "Although I could do without seeing your naked body. Didn't you bring some clothes with you?"

His dragon growled. *Why does he seem so unconcerned? He must know we're here to cart him away.*

I don't know. He's odd. That's all I can say.

Grant wanted to send a text to let the others know he'd found Max, but given the human's unpredictability, Grant wanted him in custody first.

He took a step closer. "Your slipping away put everyone on high alert. There was even a theory that you weren't working alone. You can't stay here. We need to head back."

"Of course I'm alone. I had no choice but to sneak off and come here. Word is that illegal artifact dealers are targeting this spot. If I don't find what's needed, it could be lost to history."

His beast spoke up again. *Okay, I almost admire him.*

I don't want to know.

Grant took another step. "Maybe the DDA can negotiate something on your behalf. After all, Craig Phadrig is a scheduled monument. The government will protect it."

Max never stopped his work. "Much like how they protect you from dragon hunters and the Dragon Knights? How well is that working out for you?"

Grant growled. "I don't have time to argue. I was being polite, but I'm not above carrying you back to Inverness Castle against your will."

"A-ha! This is what I was hoping for." Max removed something from the dirt. "Isn't she a beauty?"

"It looks like a dirt-covered rock."

"Maybe you're the one who can't see in the dark." He held up the object and wiped away some more of the dirt. "It's a pottery shard with an early version of Mersae on it. I'll need to clean it up more to decipher the meaning."

Mersae was the old dragon-shifter language, which in modern times was only used for special occasions or when they didn't want humans to overhear a conversation. "That's grand, but if you think I'm going to wait here while you dig up some more ancient rubbish, then you're in for a surprise."

Max picked something else up out of the dirt. "Take me back gently, so as not to damage my finds, and I'll go quietly. These pieces might be enough to convince the government to protect this spot from the money-hungry bastards who would merely sell it to a rich toff."

"Who would buy that?"

"I'm starting to understand why there aren't many dragon-shifter archaeologists. You lot don't seem interested in learning about the past."

"We are, but possessions hold less meaning. We've had everything burned or destroyed many times over."

Max waved a hand. "Still not a good enough excuse."

Grant clenched his jaw. He could toss the human across the way without breaking a sweat, but he seemed unconcerned. How Max had survived this long, he didn't know.

His dragon's voice was tinged with amusement when he said, *The human diverts me.*

I don't care if he wins your heart and you wish to sign over your unborn child. He's put the mission in danger. I won't let it happen again.

You're just grumpy because you want to kiss Faye's skin some more.

You don't want the same?

A few minutes observing the strange human won't hurt anyone.

Placing his hand on Max's shoulder, Grant ordered, "Stand up. We're heading back."

Max gently wrapped his pottery shards in some cloth and placed them in his satchel. "Remember what I said—you need to be gentle with me. These finds may change the history of Inverness."

Grant was doubtful, but refrained from commenting. "Then don't try to run away. I will tackle you to the ground, if necessary. And you'll be responsible for destroying history."

As he guided Max away from his dig spot, Grant made a loud, high-pitched whistle. After a minute, Faye's blue dragon form landed in the middle of the hill.

Once Grant and Max were close enough, he said, "Find and signal the others that I found Holbrook. To stop his whining, I'm going to take him back by car." She gestured toward his naked body. "I have some trousers in my satchel. We'll return to the B&B as soon as I can manage."

With a nod, Faye jumped into the air and slowly ascended into the sky. Before Grant could maneuver Max toward the trail that would lead to the bottom of the hill, Max's voice filled the air. "She flies strangely."

He had no idea how Max could tell Faye was a she in the darkness unless he'd been purposefully staring where he shouldn't. Grant pushed until the human started walking. "That's none of your concern."

"Was she born that way? Or was she injured? While it's not my specialty, I've always been fascinated by dragon bones. However, I've had the devil of a time studying the bones of dragon-shifters on my own. There weren't any reliable books I could find, just rubbish ones about the magical properties of ground-up bone. I could use any instruction you could provide."

His dragon chuckled. *Yes, you're such an expert. Why don't you help him? Imagine if you told him that we did have magic bones. Who knows what he'd do then.*

Grant knew as much about bones as he did baking, which was nothing. *They aren't magical. Shut it, dragon.*

He lightly pushed Max's shoulder. "Just keep walking. Talking wasn't part of the bargain."

Max continued as if Grant hadn't said anything. He gestured toward the sky, where Faye had gone. "Maybe she'll let me take a look. She's much friendlier than you."

"Friendly won't necessarily save you. Irritate her and she may kick your arse."

"So she's a feisty one. Much like the purple dragon from before. I never learned her name."

"Iris. And I'd watch out for her, too. She was close to dropping you into a loch."

"I'm not sure why. I was waxing on about gender roles of dragon-shifters through the centuries and how females were once the fiercest warriors. She should've enjoyed that."

He grunted and picked up their pace. He wasn't going to encourage the human.

However, Max didn't take his hint of silence. "It's quite fascinating, actually. If what I've discovered in ruins and by piecing together artifacts is correct, the dragon leader who faced the Roman invaders of Britain and managed to negotiate a fair treatment was a female. It's hard to tell, but I think she became queen of all dragon-shifters living on the isle of Great Britain at the time."

Grant recalled some vague history lesson as a teenager about Queen Alviva. "I hate to break it to you, but we know that already."

"Ah, but did you know she handpicked the strongest, cleverest Roman generals and wealthiest villa owners to sire her children?"

"No, but—"

"Well, then let me tell you how I came to this conclusion. It all started with a visit to the Cotswolds...."

As Max droned on about late night digs that were probably illegal, Grant decided to just let the human talk. He seemed to do it without requiring participation, allowing Grant to keep an eye out for the artifact thieves Max had mentioned.

All he wanted to do was deliver the human safely and seek out Faye. Only then could he focus back on his mission to root out the Lochguard traitors. History would do little to help him accomplish that task.

CHAPTER TEN

The next morning, Faye stretched her arms over her head and stared out the third-story window of her room. If she tilted her head just enough, she could catch more than the brick facade of the building next door and see a patch of cloudy gray sky.

Since no one had pounded on her door during the night, Grant and Max must've made it back safely. Good thing considering Faye had slept like the dead. It had been many months since she'd flown that much in a single day. Her wing would probably still ache if she shifted.

Her beast yawned. *It was good practice. You should find Grant and discover what happened. Maybe we'll see some of the others at breakfast, too.*

Rolling her eyes, Faye rose out of bed. *I know you fancy Adrian a bit, but it's not going to happen, dragon.*

Why not? He would be sex with no strings attached. I like that idea. And Grant?

What about him? You know he's still not my favorite person.

Faye sighed. She had to be the only dragon-shifter in existence who had an inner dragon that wanted to shag someone else when their true mate was within shouting distance. *Well, too bad. I'm going to talk with him before any of the others. And before you try to make a fuss, know that I'll find a way to delay seeing your dragonman of the moment as long as possible if you keep interrupting my conversation with Grant.*

With a growl, her dragon curled up and feigned sleep.

Faye quickly showered, dressed, and walked out the door. She was about to knock on Grant's room when Aaron's door opened. "He's not in there."

She frowned. "Then where is he?"

Aaron shrugged. "He dropped off the human and then went for a late-night flight. I wanted to ask him something this morning, but Grant never answered the door or his mobile phone. I was hoping you knew where he was."

Faye took out her phone, but there was nothing from Grant. "I'll look into it."

Not giving Aaron a chance to say another word, Faye raced down the stairs. She scanned the breakfast room, but there was no sign of Max or Grant.

She made a beeline for Lachlan, who was talking to his assistant. Not waiting for a natural pause, she said, "I need to talk with you, Mr. MacKintosh."

Lachlan raised his eyebrows. "By your tone, it must be important." He nodded at the female assistant. "You can handle the morning meeting and walk-through, Mia."

The human male guided Faye to the hallway and raised an eyebrow. "So? Tell me what's on your mind, Ms. MacKenzie."

Her dragon huffed. *This one is too polite. Even though he's handsome, I don't want to sleep with him.*

Ignoring her beast, Faye answered Lachlan's question. "I need to talk with Max Holbrook. Where is he staying?"

"He's being watched by my security team until a suitable dragon-shifter guard can be located."

"When was this decided?"

"Last night. Your clan member, Grant, went to fetch his candidate."

She frowned. "The bastard could've told me."

Lachlan cleared his throat. "We were trying to do it in secret. The DDA is already nervous about having eight dragon-shifter Protectors traveling the length and breadth of Scotland. Adding a ninth might stir up protest. I've been assured of your clan member's discretion."

Faye opened her mouth to reply, but Grant's voice filled the hallway. "Aye, Iris can hold her tongue."

Faye whipped around and Iris raised a hand in greeting. Faye nodded in return before taking Grant's arm and guiding him to the side. She whispered, "You could've told me what you were up to."

"Why? Were you worried about me?"

At the smugness in his tone, Faye raised her chin. "No. But others were looking for you. The last thing we need to do is create a panic, especially after Max's disappearance last night."

"Calm down, lass. You were dead asleep when I checked into your room."

"Don't tell me that you picked my lock."

He shrugged. "I wanted to make sure you were fine. That was a lot of flying yesterday."

It was on the tip of Faye's tongue to deny the aches in her body, but decided truthfulness might help her in the long run. "Aye, but it was a great chance to build up muscle. By the end of this tour, you might just allow me to fight again."

"Maybe." He turned toward Lachlan and Iris and raised his voice. "Iris, this is Lachlan MacKintosh. He can show you to Max's room."

Grant and Lachlan must've discussed the arrangement the night before because the DDA employee left without another word.

"Why Iris?" she asked.

"She already knows him and has an idea of what to expect. Besides, if he runs off, Iris can find him without batting an eyelash."

Even Faye was envious of Iris's tracking skills. "Yes, but what did she demand in return? Watching over Max can't be high on her list of love-to-do activities."

"She wanted to invite dragon-shifters from friendly countries to participate in a tracking competition."

"And Finn agreed to this?"

"Aye, although I'm not sure he'll remember. The best time to extract a promise out of Finlay Stewart is when he's just woken up and will agree to almost anything if you're not a stranger."

She would say it was evil, but Faye had done it herself a few times in the past. After all, Finn had moved in with her family when he was sixteen, the day after his parents were murdered. Growing up together had given Faye time to learn the current clan leader's quirks, much to his chagrin.

Grant placed a hand on her lower back and Faye barely prevented herself from sucking in a breath. Somehow the platonic touch of a friend had morphed into a tingly heat that made her lose her mind.

Her beast chimed in. *Ignore it and find the other dragonmen.*

Glancing up, Faye's heart rate ticked up at the liquid heat in Grant's gaze. If he leaned down to kiss her, Faye didn't think she'd push him away.

~~~

Grant hadn't slept in over twenty-four hours. If he were in his right mind, he should eat a quick bacon butty and head off to bed.

Yet all he had thought about during his flight from Lochguard to Inverness in the wee hours of the morning was how much he wanted to see Faye. Not just to talk about strategies with regards to Max's mention of artifact thieves, but to see her smile. After a long night, he could use some of Faye's enthusiasm to get through the day. Forget caffeine; Faye was fast becoming his drug of choice.

His dragon spoke up. *I know the real reason. Nothing would energize us more than to strip her naked and come inside her.*

Your logic is fuzzy this morning, dragon. Frenzies last at least a week.

Yes, but frenzies always give us extra energy.

But only for sex.

So? When Faye needed to sleep, we could work.

Not wanting to argue further, Grant took Faye's chin between his fingers and merely listened to her heavy breathing and thumping heart. He imagined her naked as she rode him, her breasts bouncing as she dug her nails in his chest. He must've been a bloody blind idiot to ever say she wasn't feminine enough.

True, she wasn't the high heels and short skirt type of female, but Grant much preferred Faye's strength. No other female's body would call to him as much as hers.

And not just because of the frenzy. She was perfectly curved in all the right places. It was taking everything he had not to cup her arse and pull her close.

Faye's husky whisper interrupted his thoughts. "You should get some sleep before we head to where the event is being held."

Her words were like someone had tossed cold water over his head, reminding him of why he was in Inverness in the first place. "I could survive another day without rest if I had to."

She raised a brown eyebrow. "This coming from the male who always bangs on about how sleep is the most important requirement for quick reflexes and a quick mind?"

He sighed. "So even though I'm in charge, you're going to scold me?"

"Of course. Remember, when it's just you and me, there is no superior. Besides, if we aren't successful with the opening night, then we won't have a chance to complete all aspects of our mission." Her voice softened. "I know how important it is to you that we succeed. Just stop arguing and get some rest, Grant. I can handle watching Cat. I'm not going to repeat my mistake from the restaurant."

With any other Protector, Grant might've lectured them about duty to reinforce their determination. But he knew Faye wouldn't make the same mistake again. Ever since she'd been shot out of the sky and injured her wing, Faye was in constant competition with herself. He only hoped one day she would allow herself to win and accept her actions as good enough.

His dragon spoke up. *You worry too much. Faye is stronger now. Strong enough to resist the frenzy if we kiss her.*

Not this again.

Although Grant secretly admitted that he'd sleep more soundly if Faye were at his side.

His dragon sat in smug silence. Grant ignored him to answer Faye. "I'll sleep for a few hours provided you don't take Cat off the premises. I'll also need you to check in with Iris and fill her in on everything."

"I can do that." She gave him a playful shove. "Now, go get some sleep. I can't keep watch over Cat and scout the surrounding areas for threats. I need my wingman."

"Your wingman? I rather thought it would be the other way around."

"Who's keeping track of nuance? We're a team, so accept it."

Being considered a team was a start, although Grant hoped he would one day be more than that.

He nearly blinked. He was spending far too much time thinking about wanting Faye or what she looked like naked. He definitely needed some sleep. Maybe then he could focus on what was important—rooting out the dragon-shifter traitors.

Releasing his hold on her, he stepped back. "Wake me in three hours. I have a few things to discuss."

"Care to give me a hint?"

"Something Holbrook said. Why I care, I don't know. But I have little respect for artifact thieves."

"That sounds promising. I could do with a good old fashioned hunt and takedown."

"Faye."

"Okay, so no solo takedown. Maybe Iris would help me." He growled, and Faye grinned. "It was worth a shot."

"Just try to focus on our current mission before thinking of another one."

"I'll try my best." She motioned with her hands. "Now go. If I could carry you up the stairs, I would toss you over my shoulder and do so. But I can't."

Grant should dismiss Faye's comment and get some much-needed rest. However, he decided not to fight the urge to tease her.

The corner of his mouth ticked up. "I'd like to see you attempt it. Maybe your hand would even slip to my arse."

She rolled her eyes. "Yes, because grabbing your behind is the most important thing on my plate right now."

He leaned forward. "Maybe it should be."

For a few seconds, they merely stared into one another's eyes. Her pupils flashed to slits and back. Maybe he was winning over her dragon.

His beast spoke up again. *Why do we need to win her over? We're true mates. She's probably begging for our cock.*

I'm not sure about that, dragon. Faye's beast has always been unpredictable.

It was Faye who finally broke the silence. "If you're that knackered, then I can call Adrian and Kaine to carry you up the stairs."

He grunted. "I would rather jump into a pit of lava first."

She grinned. "Since there's no lava in Scotland, does that mean you want their help? I know you'd never leave the country and abandon your clan."

"Faye Cleopatra, stop being ridiculous."

"How long have you known me and my family? I'm actually one of the calmest ones. I can call Fraser down here and lock you in a room with him for three hours. Then you'll understand what I mean."

Fraser MacKenzie probably had more marks on his record than anyone else on Lochguard when it came to causing trouble. Well, with the exception of old Cal and Archie, who kept trying to destroy each other's farms.

He rubbed the bridge of his nose. "I'm going to bed now. Fraser had better not be here when I wake up."

"That all depends on how long you sleep. I'm keeping an ear out for you."

On impulse, he moved close enough to take her hand and kiss it. "As long as your ear is only for me."

Faye's cheeks flushed pink. As she opened and then closed her mouth, he smiled. It seemed Faye liked some instances of him being nice to her.

With that, Grant turned and climbed the stairs. He wasn't sure if he could fall asleep easily. Faye would no doubt continue to occupy his thoughts.

But he had to try. Flirting with Faye was only part of the equation. He needed to be the strong male she required as well.

CHAPTER ELEVEN

Faye finally closed her jaw as Grant ascended the stairs out of sight.

Never in a thousand years had she expected him to kiss her hand, let alone flirt with her. Grant was brusque and grumpy; he always had been.

Maybe he just needed a little more MacKenzie magic to loosen him up further. Even her somewhat serious brother Fergus had a playful side to rub off on Grant. She definitely needed to get him and his family to dinner once everything was sorted. And not just for some fun, but to also better know his mother and brother, Chase. Since they tended to keep to themselves, she didn't know much about them.

Her dragon spoke up. *Why does it matter? He still hasn't done nearly enough to convince me to sleep with him.*

Oh, stop it. You're acting like a child. We all make mistakes, and it looks like Grant is trying to make up for them. Maybe he is the male we need.

Maybe, maybe not. The real test will be when we encounter a dangerous situation. If he allows us to fight, then maybe I will allow him to kiss us.

Allow him, aye? You forget I have a bigger say in this.

Her beast didn't respond and Faye decided not to pursue the matter. She had too much to do to stand in the hall and have an argument inside her mind.

If she didn't love her dragon so much, Faye would almost be jealous of humans not having two personalities in one body.

She reached the breakfast room and found Cat chatting with the older dragonwoman from Clan Snowridge in Wales. Waving to Adrian and some of the other Protectors, Faye finally made it to the small table at the edge of the room where her friend sat. Cat asked without preamble, "So Grant made it back, aye?"

She eyed her friend. "How do you know that he wasn't here all night?"

Cat tapped her ear. "The door was open and every dragon-shifter heard your conversation."

Faye's cheeks heated. "Well, then you don't need to ask me what happened."

"Oh, come on. Dragon-shifter Etiquette 101 requires me to ask you rather than just go off what I overheard."

Faye swiped a triangle of toast from the holder in the center of the table and took a bite. "And since when do you follow etiquette? You eavesdropped on your siblings as much as possible growing up."

Cat sighed. "Fine. Then I'll just make a mental note of you flirting with Grant, and Iris coming to watch Max. I'll seek out Iris later for details. I'd say the same about Grant, but that one can stonewall better than you."

"I'm not stonewalling you, Cat. You heard everything in the hall. You know as much as I do."

Cat studied her a second before replying, "I think there's more to it, but it's Protector business and therefore you can't share it. Just make sure that if it's going to affect me, you tell me about it."

Faye swallowed another bite. "Fine. I'm much more interested in tonight's event. Speaking of which"—Faye turned toward the Welsh dragonwoman—"if your clan's Protectors ever wish to team up with us, then let them know they just have to ask. Can you tell them that, Nia?"

"I will. But I should probably go meet with them now." Nia nodded to Cat. "I'll catch up with you later, dear."

Once Nia was gone, Faye moved over a seat closer to Cat. "So, has Lachlan changed his plans because of Max's antics? I never did find him last night to ask."

"Not as far as I can tell. Only that if we use the toilet, we have to have an escort." Cat scrunched her nose. "Since I'm the oldest sibling and used to doing things my way, it's going to take some getting used to. I never thought I'd need a babysitter in my mid-twenties."

"You probably wouldn't make such a fuss if it were that Lachlan bloke escorting you."

"Having a male follow me into the toilet is just wrong."

"Not that. You keep staring at him when he's in the room. Care to tell me why?"

Cat lowered her voice. "He's an interesting subject for my next series of paintings. I'm not about to ask him to sit for me, so I need to memorize the details of his face and hands. Those are the two hardest areas for me to get right."

Faye snatched a piece of bacon. "On the last day of the exhibition, I can tie him to a chair for you. He won't want anyone to know about his humiliation, so we should be safe from him reporting to the DDA."

Cat moved her plate out of Faye's reach and scooped up a bite of baked beans with her fork. "Yes, because Finn and Grant are known for looking the other way."

"Perhaps," Faye answered with her mouth full of bacon. "I have dirt on my cousin. And Grant, well, I'm sure I can convince him, too."

Cat looked like she wanted to ask a question, but went back to eating her breakfast. Since it probably had to do with Grant, Faye changed the subject. "At any rate, I need to find Iris and Max. Do you want to come with me? Not only will it save you a trip from seeking her out yourself, but Max seems to listen to you, so maybe if you tell him to stay put, he will."

"He only listens to me because I'm nice to him. He may be eccentric, but he's interesting. He also has some fascinating stories about history. I've been trying to convince him to write a book for secondary school students. His flair might encourage some of them to pursue history, archaeology, or something along those lines."

Faye laid her head on the table. "Please don't encourage him. At least, not until the exhibition is finished. Otherwise, he might run off to every nearby archaeological site he can find and claim it's all in the name of research for a new book."

"From what I gather, he only went to Craig Phadrig because thieves are supposed to ransack it soon," Cat answered. "I would do the same thing if a precious painting was rumored to be a target. Surely you have something that you would risk your life for."

"My family, of course. And the clan. Other than that, I don't have many hobbies or interests."

Cat raised an eyebrow. "And that is your problem. We need to find you one." She changed her voice to a whisper. "And one that doesn't necessarily involve a man."

"Maybe. Just don't suggest painting. I'm sure my months' old nephew could do a better job than me."

Amusement danced in Cat's eyes. "Oh, I don't know. We could always start you out with finger painting."

Faye tore off a bit of toast and tossed it at Cat. The bloody woman caught it. Faye gave her best glare, but all Cat did was toss the piece of bread back.

As it bounced off Faye's head, they both started laughing. Faye was the first one to catch her breath. "Maybe if we toss some bits of toast at the others, it'll lighten the mood. Everyone seems so serious this morning."

Lachlan's voice filled their ears. "I'll thank you not to turn the breakfast room into a war zone, Ms. MacKenzie. We don't need the negative publicity."

Faye glanced at Lachlan. "What? That dragon-shifters enjoy having fun and aren't different from humans in that respect? How is that negative?"

Lachlan smoothed his shirt. "It would turn into a destruction of property story in the papers and online. I'm sure the Dragon Knights would use anything as an excuse to launch another attack."

Faye raised her brows. "We wouldn't have to worry about that if the DDA did its job."

Lachlan didn't bat an eyelash at her tone. "The DDA does what it can with its limited resources."

"Caring doesn't cost anything," Faye stated.

Cat stood and moved between them. "We're all on the same side. Let's not forget that."

Faye's dragon huffed. *Maybe if we put in a complaint, the DDA will send us someone less rigid.*

I checked into MacKintosh, and he's supposed to be the best. Not only at staging events, but also when it comes to damage control. In this instance, the stuffier the better.

She focused back on Cat and Lachlan. "Aye, we're on the same side. But just a piece of advice, Lachlan. Almost everyone in this room is tense. You need to find some relaxing activities along the way or the slightest incident could start a fire. You'll have to use all of your skills then, and it still might not be enough."

"Duly noted," Lachlan answered. "For the moment, I need to persuade everyone to change and get ready. We'll be leaving in an hour."

Faye had to give the human credit. He knew how to stay focused.

She gave a mock salute. "Yes, sir."

Cat spoke up. "We'll be ready on time. Even if I have to find someone to dress Faye, she will be downstairs in an hour."

Faye opened her mouth to say she could take care of herself, but Lachlan had already moved to the next table. Turning her head to Cat, Faye stuck out her tongue.

Cat shrugged. "I got him to leave, aye? Now, we'd better hurry or we won't have time to talk with Iris and still meet Lachlan downstairs on time."

"And I'm not sure I want to see that male upset. I have a feeling his quiet nature hides something deep inside."

Cat looked at the human. "Me, too. But nothing sinister."

She studied her friend a second. "I never said sinister. But I'm curious exactly how you plan to use him in your painting. Please tell me it's as a fairy, complete with rainbow wings and a dainty wand? And maybe some cat ears?"

Cat snorted. "Don't be ridiculous. You'll just have to wait like everyone else until I'm finished."

"Some friend you are."

Cat merely smiled at her.

Sighing, Faye stood. "Right, then if you're not going to tell me, we should go."

"You're giving up fairly easily, Faye MacKenzie."

"What can I say? I don't dare upset your Lachlan by being tardy."

Cat opened her mouth to say something and promptly shut it.

As they made their way toward Max's room, Faye wondered if she should wake Grant in an hour or let him sleep. She knew he'd want to be part of the action, but on the other hand, he didn't take care of himself properly. Faye would have to be the judge of what was best for him in this case.

Her dragon sighed. *He shouldn't be our concern.*

Even putting aside your grudge, we need the best fighting force possible in case something does happen.

Her beast paused a second before saying, *I suppose.*

Taking advantage of her dragon's agreeable nature for the moment, Faye picked up her pace. First things first, she needed to prepare Iris for the day ahead.

~~~

As Grant circled around his last area to search for the day, he scrutinized the surroundings. Usually he enjoyed gliding over the land and taking in the hills and lochs of the Highlands.

However, he was anxious to finish his sweep and find Faye. After all, the devil had forgone waking him up and had left him with a message: *You needed the sleep. When you read this, do your job and then find us.*

In her note, Faye had acted if she were still head Protector. He was also a bit miffed she had made decisions for him.

His dragon said, *I agree with her, and someone needs to look after us. Besides, those few extra hours of sleep make us sharper and better able to find clues.*

What clues? All I see are trees, cottages, and more bloody trees.

Someone is impatient.

Grant was about to argue with his dragon about patience. Few dragon halves possessed it, and under normal circumstances, Grant's was no exception.

But he decided against it. After all, Grant had been denying him their true mate. That would make anyone testy.

Grant himself was wound tight after his dream of Faye naked and beneath him. While sex dreams were great, the tenderness of her curling up against his chest as he held her tight still sent a wave of longing through his body. He'd always secretly wanted to have someone he could trust completely and confide in. He loved his brother, but Chase preferred to tease and treat the world as a ride to be enjoyed. Grant wasn't sure where he got that from, but the differences in their personalities had created a type of barrier between them growing up.

Faye, on the other hand, knew how to balance fun with dependability. She would never betray him by spilling a secret. After all, she never had in the past and she'd known more than almost anyone about his time in the army.

His dragon chimed in again. *She will be ours. Stop doubting it.*

I wish it were that easy, dragon.

It could be.

Rather than wax on about what he wanted, he focused on what he could do in the present. Grant flapped his wings as the ground sped past beneath him. He'd nearly reached the village that signaled the end of his search area when he noticed smoke coming up from a large patch of trees.

While it could be humans or even a routine controlled fire, he wasn't taking any chances. His gut said to investigate the smoke.

Grant maintained his trajectory and speed. He needed whoever it was to think he was going to fly past them.

At the last second Grant folded his wings to his back and dove for the trees. As the branches broke against his body, he didn't think of the bruises he'd have the next day. Instead, he scanned the area and saw the backs of two forms near a fire.

In the next second, the male and female jumped up and faced him.

It was his father and his father's sister.

While recognition flared in his father and aunt's eyes, the realization only took a split-second. The pair turned and ran just as Grant half-crashed to the ground. Not wasting any time, he lunged for them in his dragon form. However, he could only reach his father in time. His aunt ran out of sight.

Fucking fantastic. Even if he made it out of the trees as quickly as he could, his aunt would probably take the car parked near the lone cottage he'd seen next to the trees and escape before he could reach her. If he didn't have a prisoner, he might be able to catch up to her. But that would require releasing his father.

Grant looked down at his father, Michael. He may have a way to still find the other traitors, even if his aunt warned them.

His father spoke. "Let me go, lad. You don't want to become involved."

His father's statement only piqued his curiosity. Not that Grant could ask questions in his dragon form.

No, he had to find a safe place to stow Michael McFarland until Grant could interrogate him. He wanted to do it straight away, but he couldn't risk something going wrong with the exhibition.

Then it hit him. Inverness Castle had an underground dragon holding cell. If Grant stashed his dad there, he could question the traitor as soon as the exhibition was over.

With a plan in place, Grant moved toward the clearing beyond the trees. As expected, there was no sign of his aunt.

Focusing back on his father, Grant turned him upside down and shook him a few times to dislodge his belongings. As a few things tumbled to the ground, Grant snatched up his dad's mobile phone between two talons of his free hand and tucked it gently into the small pouch around Grant's neck. He would ask Ian and Emma, Lochguard's techies, to poke around and see what they could find.

He scanned the rest of the bits and bobs and didn't see anything of value. Hopefully if his father had any sort of anti-dragon defense items, Grant had shaken them out. There was no way he would risk Michael running free by setting his dad down to shift, calling for back-up, searching his prisoner, and then finally taking off.

Since Grant had come on a mission to find rogue dragon-shifters, he carefully took out a vial of ground mandrake root and periwinkle from the small pouch around his neck. Holding the tube with one of his rear feet, he delicately tugged the ring on the top. If he spilled any on himself, Grant wouldn't be able to shift again for days.

Quickly laying his father on the ground, Grant tossed the powder at the older man. While he coughed at the dust, Grant took out the large bottle of water, ripped it open, and dumped the contents over his dad. While the powder had already been inhaled and made contact with Michael's skin thus putting it in effect, the water would dilute it enough so it wouldn't do the same to Grant.

When his dad finished sputtering, he demanded, "What the bloody hell did you do to me?"

Not answering, Grant picked up the man, tightened his hold on his father, crouched down, and jumped into the air.

As he beat his wings furiously, he was grateful for the rest earlier. He should make it back to Inverness in record time.

His dragon said, *Are you honestly going to hand him over to the humans at Inverness Castle? We haven't checked them out and they could be incompetent. Our prisoner might break free.*

It's our only option. Besides, I'll let Finn know I found our father and he can stress to the DDA the importance of watching this prisoner.

But will Finn allow us to question him? He may send someone else.

While Grant wanted nothing more than to be the one to interrogate his father, even he recognized that he might not be the best one to do so. *We could use the help. Someone unrelated won't allow their emotions to get in the way.*

And what if the DDA claims him as their prisoner? We may never be able to find Roderick and the others.

Roderick was Grant's uncle and the unofficial leader of the dragon-shifters who left Lochguard.

I have faith in Finn.

His beast huffed and remained quiet. For once, Grant wished his dragon would keep talking. It would help distract him from the dragonman in his talons.

Not wanting to allow happier memories of his childhood to affect his mission, Grant pushed himself to fly harder. The sooner he dropped off Michael McFarland, the sooner he could go to the exhibition and talk about it with Faye. She might have a plan of how to better handle the situation.

So, you're going to rely on Faye now? That's different, his dragon said.

I would be a fool not to. She has no love for our father. She can make the necessary decisions without any sort of guilt or duty hanging over her.

His dragon paused a beat before adding, *Just think if she were always at our side. We could accomplish heaps.*

He wanted that more than anything, but protecting the clan came first.

Grant flapped his wings harder and blanked his mind. He needed to secure Michael McFarland before anyone could attack and cart him away.

CHAPTER TWELVE

Faye watched as the five participants of the DDA's exhibition made the final adjustments to their displays.

Cat's paintings and photographs caught her eye the most. The vivid colors and definitive brush strokes captured both the land and the vitality of Lochguard's people. Although the humans would be most interested in the dragon paintings, Faye preferred the ones featuring the children or the broch near their land. The pile of rocks on Loch Never had once been a defensive tower of sorts, and Faye appreciated Cat's imagination in bringing it back to its original glory. Not with the people of old, but rather with a modern twist of fairy lights and of a couple stealing a kiss. There was also a faint outline of a dragon in the stars above the pair, as if it were watching over his or her descendants.

Cat noticed her staring and raised her eyebrows in question. Faye gave a thumbs-up. As her friend went back to work, Faye looked at Max's set of tables. She really didn't want to attempt a conversation with the human, but her curiosity won out and she walked over.

After waving hello to Iris leaning against the far wall, Faye looked at the tables. Odd bits and pieces were laid out. Some with labels, some without. Her eye was drawn to a photograph of a large floor mosaic that was mostly intact. It had two dragons entwined in flight in the center.

Before Faye could try to construct their story from the other images at the edges of the mosaic, Max rushed over and said, "I had hoped to bring the genuine article with me, but the British Museum wouldn't allow it. Even though I found it, they took credit for it and claimed it."

Not wanting to talk about the politics of artifact finding, she asked, "Where was it found?"

"In southern Britain, not far from where Clan Skyhunter once lived. Very few Roman mosaics survived that depict dragons. This one not only features them, it tells the story of dragons assisting the villa owner." Max pointed to one of the smaller images in the corner. "Here, the dragons are protecting the inhabitants from other dragons."

Faye leaned down. The mosaic was missing some tiles, but she could just make out a dragon standing in front of humans while another dragon roared at him.

Max spoke again. "If you like this one, I have a few other tables of artifacts from the Roman period in Britain. Some of the finds are truly extraordinary."

Before Faye could think of how to politely decline, she saw Grant striding toward her. Judging by the firmness of his jaw, something had happened.

"Excuse me, Max."

Faye met Grant halfway. She opened her mouth to ask what was going on, but he beat her to it. "Not here. Come."

"What about Cat?"

"I asked Aaron on the way in, and he said they'll keep an eye on her."

She nodded and allowed Grant to guide her to a room off the main exhibition space. Once he closed the door, he asked, "How much longer do we need to be here?"

"I don't know. Lachlan didn't specify. What's going on?"

He lowered his voice. "I found my father. He's currently being held at Inverness Castle."

"What?"

"It's true. I also found my aunt, but she managed to slip away. We need to question my father as soon as possible, before word gets out that I have him."

She studied him a second before stating, "You're telling me this because you want my help."

"Of course I want your help, bloody woman. As much as I want to singlehandedly do this on my own, there's too much history between my father and me. You would do a better job at interrogating him."

Grant's words made her stand a little taller. "I can do it, but what did Finn say? I'm all for irritating my cousin, but this is rather important."

"Finn is negotiating with the DDA. I just want to be ready as soon as he gets the green light to question him."

"Well, Iris is here. If you stay, too, then I could probably slip away without Lachlan noticing for a little while. The only question is if the staff at Inverness Castle will allow me to be alone with him."

"As long as he's chained up in his cell, I don't see why not. I dosed him with our special mixture and he won't be able to shift for a few days. If worse comes to worst, you can turn into a dragon and easily contain him again."

For a split second, Faye was stunned at how easily Grant was including her on such an important task. Then she pushed it aside. She didn't want to give him any reason to change his mind. "Right, then it's probably best if I slip away now and you take my place. I'm sure you can make up an excuse."

He nodded. She turned to leave, but Grant grabbed her wrist. She met his gaze again as he said, "Be careful, lass. Not because I don't think you're capable, because you are. My father is unpredictable and I don't know if his brethren will attack Inverness Castle to retrieve him or not."

"If they do, you'll be the first to know."

He smiled. "Aye, then you'd best leave. Don't be afraid to punch him if my father steps out of line."

Faye made a fist and raised her free arm as if to clock someone. Grant snorted at her antics and finally released her wrist.

Making her way out of the exhibition center, Faye did her best not to dwell on Grant's actions and willingness to include her. She needed all the time she could muster to prepare her interrogation questions.

Unfortunately, her dragon didn't share the same view. *Grant is trying too hard.*

She sighed. *First he wasn't trying hard enough and now he's trying too hard. I think you're just making excuses.*

Her beast paused a beat before replying, *Let me ask you this—are you ready for the frenzy and all it entails?*

Wait, you're trying to protect me?

Why is that surprising? We are one, and if something happens to you, it happens to me, too.

Putting aside self-preservation, you could just ask me. Just because Grant is earning my respect and proving how much he values us doesn't mean I'm going to jump into bed with him at the earliest opportunity.

Are you sure? You go crazy at his touch. What would happen if he undressed us and kissed every inch of our skin?

It took everything Faye had not to visualize her dragon's words. *Stop it, dragon.*

Just think about it. I'll let you carry out your interrogation, but this conversation isn't over.

Her beast fell silent, and Faye fought the urge to bang her head against a wall. She wondered how dragons ever survived finding their true mate, let alone living with them. Her dragon would probably always try to protect her.

Not that it should surprise her. She was the youngest and her entire family was overprotective. Her dragon had probably just followed their example.

Faye picked up her pace. She could debate her future and dealing with her beast later. She needed to reach Inverness Castle quickly. She wasn't about to fail this assignment. Aye, she wanted to prove to Grant she could handle important clan business. But she also needed to do it for herself. Faye missed being in charge of the Protectors on Lochguard and making delicate decisions. She might never regain her former job, but she was starting to think she could share it with Grant.

That was a future she wouldn't mind. Grant as both her lover and her work partner.

But she was getting ahead of herself. First things first, she needed to get Michael McFarland to talk.

~~~

A short time later, Faye stood outside Michael McFarland's cell and stared at the male.

While he looked like an older version of Grant with the same dark hair—albeit a bit gray—and the same brown eyes, all Faye wanted to do was punch the dragonman for abandoning his clan and family.

Faye's father had been stolen from her, but Michael had chosen to leave. To her, his act was the worst type of betrayal.

Her beast growled. *If we hit him once where no one can see, it won't cause any problems.*

As tempting as it is, no. I don't want to face the DDA's wrath. Besides, Grant's counting on us.

Hmph. Grant would approve of my plan.

Before Faye could respond, one of the guards returned from upstairs and said, "You've been granted clearance for fifteen minutes. After that, I will escort you out."

Not wanting to look a gift horse in the mouth, Faye merely nodded. The guard signaled one of the others, and the other man unlocked the cell.

Faye entered the small space and the door clicked closed behind her. As the lock turned over, she checked for anything Michael could use to overpower her. However, the cell contained a single bed, toilet, and sink. Beyond the blanket on the bed and toilet paper on the ground, there were only the chains around Michael's wrist and ankles.

Satisfied the cell was secure, she asked, "Care to tell me why you left Lochguard?"

A small frown appeared between Michael's brows. "That's your first question?"

"Just tell me the reason. I want to know."

He studied her. "I'm not going to talk, lass. You're wasting your time."

She took a step closer. "Is that so? Then maybe I should go and leave your fate to the DDA." She glanced over her shoulder. "What was it you lads were talking about doing? Oh, that's right. Keeping his inner dragon drugged silent for the rest of his life."

"You're lying. The DDA wouldn't violate its agreements."

"Ah, but you're wrong. The agreements are between the British government and the five dragon clans in the UK. Since you don't belong to any of the five clans, they have no established agreement with you. They are free to treat you as rogue dragons. I'm sure you know what that means."

Rogue dragons could be executed on sight, if deemed a threat.

Since Grant's father had never been a Protector, he didn't possess the training to keep the concern from showing in his eyes. "I still call your bluff, MacKenzie. Your entire family is good at embellishing. This is no different."

"What you call 'embellishment' I call having fun. But I can assure you, I'm not making this up. In fact, the DDA's solicitor should be here at any moment to reinforce my claim."

As they stared at one another, Faye debated her next move. She wasn't lying about the DDA's lawyer arriving soon. Still, the more information she could obtain before the official arrived, the better.

She continued. "I'm sure you know about the rogue American dragons and their attack on Lochguard this past winter. I believe they were working with you lot, aye?" Michael remained silent. Grant's Uncle Roderick, the former Protector, must be training his followers up to a point. "All I have to do is show your picture to the DDA's prisoners from that little incident. They'll confirm my suspicions, and you'll be locked away for the rest of your life. However, if you talk before I do that, you might receive a reduced sentence."

She hated the offer considering what the man had done to Grant and his family, but keeping Lochguard safe was a higher priority than punishing one male for being a horrible father and mate.

"I still say you're bluffing," Michael answered. "Maybe once the solicitor arrives and can offer me a deal, I might talk. Until then, you may as well leave. I'm not going to tell you anything."

Faye suspected the male was telling the truth. But there was one last thing she needed to find out. She stated, "You broke your ex-mate's heart when you left. Did you know that?"

For a split second, regret flashed in Michael's eyes, but it was quickly replaced by a hard look. "She made her choice to follow your no-good cousin. She has to live with her decision."

Her dragon growled. *I don't like him.*

She ignored her beast. "One thing I could never figure out was why was Finn such a horrible leader, in your opinion? All he wanted to do was reach out to the humans and work with them."

"Aye, and soon we would be bowing down to them more than we already do. Dragons were once revered and feared. It should always be that way. Only the clan leaders keep us from claiming the land and resources we deserve. They're all afraid of the DDA, the cowards."

Faye raised a brow. "So, eating people somehow makes you fierce and powerful? That sounds a bit crazy to me."

"It's not crazy to want to rule what should be ours. Especially if we obtain some of the weapons the dragon hunters are using against dragon-shifters, then no one could defeat us unless they were willing to bomb their own country and risk their precious people."

Her dragon spoke up. *The DDA needs to find him a counselor. He is delusional if he thinks the British government will turn things over to him after killing a few people. If Hitler couldn't take this country, I doubt one or two dozen dragon-shifters could.*

In his way of thinking, it was the dragons' help and not the Americans that prevented Hitler from ultimately occupying this country.

Her dragon huffed. *The Yanks were helpful, but we could've held our own. German dragons may be bigger, but they lack endurance.*

Not wanting to debate her dragon, Faye ignored her beast to focus back on Michael. "I truly hope you see the light one day. Maybe then you'll realize that giving up your family for an unrealistic power play was foolish."

Michael growled and tugged on his chains. Faye had calculated their length and stood at a safe distance. She didn't so much as flinch. She added, "Your window of opportunity is closing, McFarland. I give you until the end of the day, and then we'll step back and allow the DDA to do whatever they wish. However, if you change your mind, Finn might be able to pull some strings so that you can fly again before you die."

With that, she turned and waited for the human guard to open the cell. A younger Protector might've been disappointed in the interview, but Faye knew that planting ideas and letting them fester could sometimes do more to persuade a prisoner than punching them.

Given Michael McFarland's selfishness, he would probably want to protect himself over his compatriots. She'd bet her life's savings the male would cave.

Her dragon sighed. *I detest him. I hope his stubbornness wins out and he withers away inside a jail cell somewhere.*

And that would help the clan, how?

I didn't say it was helpful or logical. I just don't like him.

Faye snorted. *I'll make sure to tell Grant your feelings. It's nice to see you're warming up to him.*

Her dragon harrumphed and fell silent.

Faye waited for the DDA's solicitor in a small room not far from the holding cell. She paced the area, anxious to leave so she could talk with Grant. He would be less than pleased if his father continued to hold out, but her interview hadn't been a complete bust. The pieces of information she'd gathered thus far could help them formulate a plan.

CHAPTER THIRTEEN

Grant watched as Cat, Max, and the others made the final adjustments to their displays. It'd been too many years since he'd had to merely watch over anyone and he was close to climbing the walls.

His dragon said, *Maybe you understand the younger Protectors now.*

Aye, I do. But I still won't avoid giving them guard or bodyguard duty. Besides, few of them would be waiting to hear how an interrogation went with their father, aye?

Perhaps. But I trust Faye. You should too.

I trust her. I just want to know what the bloody hell happened.

Lachlan clapped, signaling it was time to depart, and everyone moved toward the far end of the room.

The only question was would Faye arrive before they left. If not, then Grant wouldn't be able to talk with her until they were safe inside the B&B.

His dragon chimed in. *A few minutes won't kill you.*

When they finally exited the room and piled into the vans that would take them back, Grant surveyed the surroundings for anything out of the ordinary. If not for Faye being away, Grant would excuse himself to do proper surveillance from the air.

However, Lachlan was already suspicious. Grant's excuse about Faye needing to find a chemist for some personal items had been met with doubt. Only because Grant offered to go into the details of a female dragon-shifter's biology and Max enthusiastically demanding to hear it did Lachlan quickly dismiss the errand.

They wound through the streets of Inverness back to their lodgings. The humans were going about their usual tasks of shopping, working, and meeting with friends. In some respects, they weren't that different from dragon-shifters. Too bad more humans didn't understand that fact.

The van finally pulled into the parking spot near the B&B and Grant spotted Faye through the front window of their lodgings. Since she was merely sitting and not pacing, the news couldn't be that bad.

Signaling to Iris to look after both Cat and Max, Grant exited the van first and made his way into the B&B. He peeked his head into the lounge where Faye sat and ordered, "Upstairs."

If the situation hadn't been so important, Faye would've probably challenged him. However, she followed him up the stairs without complaint. As soon as he shut his door, he turned to Faye. "Well?"

"It's fun to see you impatient. Maybe I'll wait a few seconds more." He growled, and she put up her hands. "Okay, I don't want to anger Mr. Grumpy too much. Especially since my news is less than ideal."

He searched Faye's eyes. "He didn't say anything?"

"Michael didn't say much, but he will if the conditions he made with the solicitor are met."

"Stop drawing it out and tell me already," he barked.

She tilted her head. "One of his conditions is that he wants to see you."

Grant clenched his fingers into a fist. "Why? I have nothing to say to that male."

Faye shrugged. "I have no idea. Just be glad he agreed to anything at all. At first, he just kept havering on about the superiority of dragon-shifters. If it were up to him, humans would treat us as gods."

"My father has always hated his lot in life. I suppose his interest in history was a subtle clue about his thoughts on dragons, since in the long run, they ruled the island more years than humans did."

Faye closed the distance between them. At her nearness, his dragon stopped pacing inside his head. Her voice was gentle as she said, "I know it's asking a lot for you to meet with him. And if it's too difficult, I may have a plan about how to draw out the other rogue dragons, although it's not guaranteed."

"I would do anything to help the clan. That includes talking to my bastard father. Still, I'm curious to hear your plan."

The corner of her mouth ticked up. "So, you're ready to follow my orders again?"

He growled, "Faye, just tell me your idea. I don't have time for your teasing."

She touched his cheek, and it took everything Grant had not to cover her hand with his. Because if he did, he might do more than merely touch her. No, he'd pull her close and kiss her to escape reality for a few minutes.

His dragon spoke up. *Yes, yes. Kiss her. She will let us.*

Just because I can doesn't mean I should. Think of the clan. They are counting on us.

His beast huffed. *We need to work on delegating or we'll never have time with our mate once we claim her.*

She still hasn't said yes.

She will.

Not wanting to argue further, Grant merely stared at Faye and raised his eyebrows. After a few more beats, she sighed. Shaking her head, she said, "Fine, I'll try not to tease you for a few minutes. However, one day I'm going to convince you it's okay to laugh, even in the direst of situations." He tilted his head in question and she continued, "Aye, well, Michael and the other dragon-shifters that left Lochguard want dragons to be treated as kings and queens. If we carefully lay the groundwork, we might be able to convince some of our allies to pose as sympathetic to their cause, gain their confidence by 'attacking' certain clans, and then infiltrate their ranks. After that, it's a matter of coordinating with the DDA and putting them in prison."

"That requires a whole lot of dependence on other clans' help."

"So? We can trust Stonefire and they have connections to Snowridge through their head Protector, Kai. I also have a feeling Northcastle might join in, too."

His dragon growled at the mention of Northcastle, but Grant ignored him. "Since when do you trust the Northern Irish dragons?"

"My dragon trusts Adrian and Kaine, and I trust her." Her eyes lit up. "And just think of it—if we gain Northcastle's trust and Stonefire has the confidence of the Irish clan, Glenlough, then we might also be able to heal the rift between the dragons in those two countries."

"Gee, you don't have big plans, now do you, lass?" Grant drawled.

She punched his arm. "Don't pretend you don't have big ideas, too. Otherwise, you're not a very good head Protector."

His dragon chimed in. *Her idea to infiltrate their ranks has merit, but I still think we should meet with our father, first.*

I was thinking the same thing.

His beast paused a second before adding, *Also, tell her she's brilliant. She deserves it.*

Faye's voice interrupted his thoughts. "What does Mister Dragon have to say now?"

"He wants to get into your pants."

His beast growled. *Yes, but tell her the whole truth.*

Faye's pupils flashed and she laughed. "I wish there was a way for our two dragons to talk directly to each other. Mine would give yours a dressing down."

The corner of his mouth ticked up. "Now, that I would love to hear."

His dragon harrumphed and curled up in the corner of his mind. Apparently, he didn't like the idea of Faye's dragon scolding him.

Faye's smile faded and he focused on her instead of his beast as she said, "But in all seriousness, we need to decide what to do and soon. The DDA's solicitor needs an answer."

"First, tell me, have you talked with Finn?"

She shook her head. "Not yet. I wanted to talk with you, first. While you gave me this task, you're still in charge."

He wanted to say they should always be cohead Protectors and lead the clan's security forces together. However, that was many steps ahead of the current situation. Until Grant knew more about his future and had a chance to better woo Faye, he didn't want to risk losing it all by mentioning his plans too soon. "Tell the solicitor that I'll meet with my father. Once I'm done with him, we'll think of the next steps and tell Finn what's going on. While I'm away, you need to watch over Cat."

"I know—"

"Not because I don't trust you, but with my father in custody, there's always a chance my uncle and the other traitors could hunt us down. They'd have no problem attacking and hurting whoever stood in their way. If they know we're working together, you'll be a target."

Faye searched his eyes. "Do you really think they would target the innocents? Cat and the other dragon-shifters here haven't done anything to merit their ire."

Grant clenched his jaw. "After the attack in January and their temporary alliance with the American clan, I think there's little they wouldn't do. Their attack signaled that they consider all of us enemies."

The temporary alliance between the traitors and the rogue members of Clan BroadBay had resulted in them bombing large chunks of Lochguard. While the casualties had been few, the deaths still sat heavy on many hearts in the clan.

Faye took his face in her hands and stroked his cheek with her thumbs. "I will die before I allow them to hurt anyone else from Lochguard."

Faye's soft skin against his helped to ease his nerves. The lass who had once ignited his temper like no other was fast becoming his best source of calmness.

Well, at least at certain moments. When the threats were taken care of and they had time, he would work his hardest to stoke her fire again.

Taking a chance, he placed his hands on Faye's hips and gently pulled her against his body. For a few seconds they stood in silence, with only the sound of their breathing filling the room.

He should pat her hip and take his leave. But Grant leaned a fraction closer to her lips. She closed her eyes. His heart skipped a beat. He wanted her to be sure, so he murmured, "Do you want this?"

"Aye," she answered breathily. "I think I can contain my beast long enough for one kiss."

His dragon roared. *Hurry up and kiss her.*

Grant closed the distance and was a hairsbreadth from pressing his lips against Faye's when Aaron Caruso's voice boomed through the door. "I know you're in there, McFarland. We need to talk."

His beast growled. *Ignore him. Kiss her.*

Faye's eyes opened. She whispered, "Anticipation makes things better, so I hear."

"Un-bloody-likely in this case. All I do is wait." With a curse, Grant reluctantly released his hold on Faye. "Sometimes, I want to murder that male."

"I heard that," Aaron answered. "Murder is illegal, but I'm game for a sparring match or flying competition at any time."

Faye bit her lip and Grant shot her a glare. "Don't you dare laugh."

She put her hands up in innocence. Aaron said, "What, did you fall asleep? I know you're getting on in age, but surely you can avoid taking another nap."

With a growl, Grant yanked open the door. "What do you want?"

Aaron looked to either side. "Do you really want me to ask out here, for all to hear?"

Grant clutched Aaron's shirt and dragged him into the room. Once the door was closed, he demanded, "Well? What's so important that you had to bellow through the door?"

Aaron looked between Grant and Faye and then smiled. "Like that, I see."

"Caruso," Grant growled.

"Aye, that's my name. And I wanted to know where Faye went today. Between you disappearing last night and Faye today, something is going on. If there's a threat, I thought the alliance between Stonefire and Lochguard was strong enough for you to share what you know."

Faye spoke before Grant could. "The alliance is important and Stonefire is the one clan we trust above all others. However, if there was a threat to your clan, you'd talk with your clan leader before us, aye?"

Aaron met Grant's gaze. "You went to Lochguard last night and I assume you talked with Finn then. Something else has cropped up between then and now?"

"Aye," Grant answered. "And once Finn gives his approval, you and Quinn will be the first to know. Until then, just be on alert and keep your eyes peeled."

"That's not much to go on, but I won't press for more right now," Aaron said. "Just know that all teasing aside, I trust you, Grant. All you need to do is ask for Stonefire's help and you have it."

Faye jumped in. "Even if we're planning a huge celebration for Finn and Arabella's triplets that involves dancing nude in the moonlight?"

"I can't say Bram will join in, but I have nothing to lose," Aaron answered.

Grant rubbed the bridge of his nose. "I assure you, it's not that. It's time for you to leave, Caruso. I have matters that I need to attend to."

Aaron raised his brows. "So, in other words, I need to get my arse out of your room? Whatever is going on is making you tense and polite. I hope you solve your issue soon or I'll have to think of ways to wind you up and get you to relax." He winked at Faye. "Or maybe Faye can do that for you."

Grant opened his mouth, but Aaron was gone before he could say a word. Faye moved to stand next to him. "Maybe we should plan a celebration like that for Arabella and forget to mention to Aaron that he's the only one who will be dancing naked."

Despite everything he had to tackle, Grant snorted. "I might go blind from seeing his arse, but it might be worth it."

As Grant and Faye grinned at each other, he took a second to enjoy the moment. He doubted he'd have much time alone with Faye until after the threat was taken care of. And not just because her family would try to meddle. That was an entirely different problem he needed to tackle.

His dragon spoke up. *If we find something from the twins' past, we could hold them for a while in a cell and then sneak off with Faye.*

As Grant debated the merits of locking up Faye's brothers, her phone chirped with a text message. She finally broke the gaze to check on it. "The solicitor needs an answer."

Pushing aside everything but his work, Grant answered, "Then tell him I'm on my way."

Faye nodded and typed out the reply. When she finished, she looked up at him again. "I'm here if you need me, Grant."

"I know, lass. I know."

"And I really hope we can finish what we nearly started a minute ago." She waggled her eyebrows and he shook his head. She asked, "What? Unless you regret what you were about to do."

"No fucking way," he growled. "When I finally kiss you, I'll be doing it properly. You might even need to lean against me to keep from falling to your knees."

"You chide my brothers for being over the top, but I'm starting to think it's a male trait. You're no better."

He took her chin between his fingers. "I'm not one of your brothers."

Amusement danced in her eyes. "Good, because that would be weird. Not to mention if we do what I think we'll do, it'd also be illegal."

"Cheeky lass." Taking a risk, Grant kissed Faye's cheek. When she leaned into his touch, a sense of satisfaction coursed through his body. She was already halfway to being wooed.

It's not enough, his dragon said.

It's a start.

Why not kiss her on the mouth now? She is willing.

Not now. I need your help with our current task. Can you stop thinking about sex for a moment?

His beast huffed and Grant took that to mean yes.

Pulling away, he smiled at Faye. "Consider that a preview, Miss MacKenzie."

She snorted. "I'm not sure what to expect when you use my surname."

"Oh, you'll like what I have planned. I have no doubt."

Before Faye could answer, he left and snuck out of the B&B. It was time to face the male who had abandoned him and his family without a word.

~ ~ ~

Half an hour later, Faye tried reading the latest paragraph of the book on her mobile phone for the tenth time and failed.

Cat was sketching in her room. A few others were also taking a breather, but the majority of the humans and dragon-shifters were downstairs laughing and having a good time. At any other time, Faye wouldn't hesitate to join them. However, she was worried about Grant and wanted to be available if he needed her.

Her dragon spoke up. *He will be fine. He knows how to keep his face expressionless and, usually, his temper in check.*

With others, yes. But this is his father we're talking about.

And worrying is going to accomplish what? We could be downstairs better knowing the others. We might need their help, after all.

Unlike Faye, her dragon seemed unaffected by what had nearly happened with Grant. If Aaron hadn't knocked when he did, she might well be in the midst of a frenzy.

Her beast huffed. *I'm strong enough to resist it, especially with him. Can you stop it? He is our true mate. Why don't you stop fighting it?*

I have my reasons.

The finality of her dragon's voice told her that her beast wasn't going to reveal what they were.

Sighing, she put down her phone and rubbed her eyes. For once, it'd be nice to have an easy, normal life. Finding a mate, kissing them, having a frenzy or at least wild sex if they weren't true mates—that was what most dragon-shifters did.

But not Faye.

However, she closed her eyes and easily remembered being pressed against Grant's warm chest. The feel of his lips on her skin had caused her body to burn in a good way.

Damn, she couldn't wait to have him naked in her bed.

Opening her eyes, she sighed. Of course, she wanted more than just sex. After talking with his father, Faye would comfort Grant. He might try to brush it off and say he didn't need it, but he would. The bloody male wouldn't take care of himself, but that just meant she would have to.

In the meantime, there was nothing she could do but wait. However, how she waited was up to her.

With Cat in her room, her charge would be safe enough if Faye snuck downstairs to join the laughter. Talking with the others might help the time pass faster, too. Aye, socializing with the others would be the best option. Who knew, she might even find out some information about the other clans. She was determined to gain the trust of Snowridge and Northcastle someday.

Before she could more than place her feet on the floor, her mobile rang. She checked the caller ID; it was Finn. Clicking Receive, Faye answered, "Finn?"

"No, this your mum, Lorna MacKenzie."

"I know your name, Mum. Why are you using Finn's phone?"

"Watch your tone, Faye. I would tsk more, but this is important. Arabella's in labor."

Faye sat up straighter. "Pardon?"

"The babies are coming. Finn's anxious to have you or Grant here to watch over the clan in case one of our enemies tries something."

"Not that I don't want to see the triplets, but why can't Cooper handle it?"

Cooper Maxwell was Grant's second-in-command of the Protectors and in charge of clan security in Grant's absence.

Lorna lowered her voice. "There have been some threats from the Dragon Knights. They have a grudge against Arabella, you know. Killing her babies would be their greatest revenge. Cooper is strong, but not as experienced as you two. I believe Cooper already sent you some of the threats to look over."

Faye cursed. When her mother didn't scold her choice of words, Faye knew her mum was worried. "I'll look at the threats and then reach out to Bram on Stonefire first and see what can be done. I want to keep Finn and Arabella safe. However, if this event is canceled because of another attack on our kind, it won't bode well for our future."

Her mother paused a second before replying, "It's nice to have you fully back, Faye."

Ignoring her mother's casual reference to Faye's long recovery from her injury, she pushed on. "Grant left me in charge, so I don't have a choice. As soon as I talk to Bram, I'll call you back at this number, aye?"

"Just don't take too long. Finn's trying his best to keep Arabella calm, but too much worry could complicate matters. She's already giving birth to three bairns. She doesn't need anything else on her mind."

"Aye, I understand. Talk to you soon, Mum."

Faye hung up the phone and checked her email. Sure enough, there was a coded message to check the secure server Arabella had set up for the Protectors.

After accessing the correct file, she read the first message:

You were meant to die at the hands of the hunters years ago. Your children are abominations. We will take care of the mistakes and realign fate.

Faye's inner dragon hissed at the same time she narrowed her eyes. Arabella had been set on fire as a teenager by a group of dragon hunters, but she had survived, thanks to her mother's sacrifice.

And yet, in some kind of twisted logic, the Dragon Knights thought Arabella surviving the horrific ordeal to start over was a mistake that needed to be corrected. Faye would never understand how strangers could harbor such hatred for someone they'd never met.

She forced herself to read the rest of the threats and Cooper's notes before dialing Bram's number. He picked up on the third ring. "I'm not sure why you're calling me, Faye, but hurry up. I'm late for a meeting."

"You might have to cancel your meeting. Arabella's in labor."

"I'm not sure I follow, lass. She's hale and hearty. She should do fine."

"No, it's not having the bairns that's the problem. The Dragon Knights are making threats and many of them mention targeting her children."

Bram's voice turned steely. "Tell me what you know, Faye, and I'll see what I can do. I'm not about to allow those bastards to ruin what should be a happy time for Ara. She may be Lochguard now, but she'll always be like a little sister to me."

As Faye explained the situation to Bram and worked on a plan, she kept her eyes on the door. She would make the necessary decisions if she had to, but she hoped Grant returned before anyone had to leave.

CHAPTER FOURTEEN

Per the DDA guard's request, Grant had handed over his phone before entering the part of the castle that held his father. He didn't like being cut off from Faye and the others, but the meeting was too important to risk making demands. Besides, he'd be done soon enough. He didn't expect the conversation to take long.

He didn't have much to say to his father.

At one time, Grant had wanted to punch the bastard and yell his question of why he'd left. Not for the sake of Grant or his brother, Chase, as they had both been grown when their dad left, but for his mother.

Gillian McFarland had only recently started to get out of bed and leave the cottage. For all his dad's faults, his mum had loved the bastard to the end.

And probably still did.

Clenching the fingers of one hand, Grant pushed down his anger. He couldn't allow emotion to derail him from his goal.

His dragon spoke up. *I wish we knew more about his deal with the solicitor. After what he did to our clan, Michael McFarland shouldn't be treated lightly.*

Not wanting to fall into yet another argument with his dragon over the matter since his beast always wanted to drop their father from a great height, Grant constructed a complex maze and tossed his beast inside.

Without someone questioning him inside his head or devising ways to eviscerate his dad, Grant focused on clearing his mind of anything but extracting information that could help secure Lochguard's safety.

The DDA guard finally stopped in front of a door and swiped a keycard. As soon as they entered, Grant spotted Michael McFarland sitting inside a cell.

He approved of the chains around the male's wrists and ankles. His dad shouldn't be able to shift for a few days because of the concoction Grant had used on him, but even if Michael managed to do so early, the specially made cuffs and chains would break his bones if he tried to change into a dragon. In other words, his dad wouldn't be able to fly away.

The guard stopped in front of the cell entrance and said, "You have five minutes. We'll be back after that to let you out."

"What about the DDA's solicitor?" Grant asked.

The guard shook his head. "She's not coming until the meeting is complete. That was part of the deal."

Grant wanted to lecture the DDA staff about being too cocky in their abilities, but he bit his tongue lest he lose his five minutes of interrogation time.

He stepped into the cell, but his father continued to look at the ground until the guards left and they were alone.

Michael raised his head slowly. Grant didn't know what to expect, but his father's expression was blank. The once familiar face now belonged to a stranger.

Grant's dragon banged against the walls of the mental maze, but it held.

Since his father said nothing, Grant asked, "Well? You made a fuss about seeing me. Are you going to remain silent the whole time?"

Michael finally answered, "I just wanted to take a moment to look at my son."

"Bullshit. If you're looking for a way to tackle me or for anything that might help you break out, you won't find it."

His father stared for a few seconds before saying quietly, "You have such potential, Grant. Why would you follow Finn and bow down to the humans?"

"We're not bowing down. It's called working together."

Michael shook his head. "Roderick was right about you."

Grant wasn't going to rise to the bait. "Speaking of your brother, do you want to make things easy and tell me where to find him?" When his father said nothing, Grant added, "So you're ready to rot in a jail cell for him, aye? I never would've pinned you as the loyal type."

"There's too much at stake."

For a split second, worry crossed his father's face, but then it was gone. The action reminded him that Michael McFarland was just a regular bloke, with little to any training. Maybe if Grant stirred his anger, he could find out more.

Glad to finally be acting like a head Protector and not a disgruntled son, Grant asked, "You're aware that if the roles were reversed and Roderick were here, he'd give you up without pause. If anything, you're a burden to him because of your lack of training or military experience." His dad remained silent, so Grant pushed harder. "Not to mention the Americans you worked with can verify your identity and add time to your sentence. Your best bet is to talk with me."

"Aye, and what would you do? Throw flowers over my head and welcome me back with open arms? I doubt it, son."

Grant wanted to tell the male not to call him son, but managed to restrain himself. He needed to keep a cool head. "Perhaps a shorter sentence. And when you're finished serving it, the DDA might help relocate you with a new identity. That way you can pretend you don't have a family and you'll never bother Mum again."

"I tried to get your mother to go, but she refused. She made her choice."

His father still wasn't riled up enough, so Grant said, "You and she weren't true mates and time has shown why not."

"Listen, lad. Some things are bigger than love or family. You left us to serve in Afghanistan, to fight for the British and other humans' war. You should understand that."

Grant raised an eyebrow. "Me joining the army and learning the skills necessary to protect the clan is nowhere near the same thing."

"Wasn't it? You made the selfish decision without asking us. You're not so different from me, son."

"I never would've attacked my own people, and I was thinking about the clan's future. That's a bloody big difference." Grant had an idea. "Your actions eventually helped to kill Nora and Isla Chisolm during the attack in February. Isla was just a wee lass who had done nothing. You're going to tell me she deserved to die?"

For a second, regret flashed in Michael's eyes, but it quickly vanished. "That is on Finn's leadership. A better clan leader would've evacuated everyone to safety on time."

It seemed his father had an excuse for everything.

Aware that Grant's time was running out, he played one last card. "If you're so dead set on dragon-shifters being superior, then why did Roderick work with the Dragon Knights?"

Before Roderick's band of traitors had left Lochguard, they had worked with Duncan Campbell to pass on the codes to Lochguard's security gates so that the Dragon Knights could infiltrate Lochguard. Finn and the loyal members of the clan had ultimately defeated the Knights with the help of the DDA, but it was the event that had triggered the banishment of the dragon-shifters turned traitor.

"Using humans as a tool doesn't violate our way of thinking or ultimate goal," Michael answered. "Once we have convinced enough dragon-shifters to join our cause, we can also rule over the Knights."

"So that's your ultimate plan, aye? I'll find a way to pass that information on to the bastards. They won't be helping you again in the future." Michael fidgeted in his seat but remained quiet. Grant added, "This is your final opportunity to tell me everything you know. Otherwise, you will be dealing with the DDA on your own."

"I'm not about to go back to a shit life and do what others tell me. The DDA may imprison me for a short while, but that just gives me time to make friends with the other dragon prisoners. They should be easy to sway to our side."

Grant was careful to keep his face expressionless at the statement. His father probably didn't realize how valuable that information would be.

The door behind him opened and the guard walked up to the cell to unlock it. Grant looked at his father one more time before he turned and left.

From here on out, Grant didn't have a father. But he did have information that could prove useful to the clan and the DDA in general. He needed to get back to the B&B and talk with Faye. They might just have to use her plan after all.

~ ~ ~

Arabella MacLeod slumped to the bed as another contraction ceased. "I thought the bloody things were supposed to help me push out the babies."

Dr. Layla MacFie, Lochguard's recently appointed head doctor, smiled up at her. "They do, but if you push now, all it'll accomplish is to make you tired. The bairns have to be in the right position to cooperate. Yours are being stubborn devils."

"Of course they are. Finn is their father," Arabella muttered.

Finn wiped her forehead with a wet cloth. "They'll be here soon enough, love. Just think of it this way—the longer they stay inside, the fewer nappies we have to change."

Arabella glared at her mate. "I will gladly change nappies if it means this can be over. And I meant it, Finn. No more children after this. I can't handle being pregnant again."

Even a year ago, Arabella would've had a hard time admitting a weakness. But after falling in love with Finn and the male proving time and again she could trust him, she always spoke her mind.

Her dragon spoke up. *Tell him he needs to work harder at distracting us from the pain.*

Do you really want to encourage him?

Normally no. But another contraction is about to hit and it should remind you of why his humor can help.

149

Arabella didn't have a chance to reply before a contraction rippled through her uterus. Gripping Finn's hand in hers, she clenched her teeth. She needed to be strong and not scream. She was the clan leader's mate.

Finn whispered into her ear, "It's okay to yell, love. Half the clan already knows what it sounds like when you scream my name when you come."

She growled at Finn and rode out the contraction. When it finished, she whispered, "That is what got us into this situation in the first place. Don't remind me."

Before Finn could reply, Aunt Lorna MacKenzie rushed into the room and went to Arabella's other side. The woman had been like a mother to Arabella and she smiled at Lorna's familiar face. "Good, you're here. Maybe you can tell Finn to tone it down."

Lorna raised her brows and looked to Finn. "What have you been saying?"

"Nothing, Aunt Lorna. I was just trying to lighten the mood."

Lorna tsked and looked back at Arabella's face. "He means well, child. Finn is trying to hide it, but he's worried. The humor helps distract him as well."

Looking to Finn, Arabella said, "It'll be okay, Finn. Despite your antics, I'm not going anywhere. I love you."

Finn smiled slowly. "I sometimes wonder about that."

"Finlay," Arabella and Lorna said at the same time.

Thankfully, Layla's voice prevented any of them from saying more. "Lorna, you should go wait with the others."

From experience, Arabella knew that Lorna MacKenzie didn't take orders from many. But she smiled once more at Arabella and said, "If you need me, child, I won't be far away."

Arabella bobbed her head and Lorna exited the room. Layla didn't miss a beat as she spoke up again. "Okay, Ara. I need you to focus and push on this next one. The first bairn is ready to come out." Arabella nodded and Layla added, "But stop when I tell you to stop. I need to make sure the next lass or lad is in the right position."

Arabella and Finn had followed dragon-shifter tradition in that they wouldn't know the genders of their babies until they were born.

Her dragon chimed in. *Three boys would be easier. Then Finn wouldn't threaten the lives of other males wanting to court a daughter.*

It also means being surrounded by protective males.

Good point.

The pain returned, but at Finn's firm grip in hers, Arabella drew on his strength and pushed with everything she had.

Trying not to think of the details, something stretched her in ways she couldn't imagine. What she wouldn't give for pain medication, but it was risky because of the amount of dragon-shifter hormones in her body due to carrying three babies.

When the contraction finally stopped, Layla beamed at her. "We have a head."

"You mean I have to push five more times just to have three babies?"

"It may be less or even slightly more. The first one will be the hardest, most likely."

Arabella barely had the strength to keep her eyes open. She had no idea how she was going to make it through who knew how many minutes or hours of labor. As it were, she'd barely been able to keep anything down her entire pregnancy, and the result was that she was always a bit lightheaded.

Finn nuzzled her cheek and murmured, "We'll do this together, Ara. I'll take care of you for as long as it takes you to fully recover. Let's just meet our wee rascals first."

She leaned into his touch. "Then help support me, Finn. My strength is waning."

Finn moved to wrap an arm around her shoulders. The solidness of his muscles and his familiar scent helped her to relax a fraction.

He kissed her head and murmured, "You can do it, Ara. I know you can."

Pain raced through her body with another contraction, and somehow Arabella followed Layla's command to push. After what seemed like hours but was probably seconds, a baby's cry echoed inside the room right before Layla said, "Stop pushing, Arabella. It's time to meet your son."

One of the nurses, a male named Logan, took their son and brought him over. "Just for a second. Say hello, wee one, before I clean you up."

Arabella looked at the tiny red face topped with dark hair like hers and tears prickled her eyes. She was now responsible for a tiny dragon-shifter. "I'm a mum."

Finn kissed the boy's forehead. "Hello, son. Your mum is a bit worried right now, but I know she'll do a fantastic job."

As Finn grinned at Arabella, she nearly started crying. "Don't be too nice or I'll never finish this."

Logan moved away, and Arabella wanted to scream for him to come back. She hadn't even had a chance to hold her firstborn child.

However, Layla's steely voice garnered her attention. "The next one feels as if he or she is in the right position. I'm going to need you to push again."

THE DRAGON WARRIOR

When the contraction hit, Arabella followed Layla's order. She only hoped she could last long enough to deliver all three of her children safely before she passed out from exhaustion.

Then Finn squeezed her hand and she knew she would. Arabella might be knackered at the end, but she wouldn't give up. If she could survive being tortured by dragon-hunters as a teenager, she could handle birthing three babies, no matter if they inherited Finn's stubbornness and penchant for causing trouble.

Her dragon's voice was weak, but gentle. *I am also here.*

Drawing on the combined strength of her mate and dragon, Arabella pushed with all she had.

~~~

Finlay Stewart might be teasing and strong on the outside, but inside, he felt guilty. He was the cause of Arabella's pain and suffering in the moment. She would forgive him, of course, but given her past, he'd never wanted her to suffer ever again in her life.

His dragon spoke up. *It is temporary. Besides, the pain will give us a family. That is something Arabella yearns for, but rarely voices.*

Aye, she's stubborn. Still, I wish I could take her suffering away.

Even though it was minor in comparison, Arabella squeezed his hand and pain radiated up his arm.

Thankful for his experience as clan leader, Finn never showed his discomfort. "You're doing well, love."

"Harder, Ara," Layla ordered. Soon, the doctor shouted, "Another boy!"

He grinned. "We have two sons, love. I'm rooting for lucky number three, too."

"I hope not. Living with four males in one house would drive me mad."

Logan brought over their second son. He was tiny and pink with dark hair, just like the first. The thought that Finn had helped make the wee one sent a rush of pride and love through his body. He couldn't wait to see how their bairns turned out. For Arabella's sanity, he hoped at least one of them took after her and not him.

Finn was no expert, but their second child looked to be the same size as his other son, not to mention he had the same nose and face shape. "Hello, younger devil." Finn maneuvered their clasped hands so that Arabella could touch their son's head. "You're handsome, just like your brother."

Logan said, "Aye, he and his brother look alike. I'll have to check more closely, but you might have identical twins on your hands."

Finn smiled as Arabella said, "At least they have dark hair and not ginger. We don't need two sets of ginger-haired twins."

Finn's cousins, Fergus and Fraser, were identical twins with red hair. "If our sons did, I might just have to question the parentage. Ginger hair is a MacKenzie trait, not a Stewart one."

Arabella sighed. "Finn."

At the exhaustion in Arabella's voice, Finn nodded and refrained from teasing his mate further. Logan took their second son away to be checked and cleaned up. His beast said, *Why do they keep taking our bairns away? I want to see them and hold them. They are ours.*

In time, dragon. We need to make sure they're healthy first. And we also couldn't lend Arabella the support she needs if we had to look after the bairns, aye?

His beast grunted at his logic and fell silent again.

Finn focused back on his mate. "You're nearly there, love. Just one more. Our third son is eager to join his brothers."

Arabella shook her head. "Our daughter wants to wait as long as possible. She knows already that her brothers are overprotective. They probably growled in the womb."

Finn chuckled. "Aye, I could see that. Even if it's another boy, he'll be the youngest and the other lads will look out for him."

He watched as Layla felt around Arabella's abdomen. While working, Layla said, "Don't push on the next contraction, Ara. I need to get the last one in position."

As if on cue, their boys started crying in unison. Logan murmured, "It's okay, lads. Your sibling will be along shortly."

While Finn trusted Layla and Logan with his children's lives, he missed the former head doctor, Gregor Innes, who had mated Stonefire's doctor and had moved to Northern England to be with her. If he were still part of Lochguard, Arabella would have both Layla and Gregor watching over her. Two doctors were better than one.

His dragon spoke up. *Gregor is finally happy again and will have his own child before long.*

I know. Still, he was much better at getting Ara to rest and listen to him.

Layla is still earning her marks as head doctor. It won't be long before the whole clan adjusts.

Finn could spend an hour thinking of how to better support Layla, but Arabella sighed and he zeroed in on his mate. "Is the pain worse?"

"No. But I feel as if I could sleep for a week and still be tired."

Because of the circles under her eyes, he refrained from mentioning that the triplets were going to keep them busy. Finn would shoulder what he could, but Arabella was the food source and would have to help.

He merely hummed a tune and Arabella smiled at him. "That's your mum's tune. The one you've been using with little Jamie."

"Aye, I practiced humming it with my nephew. I wanted to have it perfect for our bairns. Singing is not one of my specialties, despite my best efforts."

She nuzzled against his arm. "If the babies start crying, then you can worry about being tone-deaf. Until then, it's just a sign of love and tribute to your mother."

Not wanting to think of his parents and how much he wished they were still around, he looked to Layla. "Any progress?"

Layla nodded. "Let's try with the next contraction. We're nearly there, Ara."

It wasn't long before Arabella was pushing again. He barely noticed his bruised fingers. He was anxious to meet his last child.

Last? His dragon echoed.

Aye. I'm not doing this to Arabella again. We're going to get snipped.

Arabella strained as she tried to push their third bairn out. After what seemed like two lifetimes, a baby's cry pierced the air, followed by Layla's declaration. "You have a daughter."

Arabella slumped onto the bed and leaned heavily against Finn. "A daughter."

Kissing Arabella's nose, he answered, "Aye, and her Auntie Faye is going to have to teach her a few things about being the youngest and holding her own."

Logan brought their little girl over. She was smaller than the other two with fair hair, just like Finn as a child.

"She's so tiny," Arabella murmured.

"Aye, but she's braw," Logan answered. "I still need to check her thoroughly, but she looks healthy to me."

Finn guided their hands to their daughter's cheek. The soft skin under his fingers brought tears to his eyes.

His dragon spoke up. *Why are you emotional now? All three children are precious.*

Of course they are. But this is the last one we'll be greeting for the first time. Allow me to enjoy it.

Finn murmured, "Thank you, love, for the precious gifts."

His mate merely snuggled against him and continued to stare at their daughter.

After Logan finally took away their youngest child, Finn looked at Arabella. "Two sons and a daughter. Aunt Lorna will be pleased. It's as if we paid homage to her own brood."

"Yes, that was my first thought," Arabella drawled.

"Oh, come on, love. It is a bit amusing. Fate has a sense of humor."

Amusement danced in Arabella's eyes. "In more ways than one."

With a growl, Finn kissed his mate and whispered, "Despite your cheekiness, I love you, lass."

"You should. The cheekiness is thanks to you."

As they smiled at one another, Layla's voice broke the moment. "Sorry to interrupt. But I thought you might want to hold all of your children before we deliver the afterbirth."

Finn reluctantly released Arabella's hand as Logan deposited one blue bundle and then another into Arabella's arms. Layla brought the pink bundle and laid it on Arabella's chest and Finn kept her in place with his free hand.

He laid his cheek against Arabella's as they stared at their three children. From this moment forward, their lives would never be the same. But Finn wouldn't have it any other way. Arabella had given him a family. Since both he and Arabella had lost so much, it was just the fresh start they needed.

And fuck any Dragon Knights or anyone else who tried to steal away their happy future.

CHAPTER FIFTEEN

Faye checked her mobile phone yet again. She still hadn't heard anything from bloody Grant.

Her dragon spoke up. *He will respond as soon as he can. Besides, Bram has people going to help guard Arabella.*

I know, but I feel as if either Grant or I should also be there. Cat doesn't need us plus Iris and the DDA security team to watch over her, provided she stays inside our accommodations.

Then just tell Iris you're going and leave. Grant will understand.

He probably would, but Faye still didn't want to make such an important decision without his knowledge. *He is head Protector and if I start breaking the chain of command, others might follow suit and compromise Lochguard's security.*

Her dragon huffed. *This is different. You used to be in charge. You know when to bend the rules.*

She decided how to respond to that since technically, it was true. Being a former head Protector gave her a unique perspective on things.

However, Grant's authority needed to be absolute, except for the clan leader's say. *Maybe next time he can designate me as in charge. Then we won't have this problem.*

Faye's phone beeped with a message. It was from Grant: *I'll be there soon.*

She'd been cryptic in her earlier message, but the fact he trusted her and didn't question her urgency meant more to Faye than she would ever say. She was starting to think she and Grant might work out, after all.

What about the frenzy? her dragon asked.

So now you're open to him again?

I didn't say that. But he is proving himself. It's a start.

Faye sighed. *Let's not argue about this right now. Kissing Grant is the last thing on my mind, at least until we know Arabella is safe and no one is about to attack Lochguard.*

We only just received word from Mum that Ara had two boys and a girl. Even if the Knights have someone working at the surgery, it would take time to mobilize.

You seem to forget that we still have to fly back.

Someone knocked on the door and Faye answered it. Cat stood there and studied her. "Are you okay? They're serving supper here tonight, and you're usually the first one to round us all up and head downstairs."

Faye motioned for Cat to come inside. Once the door shut, Faye answered, "Arabella just had her babies."

Cat looked at her askance. "That should be wonderful news, so why aren't you happier about it?"

She lowered her voice. "Because we might have a situation."

"Does that mean we need to leave?"

Faye loved the fact Cat asked that question without any hint of disappointment or disgruntlement. "You should be able to remain here with the other participants. We need all of the good publicity your event should bring this evening."

"What aren't you telling me, Faye MacKenzie? If it's classified, I understand. But if not, I'd love to know what's going on. I may not be a soldier, but I'm sure there's some way I can help."

"Thanks, but your place is here. Your presence and interaction with the media will do the most good." Faye paused and then added, "As for what's going on, I promise to tell you as soon as I can. Just know that it has nothing to do with anyone here."

"Okay, that's a bit cryptic, but I trust you. Would you like me to bring something up for you to eat? It's not as good as my mum's, but it's passable."

Faye smiled. "Nothing is as good as your mum's cooking, except for maybe mine. But anything will be great. If you could nab some for Grant, too, that would be perfect."

Cat opened her mouth to reply, but a furious pounding on her door interrupted her. Faye said, "Come in."

Grant rushed into the room but paused a second when he saw Cat. "Cat."

Cat smiled. "I was just leaving."

As soon as Cat was gone, Grant blurted out, "What's going on? Your message only signaled that something was happening back home, but that it was immediate."

Faye filled Grant in on the situation with Arabella and the threats before adding, "No one has attacked Lochguard yet. Although Bram is sending a few of his Protectors to help us out. We need to decide which of us is going back to Lochguard to oversee security until the threat is no more."

Grant didn't hesitate. "Both of us. Iris can handle things here."

"Are you sure?"

"Of course I'm bloody sure. Don't start second-guessing yourself now, Faye Cleopatra."

She narrowed her eyes. "I'm not second-guessing myself. I'm not in charge anymore. Unless it's common practice for anyone to defy you and make their own rules, I thought it best to wait for your order."

"You shouldn't have to. Once things settle down, we're going to talk about sharing the responsibility of being head Protector."

~~~

Grant could've picked a better time to share his plans for Faye, but the words had spilled from his lips before he could stop it.

Faye's eyes widened a fraction before she whispered, "Truly?"

"Yes, bloody woman. We can hash out the details later. For the moment, we need to make preparations and head back to Lochguard."

Faye shook her head. "Leave it to you to make a grand announcement and then dismiss it. We're going to have to discuss your timing." She reached out and touched his arm. "But before we leave, did you learn anything from your father?"

The warmth of Faye's hand on his arm helped ease his tension a fraction. "Michael shared some valuable information, but it's not anything that can't wait."

His dragon spoke up. *You shouldn't be so abrupt with her. Time is of the essence, even with Faye.*

However, Grant didn't want to completely dismiss Faye and have her take it the wrong way. He covered her hand on his arm with his. "Once things settle down on Lochguard, I promise to tell you everything, lass."

She smiled. "You're just worried about our home, which is as it should be."

As Grant stared into Faye's brown eyes, he wished he had time to hold her close and tell her how bloody wonderful she was. She understood him on a level few would.

Unfortunately, head Protector meant putting his personal desires to the side when needed.

His dragon added, *Hopefully not for much longer.*

Grant agreed. He nodded at Faye. "Aye, so let's get going. I talked briefly with Iris before I came to your room. She'll handle Lachlan, so we're free to leave straight away."

Faye moved to her bed and picked up a satchel. "I'm already packed. Let's go protect the clan."

She rushed past him, and the corner of Grant's mouth ticked up as he followed. Faye was indeed a leader. The sooner he made her coleadership role official, the better.

His dragon chimed in. *You might want to confirm the details with her first. Faye isn't the type to like things decided for her.*

Aye, I know, dragon. Let's sort out all the crap happening as quickly as possible so that we can corner Faye and talk about the future.

You're the one being slow. The sooner we reach Inverness Castle, the sooner we can shift. I'm much faster than you.

He and Faye snuck out of the B&B carefully and had managed to step outside when a voice asked, "Where are you going?"

It was Max Holbrook.

Grant turned around. "Clan business. I'm sure you understand."

Max's eyes widened. "May I accompany you? I love flying and don't have the opportunity very often."

Faye replied before he could. "Maybe some other time, Max. I'm sure if you listen to Iris and follow her orders, she'll offer you a ride."

Grant could just imagine the look on Iris's face if she heard what Faye was saying.

Max said, "I'm not so sure about that. She thinks we need to stay here and never leave."

Grant kept his voice free of impatience. "You can discuss it with her. But no, you can't come with us. For your safety, go back inside."

Faye added, "It's nearly time for you to leave for the exhibition opening. You don't really want to deprive all of those people of your wonderful finds, do you?"

"You're right. It's my duty to share." Max turned back toward the house. "But I'll remember your words about Iris. I'm going to fly again by any means necessary."

The human went back inside. He was glad that Max wasn't his problem.

Grant took Faye's hand and gently pulled her down the pavement. "Let's hurry before he changes his mind and tries to follow us."

As they jogged toward Inverness Castle, he squeezed Faye's hand in his and she did the same. He knew she'd have his back. Always.

His dragon sighed. *We still need to ask and make it official.*

Even if for some strange reason she wants to delay the frenzy, she will always still have our back. If you question Faye's loyalty, then I wonder if you've paid attention.

Of course I trust her. But I want the right to protect her as our mate. I'm impatient.

Then help me secure the clan as fast as possible.

Faye's voice prevented his beast from replying. "I wouldn't underestimate Max. If he's managed to stay out of prison this long despite his illegal digging, he has some sway somewhere."

"I don't bloody care. I just want to reach Lochguard as soon as possible."

"And we will. You need to learn to multi-task."

Faye released his hand and rushed ahead of him. With a growl, Grant pushed himself to catch up. Even though Faye was shorter than him, she'd always been quicker.

His dragon spoke up. *I'd love to chase her when there's no danger.*

Aye, so would I. So let's rid Lochguard of any threats and we can work on it.

Someone's changed his tune from a few days ago.

Taking care of the traitors may involve a more long-term plan. As long as we can ensure the clan's safety from the Knights for the foreseeable future and put our plan into motion, Faye may be open to some kissing.

Then hurry up and run faster. I can't do anything to help us succeed until we shift.

He smiled at his beast's impatience. Not that Grant didn't feel the same.

However, as he watched Faye's body move as she ran, he rather enjoyed being a second behind her. The view provided him with motivation to finish their current task as soon as possible.

~~~

Finn swapped his daughter, Freya, for his youngest son, Declan. Careful to keep his tone light, he said to Fergus, "What are the latest reports?"

"So far, the forest is quiet. The loch, too, looks free of invaders. Our biggest concern is that drones will suddenly appear and attack everyone," Fergus answered.

Arabella's voice was tired as she said, "Is everyone inside?"

Fergus nodded. "Aye. But we can't stay this way for long. Even with most of the cottages now having a bomb shelter stocked with supplies, we can't live this way long term."

As Declan squirmed a second in his sleep, Finn quietly cursed the Dragon Knights. He should be enjoying time with his new family, not worrying about a possible attack.

His dragon chimed in. *It's better to be cautious than to lose more people.*

Finn looked down at Arabella holding both Freya and their oldest son, Grayson. Despite everything going on, he took a second to memorize the love in Arabella's eyes as she stared at one of their children.

His beast spoke up. *We fight for them.*

Finn looked to his cousin Fergus. "You can go back to monitoring contacts with the others. Although, when you have the chance, could you bring one of Ara's computers here?"

Fergus frowned down at Arabella. "Ara just gave birth."

Arabella smiled. "Believe me, I would rather be sleeping in a big bed with my mate and children, but I can't do that until the clan is safe."

"You're a strong one, Arabella MacLeod." With a nod, Fergus left them alone in the delivery room.

Finn sat at the edge of Arabella's bed and looped an arm around her shoulders. "Are you sure you want the children to only carry my surname?"

Arabella glanced up at him. "You want to discuss that now? I thought we decided weeks ago to give them Stewart."

"Aye, but it feels wrong for them not to carry a piece of their mother's name."

Leaning her head against his shoulder, Arabella said, "We'll discuss it later. As it is, I'm glad we had two boys and a girl. That simplified naming rights."

He and Arabella had each picked out a male name. Finn had selected Declan and Arabella had wanted Grayson. Freya had been the only female name they'd both agreed on.

Finn lifted Declan and kissed his youngest son's cheek. "We'll get you home soon, wee Dec. Your uncles Fraser and Fergus promised a surprise."

Declan scrunched his nose as if he knew the surprise would be outlandish. At least his children would be initiated into the MacKenzie family antics from the get-go.

Arabella's voice filled the room. "I hope by the time they're old enough to walk, the Dragon Knights will be a distant memory."

"Me too, love. Me too."

Finn gently switched Declan for Grayson before whispering into his oldest son's ear, "But even if that's the case, you're the oldest, lad. It'll be up to you to look out for the others."

Grayson didn't so much as move a finger.

Arabella adjusted her children so that they lay on the bed to either side of her. "I need to take a nap, no matter how short, Finn. Make sure the babies don't roll off the bed?"

He smiled down at his mate. "Never fear, Gray and I will keep watch."

"Gray and Dec," she murmured. "I already see the twins getting into trouble with you."

Her eyelids closed and Arabella was asleep before Finn could say anything.

As he took in each member of his family, Finn whispered, "I will keep you all safe, no matter the cost. Your dad will never allow harm to come to you."

As his three bairns and Arabella snored slightly, Finn only hoped he could keep his promise.

His dragon chimed in. *Of course we will. The Knights are sloppy. We can defeat them.*

Just don't underestimate them.

His beast fell silent, and Finn enjoyed what precious moments he could with his family. Shit would probably hit the fan soon enough.

CHAPTER SIXTEEN

Faye and Grant had decided to take the less direct approach to Lochguard by flying apart but close enough they could call out to each other. That way they could survey some of the past hiding spots of the Knights, if they were indeed there.

So far, Faye only saw the usual cottages, trees, and animals in the late evening sunshine. Thanks to it being early summer, the sun set late. That would work to Lochguard's advantage. Large groups could easily be spotted. If there were enemies, they definitely were moving in small groups under the cover of the trees.

I can't wait to hear an update from Cooper, Faye said to her dragon.

We're nearly there.

The landscape below told her they would arrive in a few minutes.

Ignoring the growing ache in her wing, Faye tried to tamp down her excitement. Not for the threat to the clan, but rather at seeing Finn and Arabella's children. She'd loved being auntie to wee Jamie and looked forward to putting ideas into the heads of Finn's kids. She could then sit back and watch it play out.

Her dragon spoke up again. *You might want to be careful. Whatever you do to the others' children, they will retaliate with our own.*

Faye's wings missed a beat. *You're getting ahead of yourself, dragon. I haven't even kissed Grant. Let's see how that goes before you start plotting out our future.*

A kiss is all it will take. I hope you remember that.

She was about to reply when Faye noticed a quick, bright flash of light in one section of the Naver Forest. Since the forest was partially along the Strathnaver Trail, which was a series of stops related to local history, the light could've been a camera flash. But Faye wasn't taking any chances.

Gliding down, she scanned the road for parked cars or motorcycles. There weren't any.

That most likely ruled out tourists.

Faye wanted nothing more than to land, shift into her human form, and check out the light herself. But she wasn't naïve. Since no one knew her exact location, she needed to land on Lochguard and set things in motion there.

She turned and quickly flew across Loch Naver toward Lochguard's rear landing area.

Grant was already on the ground in his human form when she arrived. He spotted her in the air, moved to the edge, and Faye slowed her descent until her hind legs touched the ground.

Imagining her snout shrinking into a nose, her wings disappearing into her back, and her limbs changing into arms and legs, she soon stood in her human form. Grant strode over with a blanket he'd snatched from somewhere. He quickly laid it over her shoulders and said, "I didn't see anything. For a second, I thought someone was swimming in the loch, but whatever it was dove down and remained there far too long for a human."

"Unless they're using scuba gear."

"Aye, that's true. We'll keep an eye on it. If so, they won't have enough air to stay down there too long and will have to emerge. I can send a few of the younger Protectors to take a cold swim and investigate." He rearranged the blanket until it better covered her body. "What about you, lass?"

"I saw a flash of light in the forest. It could be a strong camera flash or it could be something else. I think we need to send a team over there to investigate, too."

"After we check in with Cooper, I'll send a team." Grant paused a second before adding, "If you have some candidates in mind to check the forest, we can use them."

Grant was yet again sharing his role with her.

Pushing aside her curiosity as to whether he would continue to share his responsibilities or not, she nodded toward the central command building. "Let's hurry. If there is someone out there, they might've seen my dragon form. If we give them too much time, we might lose them."

Grant nodded, and they both hurried toward the most fortified building on Lochguard.

~~~

Grant waited for Cooper to finish his report before saying, "I wish there was a better way to confirm there isn't a large group of drones waiting to attack."

Cooper replied, "We don't have the funds for the expensive radar that can detect them. However, there hasn't been any sign so far. And given that you and Faye just flew in, which would've been a perfect time to attack, we should be safe for the moment."

Faye asked, "Any word from the DDA?"

"They received our concerns, but until we have proof, there's nothing they will do," Cooper answered. "Dragon-shifters have received threats for centuries. Besides, they don't even take all of the threats towards their employees seriously. I doubt ours

171

will receive any more attention without an attack or some other proof."

Uncrossing his arms, Grant stood tall. "Aye, well we can look after ourselves for the time being. Send the two teams to investigate the forest and the loch before the sun sets."

Cooper nodded. "Of course. Once you see Finn and check with Arabella, come find me. There are a few other ideas I'd like to share."

Grant studied Cooper a second. The male had so far proved himself in a tense situation. Grant needed to delegate more to the dragonman in the future. "We shouldn't be long. I'll have my mobile if anything comes up."

After waving good-bye, both Grant and Faye exited the room and headed toward the surgery. Grant spoke first. "I can't believe they're making Arabella work so soon after giving birth."

"She, more than anyone, wants to ensure the safety of the clan. Ara didn't just spend who knows how long birthing three bairns to have it all taken away from her. If she overtires herself, Finn will make her take a break. He wants the clan safe, but not at the expense of his mate's life." She paused a second before asking, "Are you one of those males who believes a female should give everything up once they have children?"

Grant had known the question would come eventually but had expected a little more time to think it through.

His dragon grunted. *You already know the answer. Just tell her.*

While Grant never slowed down his pace, he did look over at Faye. "No, but just as a new father needs to be more careful for the sake of his family, a new mother should do the same. That means no unnecessary risks to prove one's self."

She raised an eyebrow. "You think I'm out to prove myself?"

"Up until a few days ago, aye, I did. You've been in competition with yourself since the attack, Faye. I'm glad you've embraced your confidence again and aren't second-guessing yourself."

She opened her mouth and then closed it. As the silence dragged on, Grant wondered if he'd made a mistake in telling the truth.

Never, his dragon said.

Faye finally sighed before she replied, "I thought I'd done a pretty good job at hiding that fact, if I'm honest. I'm starting to think you're a mind reader."

"I may not know you as well as your family when it comes to how you toss a roll across a table, but no one knows you better when it comes to your Protector-related skills. Confident Faye is someone I'd entrust my life to. I'm glad she's back."

She paused a second before asking, "So when you said earlier you wanted to share the head Protector role with me, you were telling the truth?"

"Of course I was. I've never been good at lying or placating you, lass. I'm not about to start now."

She paused again. Each time she did, his dragon paced and swished his tail a little more inside his mind.

Grant said to his beast, *Calm down. You're the one who wanted me to tell the truth.*

Aye, but if I had my way, I'd get straight to the point.

I'm easing her into the idea of being our mate.

So now you want her.

I have for a while now. If you don't know that, then you haven't been paying attention.

His dragon huffed but didn't say anything else.

Faye's voice finally filled the air. "Then answer me this, Grant. If I allow the frenzy to happen, what then?"

173

He didn't miss a beat. "I would protect you with my life. However, I would also understand that you need to be who you are. I won't keep you in a locked cage like some males, Faye. But you also need to promise to be careful. No more pretending your wing is as good as new. You have limits and I need you to share them with me."

"Only if you share yours with me."

"So, did you just agree to kiss me once the clan is safe again?"

She smiled. "Maybe. Although I have one other condition."

"Do I want to know?"

She lightly hit his arm. "I should say I want you to join Aaron Caruso in dancing naked at Arabella and Finn's triplets' celebration, but my request isn't just about you. I was serious before about you, your mother, and brother dining with my family. Only after that will I kiss you. I think that's good motivation."

He growled. "Just don't expect me to kiss you for the first time in front of your family." He lowered his voice. "I'm not going to hold back. We'll see if you can handle me."

"Those are fighting words. Maybe you can't handle me."

"I accept your challenge." He leaned over and whispered, "Oh, and lass? You know I'm competitive. I intend to win."

Faye shivered at his words and both man and beast wanted to haul her into the nearest empty space and kiss her straight away.

Too bad they were nearly to the surgery.

His beast spoke up again. *We just need to vanquish the threat as soon as possible.*

You mean the Knights. I'm not so sure about the rogue dragon-shifters. That's going to take a more involved plan.

So be it. As long as it's in motion, we can finally kiss our true mate. After all, she never said anything about capturing them before she'll kiss us. The clan only has to be safe.

And if we groom Cooper a bit more, it should put Faye's mind at ease.

Exactly.

Faye's voice prevented him from replying to his beast. "Let me guess, your dragon is happy now?"

"A bit. I hope yours doesn't attempt to dress him down once I kiss you."

Her pupils flashed to slits and back. "I can't make any promises. However, I think it'll be good for her to make your dragon work harder."

His beast huffed. *I now have my own challenge.*

Good luck, mate. The frenzy will give you lots of time to sort things out with lady dragon.

Just as they approached the main entrance to the surgery, Lorna MacKenzie strode out and headed straight for them. She pulled Faye into a hug. "I've missed you, Faye."

"Mum, it's only been a few days. You act like I've been gone for years."

Lorna released her daughter and patted her arm. "I know, child. But what with Arabella having her bairns, it reminded me of the last time I gave birth." Faye opened her mouth to reply, but Lorna beat her to it. "But enough about me. You two need to hurry up. Arabella needs rest, and the sooner we sort out the bloody Knights, the better."

Grant blinked. He had never heard Lorna MacKenzie swear in his life.

Lorna fixed her gaze on him. "You've heard worse from my own children. Now, let's not stand out here all day. Come on."

Faye tugged Grant through the door and down the hall. Because the clan was staying indoors until told otherwise, the waiting area was empty. Grant murmured, "Maybe we lucked out and your brothers are at home."

Lorna's voice carried down the hall. "Why would they be? Everyone's here."

Faye winked at him. "You know you love them." She lowered her voice. "My advice is to give as good as you get. Otherwise, you won't ever stand a chance. You can't be aloof and growly forever. That will only encourage Fraser and Fergus to try harder."

Faye dashed into the room as his dragon chimed in. *Maybe we should allow them to underestimate us. After all, we're the one with military training. They don't stand a chance in the long run.*

I agree, but let's not best them too early. They could become allies in the future.

Grant entered the large room and wondered how so many dragonmen and women could fit into it. In addition to Finn, Arabella, and their three bairns, there was her whole family and their mates—Lorna and Ross, Fergus and Gina, Fraser and Holly. To round it off, there was also one of Lochguard's nurses, Logan Lamont.

Whether he liked it or not, Grant was going to have to get used to being around a large family if he wanted Faye as his mate.

His dragon spoke up. *That should be easy enough.*

I'll remember that when you start moaning later.

Huffing, his beast fell silent and retreated to a corner.

Faye was already at Finn and Arabella's side, scooping up a pink bundle. "There's at least one more female in the family. This must be wee Freya."

Finn answered, "If not for the possible threat, I would've switched the blankets before you lot arrived. Then I could've told my children how you couldn't tell the males from the females."

Arabella rolled her eyes. "Ignore him. If I ever want to take a long nap, then we need to deal with the threats." Arabella motioned toward the laptop in front of her. "I never pegged the Knights as intelligent, but it appears as if they've learned not to post their content on the dark areas of the internet. I haven't found anything there to help us."

Grant spoke up. "We're investigating a few things nearby. If my people find nothing, then we might all be able to relax a little."

Holly Anderson, the human female mated to Fraser, sighed. "I hope so. I'm tired of people taking away our happy memories."

Fraser rubbed his mate's back. "I know, honey. I'm tempted to go on holiday for our child's birth just so we can enjoy it."

Lorna frowned. "You're not going anywhere. I want all my grandchildren born here. I'm getting on and don't want to fly long distances, especially if I have to carry Ross around."

Ross patted his belly. "You're the reason I've gained a stone since our mating."

Lorna tsked. "We can discuss how it's your own fault later. Arabella needs to finish talking so she can get some sleep."

All eyes turned toward Arabella. Grant couldn't be the only one to see the circles under the lass's eyes.

His dragon said, *We need to capture the traitors from the clan before the birth of our child. I don't want Faye to be forced to work when she should be sleeping.*

Give it a rest. We haven't even kissed Faye yet.

Arabella's voice filled the room and garnered Grant's attention. "There's not much else to share. I've put out some feelers, but until any of my fellow, er, computer experts get back to me, it's up to you lot to protect us."

Finn nodded. "Then you've done all you can do for now, love." Finn looked to Grant and then Faye. "Let's have a word in the hall."

Finn reluctantly handed over one of his sons to Lorna and exited the room. Grant and Faye followed. Once they were alone, Finn kept his voice low as he said, "The reason I wanted you two back is because while Cooper is improving, I don't think he's ready to handle a possible attack. I'm entrusting you two with the leadership of the clan until it's absolutely necessary for me to resume command. Ara is putting up a strong front, but she needs me. Is you two working together going to be a problem? I know you weren't on the best terms recently."

Sometimes Grant forgot how observant Finn could be. "Aye, we'll be fine. We've been working together well the last few days."

Finn raised his brows. "And I trust you can keep from snogging each other until this is over?"

Faye blinked. "What?"

"Don't play daft with me, Faye," Finn replied. "I know you two are true mates and I'm happy, I really am. But it needs to wait until this is over. Can you do it?"

"I should be offended at your implication," Grant stated. "But what is between Faye and me is our business. Even so, we've kept our heads so far. I doubt a pending threat is going to suddenly make us want to shag in some corner."

"Grant," Faye scolded.

He shrugged. "The truth expedites things."

She rolled her eyes. "I swear I'm surrounded by males who love to irritate me."

"Aye, and we can team up to give you a bigger dose later," Finn said. "For the moment, I'm entrusting the clan's safety to you. I know you'll do well."

With a wave, Finn went back into the room to his mate and children.

Grant turned toward Faye. "Don't worry. If Finn becomes my kin, then I have some ideas about how to retaliate."

Faye placed a hand over her heart. "Is Grant McFarland showing his playful side? I might have a heart attack."

He ignored the fact Faye hadn't protested about his becoming Finn's kin and replied, "There is much about me I only show to those I trust and care about. However, if you're going to tease me about it, I can remain growly and a closed book."

Faye leaned against his chest. "You do that and this will be the last time I do this."

She stood on her tiptoes and kissed his jaw. The light brush of her lips against his skin sent a wave of heat through his body. What he wouldn't give for half an hour alone with Faye.

His dragon growled. *We need more than half an hour.*

Not the frenzy, dragon. I merely want to taste between her thighs.

Don't tease me if we're to focus.

You always boast about being strong. Contain yourself for the next minute or two.

While the clan needed them, he was going to take a few seconds to drive Faye crazy, too.

Grant placed a hand on her back and slowly lowered it until he gripped her arse cheek. Faye sucked in a breath and he smiled. His voice was husky as he murmured, "Two can play that game, lass." Since Faye had wrapped the blanket around her chest to drape down, Grant released her arse and moved his hand to the edge of the blanket. "Consider this some motivation for telling me your limits and never hiding anything from me that's important."

He slowly ran his hand up under the blanket until he reached the juncture between her thighs. He paused to give Faye enough time to tell him to stop. But she remained quiet except for her pounding heart, so he lightly ran his fingers between her folds. He barely restrained a groan at how wet she was. "Faye."

Rather than beg or whimper, Faye placed her fingers over the outline of his hard cock. Despite the fabric of his trousers between them, her touch sent a jolt of electricity through his body. His dragon was barely restraining himself in the back of their mind.

If a mere touch drove him crazy, what would her lips closed around his cock do to him?

Faye's voice filled his ear. "Let's make a deal. Whoever finds the most important information related to stopping the threats will have first go at devouring the other's body."

The image of Grant restrained on a bed as Faye took his cock into her mouth filled his mind. His dragon growled. *I much rather it be the other way around.*

Are you sure? I look forward to Faye teasing us with her tongue.

His dragonwoman's voice cut through his thoughts. "So? Is it a deal?"

"Fine. But just know that if I win, this is just the beginning." He lightly brushed the hard little nub between her thighs and Faye leaned more against him. "There's much we can do without a frenzy, just to make sure you know what you're getting into."

As he teased her opening with his fingers, Faye groaned. "Grant."

"Aye, that's my name." Reluctantly, he removed his hand. "Now, let's get started. The sooner we protect the clan, the sooner I can give you more than a preview of what's to come."

Faye leaned another few seconds against his chest, and he wanted to wrap his arms around his female and never let go.

But he needed to stem all temptations from here on out until he finally had the time to make Faye come and scream his name. Merely touching her wasn't enough for man or beast.

His dragon spoke up. *Then why are we standing in the hall? Let's oversee the two teams investigating the surrounding areas and see what we can find.*

Faye finally pulled away and put a few inches between them. After taking a deep breath, she nodded. "Right, let's go."

As she swayed her hips and headed toward the exit, Grant memorized every detail. He would use it as motivation. Because if he had his way, Faye would be in his bed within the day.

CHAPTER SEVENTEEN

In the interest of expediency and to help each of them concentrate, Faye and Grant had each gone with a team to search the surroundings. Since Faye had seen the light in the forest, she was flying at the head of the V-formation of that team.

Even though leading a team for a mission should make her giddy after so many months without, her thoughts kept trailing back to what Grant had done in the surgery's hallway.

His fingers were rougher and warmer than she'd imagined. And what he did with them, oh boy, that would make her blush if she were in her human form.

Her beast huffed. *Why? We've slept with men before.*

Yes, but it's different with Grant. There's attraction, aye, but I've also known him my whole life. Combined with his skill as a Protector, and the whole package sets me on fire in a way no other male has before.

You think too much. We just need to win.

So, you're on the "shag Grant" bandwagon now?

Perhaps. He's more interesting than I thought. I'll now accept a few other things besides groveling for him to get into my good graces.

Faye mentally sighed. *His poor dragon has no idea what he's getting into if there is indeed a frenzy.*

Her beast sniffed. *If he can't handle me, then he's not worthy enough to be the father of our child.*

Not wanting to think of children and risk missing something important, Faye focused on the final approach to where in the forest she'd seen the light. There were a few dragon-shifters also approaching via the ground in their human forms, which made Faye and the two other dragons with her the distraction, if need be.

She motioned with a hind leg and all three of them dove down toward the trees. She pulled up a split second before she'd crash and skimmed the tops with her talons.

The forest wasn't as grand as it had been in the past, but there were still enough trees to block out large sections of land. Sometimes the ruins of the cottages used by the humans before the Clearances would break the tree cover, but not always.

She finally found a large enough spot to gently descend and put her feet on the ground. The other two members of her team remained in the air.

Listening carefully, Faye only heard the beat of dragon wings, the buzz of midges, and a few small animals scurrying away. She also smelled the forest, dirt, and decay of both plant and animal, but nothing related to recent human activity.

As agreed upon earlier, Faye waited for Brodie MacNeil, one of Lochguard's Protectors, to rendezvous with her.

Speaking of the devil, he appeared out of the trees in his human form. She would have to commend him later for his stealth. It also reminded Faye that if she were to help Grant run the Protectors, she should go out into the field with each of them in turn to reassess their skills and placements.

Brodie's tall, ginger-haired form approached her. She lowered her head. Only when he could whisper in her ear did he say, "There were traces of humans in the forest about a hundred yards from here, but all I could find were some empty bottles of alcohol. They probably were just young folk having a good time."

She bobbed her head a fraction, and he continued, "Regardless, we'll keep looking. I'll meet you at the next checkpoint."

Before she could do anything, Brodie headed back into the trees.

Her dragon grunted. *I hope Grant isn't doing better. I don't like to lose.*

Neither do I, dragon. But we need to be thorough. You know that.

Just because I know it doesn't mean I have to like it.

Methinks you are anxious to see Grant again.

Of course not. Now, are you going to chat all day or can we finish our mission?

With a mental sigh, Faye crouched down and jumped into the air. It took a few extra beats of her wings to get back above the trees, but her wing didn't ache too much and she accomplished it with little trouble.

As she glided on the air currents, Faye continued scanning the trees and wondered if Grant had fared any better.

~~~

Needing the cold water to cool him down after teasing Faye with his fingers, Grant had volunteered to lead the group who would swim in the loch.

As he currently made his way through the water in his dragon form, he arrived at his designated search location. Taking a deep breath, he dunked his head under the water. Since the loch was only about five dragon lengths deep, he only had to dive a few seconds to see everything around him. Thanks to the waterproof light strapped around his neck—dragon eyesight needed at least a little light to work properly in the dark—he could see every nook and cranny even at the deepest section of the water.

There was little beyond vegetation, some rubbish, plenty of rocks, and fish swimming by. Finishing his scan of the current section, he rose to the surface. His head broke the water, and he looked to the other two dragons helping him. They both shook their heads to signal they hadn't found anything and everyone moved to their next area to search.

Grant glanced to the forest on the side opposite from the clan, but didn't hear any sort of alarm. Faye must not have found anything yet either.

His dragon spoke up. *Finding nothing is good. Not only because it eliminates threats, but also because our competition becomes a draw. That could work to our favor.*

Ignoring his dragon, Grant arrived at his next section. The area was near the shore, but was one of the few places where there was a tall rock formation and a sharp drop off; most of the loch had a rocky, relatively flat shoreline.

Taking another deep breath, he dove down again. He surveyed the floor first, but he didn't spot anything out of the ordinary. Next, he went to the almost sheer drop and examined the rock face. At first, all he saw were ridges and crevices that looked natural. But at the bottom, he found a circular outline in the rock, one that had been made by man.

Just in case something waited on the other side, Grant quickly swam to the surface. As soon as the other two dragons also appeared, he motioned for them to come over. Once they arrived, he dove back down. The other two dragons followed.

He guided them to the same suspicious location and pointed out the anomaly. He then extended a talon and tried to pry the circle covering loose.

At first, nothing happened. But as he worked his talon around the outside of the circle, Grant was finally able to pry the covering away. He shined his light inside, and it highlighted a small alcove containing a waterproof-looking sack. Checking to ensure there weren't any traps, Grant extracted it gingerly and made his way back to the surface.

Not wanting to risk ruining what was inside, he swam as quickly but gently as he could to Lochguard's side of the water. Once ashore, he laid down his find and imagined his body shrinking back into its human form. After he finished shifting, Grant crouched down and examined the bag.

It was black and partially rolled up and sealed at the top, which meant it was probably waterproof. The bag looked to be high quality. Of course it had to be if the owner didn't want anything ruined. After all, it had been submerged for who knew how long.

His dragon chimed in. *Can we open it now? We're losing precious time.*

I'm trying to make sure it's not a bomb or a booby trap. I won't open it until I know it's safe.

Then hurry and bring it to one of our scientists. Although it is fairly far from the clan to cause any damage.

Maybe, maybe not. It depends on what's inside.

Grant stood and faced the two members of his team. He pointed to the red female dragon named Zoe Watson. "Go to Lochguard and find Alistair Boyd. We need to make sure that whatever is inside won't hurt the clan and he should be able to verify its contents. I'll carry it to the forest at the back entrance, about two hundred feet away." Zoe nodded, and Grant looked to the black dragon next to her. "Find one of the Protectors on duty who can help you finish checking the loch. I want to ensure there are no other surprises lurking. Pay special attention to the perimeter and the floor. Now that we know someone stashed at least one bag, there might be others hiding in objects that look natural."

The black-colored Protector jumped into the air and followed Zoe back to Lochguard.

Grant looked back down at the black bag. Taking a deep breath, he picked it up slowly and made his way to the back entrance.

His dragon chimed in. *Why not just call the DDA? They have the resources of the British government and can easily check it for us.*

Given the recent betrayal involving the former DDA director, I'm trying to rely on them as little as possible.

But the new female in charge is different.

Even so, the exhibition is about to open in Inverness. I don't want anything to overshadow what should be good publicity.

Publicity is a human affair. It seems like a waste of time to me. Not everyone will like us, no matter what we do.

Then think of Cat. She's worked hard for this moment. We can't spoil it.

I suppose. She has been nice to us, even if she was a wee bit annoying as a child.

He didn't reply to his dragon and picked up his pace a little. Grant needed to be careful, but he also wanted to let Iris and the other dragon-shifters down in Inverness know to be on the lookout for anything unusual. If the Dragon Knights were stashing dangerous objects for later use, they might've done it near the exhibition's location as well.

~~~

Faye touched down at her third checkpoint. But with her first deep inhalation, she instantly detected the scent of human mixed with something chemical.

Her dragon perked up. *Finally. Let's investigate.*

Not until Brodie shows up.

Still, Faye surveyed the area around closely. The trees and their shade made it more difficult to see things clearly.

Her little clearing was free of rubbish or other signs of recent activity. Whatever she smelled must be further inside the forest.

A few seconds later there was a human yell and the sound of fighting. Faye roared in alarm to her comrades in the air before imagining her body shrinking. Once she was standing on two human feet again, she dashed toward the sound, careful to avoid breaking branches so as to not make her location obvious.

Her heart pounded as she drew closer. Pushing her body harder, Faye finally found Brodie wrestling one human male. Two others were engaging the other Protectors in human form.

She barely noticed the tent beyond the scuffle. Since Brodie was one of the best hand-to-hand combat fighters in the clan, Faye dashed over to one of the younger Protectors, Shay.

Shay struggled to get out from the human pinning him. Faye scooped down to pick up a grapefruit-sized rock and closed the distance. Before the human noticed her, she swung the rock against his head hard enough to knock him unconscious but not kill him.

After a quick check to ensure Shay was conscious and alive, she went to help the other Protector. However, Brodie had already taken care of his foe and was assisting their clan mate. Satisfied that Brodie would handle it all and tie up the humans,

Faye approached the tent. She paused a few seconds but didn't hear anyone moving about inside.

The smell of chemicals was stronger here. Just in case they were deadly, she took a deep breath and peeked inside.

She spotted a table with a variety of beakers, electronic parts, and some tools she couldn't identify. A stack of gas masks was at the entrance, so she took one and turned back toward the forest.

After a few deep breaths, she donned the mask and went inside the tent.

Faye had no biological or chemical training beyond the basics from her time in the army, but as she surveyed the table with half-completed gadgets that looked like giant eggs, she knew it wasn't anything good. She needed to find someone to take a look and ensure the forest wasn't about to go up in smoke.

She wondered how the bloody hell anyone had constructed a lab in the forest without anyone noticing. Lochguard might need to include forest sweeps in human form to their daily rotations.

Exiting the tent, she made a beeline for Brodie and the others. The three humans were tied up, so she took Brodie aside and whispered, "I want you to stay here and see what you can find out from them. In the meantime, I'm going to fetch someone who can make sense of what's in that tent."

Brodie kept his voice low as he replied, "Aye. I still have my mobile, so keep me in the loop. We're going to need Dr. MacFie as well. Shay is hurt."

"Have the other member of your team call her. I'm going to have my hands full trying to round up what scientists I can find. I may even need to reach out to Stonefire."

Stonefire had recently acquired a male dragon-shifter named Dr. Trahern Lewis, who was a genius with biochemistry.

His human friend, Dr. Emily Davies, also lived on Stonefire and was just as brilliant.

She glanced at the prisoners and asked Brodie, "Did they attack first?"

"Aye. I asked what they were doing and they jumped us. One tried to use a stun gun, but it was a projectile type and he missed. I figured asking questions could wait. Even the DDA should approve of self-defense."

"The DDA can be unpredictable, but I would've done the same." She gestured toward the tent. "What's in there will probably ensure the three humans are locked up for quite a long time." She handed him her gas mask. "Try to stay out of there, but if you absolutely must go inside, wear this. For all we know, there could be something deadly to only dragon-shifters in there. After all, the Knights were using a specific poison in the drones that attacked Stonefire."

Brodie took the mask. "I may be able to get a little information about what's inside from the smallest bloke. He was giving orders and appears to be the leader."

Faye moved her gaze to the short, skinny human with thinning hair. He remained unconscious.

"Just don't wake him early. I want to try to have as many people as possible here to help in case the human leader activated some sort of panic device." Brodie lingered a second and so Faye asked, "What? Is there something else?"

Brodie smiled. "It's just nice to be taking orders from you again, lass. If McFarland knows what's good for him, he won't try to keep you away any longer."

Not wanting to get into the specifics of what had already transpired between her and Grant, Faye merely said, "Aye, let's hope so. If you find anything, contact Cooper back at central command. He'll be able to pass the word along to the rest of us."

As one of the human males stirred, Faye took that as her cue to head back to the clearing and shift. However, thanks to her alarm, there were already a few Protectors and one nurse standing there. Faye motioned behind her. "Shay needs some medical attention. Brodie has the intruders restrained, but will need help transporting them. You can ask Brodie for the rest of the details."

As her fellow clan mates started moving in the direction of Brodie and the others, Faye imagined her arms and legs stretching, her nose elongating into a snout, and wings sprouting from her back. Once she was in her blue dragon form, she crouched and jumped into the air.

She'd barely had a chance to flap her wings a few beats above the trees before something boomed across the loch. A second later, a giant plume of smoke rose into the air.

Refusing to think Grant and his team had encountered an attack or worse, she made a beeline for the smoke to find out what happened.

Chapter Eighteen

Cat MacAllister tapped a pencil against her thigh. She always carried a small sketchbook with her in case inspiration struck, but even though she had a new idea, she'd given up trying to get it down. Three attempts and she still couldn't get the lines right.

Her dragon spoke up. *Why are you nervous? You are brilliant. The others will see it too.*

The quality of my work isn't the issue. How this event goes tonight affects all dragon-shifters in the UK. That's a huge weight on my shoulders.

Everyone here is nice. The human Max is a little odd, but not in a bad way. Everything will be fine. Try penciling out your latest idea again. We have time.

Glancing at the time on her mobile, Cat noted that she had ten minutes before anyone would be allowed inside. She stretched her arms above her head and circled them wide to loosen up her shoulders. Just as she put pencil to paper, Lachlan MacKintosh's voice filled her ears. "I hope you don't plan on sketching the whole evening. Part of our success will be judged upon how you and the other dragon-shifters interact with the public."

She met Lachlan's gaze. "You like to plan events, aye?"

"Yes."

Emboldened by her actions the day before, when he'd reacted to her candor, Cat asked, "Do your ideas always come on a predetermined schedule? Because if you say yes, then you're lying."

"True, I can't control all of my ideas. But for a night like tonight, I would find a way to put them aside. You have an inner dragon. Let her remember what to draw later."

Her dragon sighed. *He really has no idea how this works.*

I don't think most humans do. Let's find out what he knows.

Cat tilted her head. "Since you work for the DDA, you should have a better understanding of us as a species, aye? So, what do you know about how a dragon-shifter interacts with both halves of their personality?"

Lachlan clasped his hands behind his back. "I didn't realize there would be a test this evening."

Her beast chimed in. *I can't tell if he's joking or not.*

Cat replied to the human, "Aye, well, if you have no idea, then just say so and I'll enlighten you. Think of it as an opportunity to expand your knowledge."

He raised an eyebrow. "Dragon-shifters possess two personalities in one body. The human is more in control and understands human ways whereas the dragon half is more instinctual. When the dragon half ends up taking true control for an extended period, a dragon-shifter is considered a rogue dragon. Rogue dragons rarely occur before a dragon-shifter is a teenager. I could go on if you like."

Her beast huffed. *If he knows that much, then why suggest to me that I do something I have no interest in?*

Knowing the basics and the details are two very different things.

Cat cleared her throat. "That'll do for now. However, while you have the basics, just know that my dragon isn't the artistic one of us. If I don't get an idea down, I may lose it forever."

"Have you ever allowed your dragon to paint? You never know, she may surprise you."

Her beast spoke up. *I've never tried because I don't like to get dirty and paint usually ends up everywhere when you do it. However, if he would pose nude for us, I might be open to trying.*

Cat snorted and Lachlan asked, "Care to share what's so humorous?"

"Believe me, you don't want to know. Although I have another question for you."

"Make it quick as I need to check on the others."

"Why are you so formal all of the time? I can assure you that all of the dragons from Lochguard prefer casual."

He stood taller. "I've heard of Lochguard's reputation. But this is my job. I must perform to the highest standards." He bobbed his head. "I will check on you later."

Cat said to her dragon, *I wonder what Lochguard's reputation is with the DDA. I wasn't aware we had one.*

As long as it's something along the lines that we're brilliant, I can live with that.

Smiling, Cat focused back on her sketchbook. The conversation with Lachlan had given her a new idea. As she drew the first lines, she couldn't wait to show him the finished product. If it didn't make him laugh, nothing would.

She managed to put the finishing touches on the rough sketch just as the doors opened. Cat hadn't known what to expect, but as a throng of humans streamed in and visited the various tables, she soon found herself explaining one painting or another to a rapt audience.

Of course, it was just the start with a few hours to go. She only hoped their good luck and warm reception continued.

THE DRAGON WARRIOR

~~~

Faye finally reached the area where the smoke was coming from. There was some yelling below, but she couldn't make out the words amid the chaos.

Please let Grant be okay. She hadn't seen him in or near the loch and that worried her.

Her beast replied, *Grant is strong. He's been through tougher times in the army.*

True, but back then he was only a comrade.

And now?

You bloody well know what.

Ignoring her dragon, Faye found an opening big enough for her dragon form and maneuvered her way down. The instant her back legs touched the ground, she shifted into her human form.

Making her way through the trees, Faye focused her mind and pushed away her fears. One of the first parts of her training had been about how emotion could jeopardize a mission and cost lives.

She soon approached some of her clan members who were attempting to put out the remaining bits of fire licking the trees and underbrush. Not wanting to distract them, she pushed past until she spotted Dr. Layla MacFie checking over someone on the ground.

Faye couldn't make out who it was because of the people surrounding the male or female. She closed the distance and managed to take a peek at the unconscious dragon-shifter.

It was Grant.

Seeing him motionless and covered in scrapes and a few burns twisted her heart. Still, Faye took a deep breath. She needed to keep her head.

She asked Layla, "Is he okay?"

The female doctor never stopped her ministrations. "He's alive and appears stable, but I won't know more until I take him back to the surgery."

"Then why haven't you moved him?"

Layla didn't miss a beat. "I'm concerned about his spine. I won't move him until I have a proper stretcher."

The dominance in Layla's voice made Faye blink. It seemed Lochguard's new head doctor had finally embraced her position of authority within the clan.

Faye itched to push everyone but the doctor aside and stroke Grant's forehead. She wanted him to know she was here.

And yet, with Grant out of commission, it was more important that she find Cooper and ensure everything was handled properly. Grant would expect it of her and she wasn't about to let him down.

She took one last, long look at Grant's body and willed him to know she'd be back later. After touching Layla's shoulder in parting, Faye searched the area until she spotted Cooper standing with Alistair Boyd. Alistair had once been Lochguard's head scientist until a few years ago. To be honest, Faye was surprised to see him out and about. The male always had his nose in a book these days.

Still, she headed over to the pair and demanded, "What do we know?"

Cooper didn't so much as blink as he answered, "Grant was waiting in the forest for Alistair and a few of his colleagues to examine a suspicious bag Grant had found in the loch. However, before anyone arrived, there was an explosion. We won't know for certain what happened until Grant wakes up."

She liked that Cooper said "until" instead of "if" Grant woke up.

Keep it together, Faye. Grant is counting on us. After taking a deep breath, Faye moved her gaze to Alistair. "Any guesses as to what caused this?"

Alistair replied, "I can't say for certain until I better examine the fragments here and inside the ad hoc laboratory across the loch, but it looks like a run-of-the-mill explosive. We checked to make sure there wasn't any radiation or dangerous elements in the air. Lochguard might not have the most sophisticated equipment, but it served its purpose. We'll just have to wait and see if there are any lingering effects."

"Maybe you should go visit the tent we found across the loch and see if you can learn anything else. The more information we have, the easier it'll be to pinpoint the creators, especially if we can't get our prisoners to talk. I can take you there if need be," Faye said.

Cooper jumped in. "That won't be necessary. I already have one of the younger Protectors waiting in the landing area with some of Alistair's old equipment." Cooper motioned his head. "Go, Alistair. We won't touch anything here until you return."

Alistair left and Faye tamped down her curiosity. Alistair had sworn off science completely and had resorted to teaching a few years ago. She wondered what had convinced him to assist the clan again.

Her dragon spoke up. *Even if he has reservations, most anyone on Lochguard would face their fears if it meant helping the clan.*

Aye, I suppose. We can talk to his mother Meg later. She might know and loves to gossip with a friendly ear, especially when the ear belongs to a single female.

Her dragon sniffed. *I don't care for him. He would break too easily. Stop wasting time. We need to help Cooper and then sit with Grant.*

197

Faye decided against probing her dragon's change of heart toward Grant. Instead, she looked back to Cooper. "What do you need me to do?"

The younger male sighed. "I was hoping you could take over. I've never had to handle something like this before."

She slapped his arm. "No worries. It takes a strong male to realize his limitations." Faye pointed toward the clan members fighting the fire. "Go help them and assess the damage. Once you're done, report your findings back to me." Cooper nodded and Faye continued, "Is there anything else I should know before you go?"

"Only that everyone is in a bunker or shelter until we give the word it's safe. Finn also wants an update every ten minutes. My last call was a few minutes ago."

"I'll ring him in a bit. Now, go help the others."

Once Cooper left, Faye surveyed the area. Layla had Grant in hand and now Cooper would oversee the fire brigade. Faye headed toward the taped off area. Inside were a few scientists she knew by face and name, but not much else. They had to be cataloging data and shrapnel. She made her way over. While not an expert, she'd experienced a few IEDs detonating during her time in Afghanistan. And if nothing else, she could help record data. The task would help her forget about Grant.

Because if she thought too hard about him never waking up again, she might start crying.

Her dragon's voice was strong yet gentle as she said, *Grant will wake up.*

You're fairly certain, especially for a male you don't completely like yet. We could do worse.

Is that your way of saying you approve of him now?

Perhaps. If he set off the bomb himself because of impatience, my opinion will lower again.

And if it went off by itself?

That depends. If he is raring to join the Protectors again, then maybe we should kiss him when he wakes up. A male willing to do whatever it takes to protect the clan, even after nearly dying, is one I can admire.

In agreement with her dragon, Faye asked what she could do to help. As she set about recording data, she willed Grant to be okay. Because if he decided to be stubborn and not wake up, she might just have to kick him and see what happened.

CHAPTER NINETEEN

The next day, Faye sat in Grant's hospital room and tried to focus on the data on her tablet. Alistair and his team had been thorough and while the results were still preliminary, the main components inside the tent she'd seen had indeed been for making explosives.

However, there were still a few unidentified elements that not even Alistair could pinpoint. Finn had reached out to Bram for help, and after some negotiating, had come to an agreement. Dr. Lewis and Dr. Davies from Stonefire would be arriving shortly to help Alistair with his work.

Her dragon spoke up. *They will handle it. We don't know much about that kind of work and would only get in the way.*

I know, but I wish I could help. A face-to-face battle is much more my style. I know how to approach it.

We have our own battle here. Grant needs us.

Peeking a glance at Grant, Faye resisted the urge to climb into his bed and snuggle against his side. Layla was still concerned about his back, even if it wasn't broken. Until Grant woke up and Layla could better assess the damage, everyone had to be careful not to jostle him.

Being delicate around Grant wasn't going to be easy, but if she didn't follow Layla's orders, there would be hell to pay. Faye would never be able to concentrate on the investigation into the incident if the doctor banned her from Grant's room.

What she needed was a distraction.

Faye was about to pull up Brodie's notes from his interrogation with the three men who had turned out to be Dragon Knights when her mother, Lorna MacKenzie, strode into the room. Before Faye could do more than open her mouth, her mum said, "I know you have important work to do. But even Finn manages to take a few minutes for his family when needed. And right now, it's needed. How are you holding up?"

She wanted to make a sarcastic quip but had long ago learned what battles to fight with her mother. Instead, Faye sighed. "All right, I guess. Sitting still isn't my strong point, but I'm trying. It'd be easier if I had more information to keep my mind occupied."

"You've done all you can for the moment with regards to the clan. How are you holding up with regards to Grant?"

"I'd rather not talk about it."

Lorna raised her brows. "I gave you space after your accident, but I won't do it again with this." She motioned toward Grant. "The male you fancied, then hated, and recently came to care for is unconscious with an injury that could put him in a wheelchair for the rest of his life. You are hurting, don't deny it. What you need to do is let it out and allow your mum in. You'll be able to concentrate better after you do."

"Mum."

"Aye, that's me. But while you remember that fact, you might not remember that I was in a similar place to you once. Only in that instance, your father was dead. I originally tried to keep everything bottled up inside to care for my children, but it nearly tore me in two. If not for Meg Boyd's kindness and willingness to listen, I would be a different dragonwoman today.

Mind you, if you ever tell her that I said that, I'll pretend you're not my daughter."

Faye and her mother had rarely spoken of her father in the past. Her mum was giving her the option to brush aside the sadness with humor, but for once, Faye wanted to have a serious conversation with Lorna MacKenzie.

Putting down her tablet, Faye leaned forward. "I wish it was as easy to define Grant and me, but I don't know what we are right now. Especially since we don't know the extent of his injury. Grant's a stubborn devil and if he can't be a Protector, he might try to push me away."

"And how did that work for you when you tried the same thing with him?"

She looked to Grant's face. "I eventually gave in and allowed him to help me with my recovery."

"Aye, so unless you're saying the McFarlands are more stubborn than the MacKenzies, which is poppycock, then you know what you need to do. If you want him, fight for him. It's that simple. As I learned with your father, you never know how long you have with someone. They could be taken from you tomorrow."

Faye could make up a hundred different excuses as to why she should wait until Grant woke up, until the clan was safe, or until she was comfortable with the idea of becoming a mum. It would be easy to brush everything off and avoid answering her mother's question. After all, the MacKenzies were all hardheaded and if Faye put her mind to it, she could be more tenacious than her mother.

Her dragon huffed. *Stop with the excuses. Tell Mum the truth. She deserves better than a lie because you're scared.*

And damn her beast, she was correct. Faye was afraid of jumping in with everything she had. Because if she did, she'd probably soon be in a frenzy with Grant, which would result in a child.

However, as she stared at Grant's face, she knew he would never force her to be something she wasn't ready for. Few males, especially of the Protector variety, would have given Faye any Protector-related assignments after her injury like Grant had, let alone suggested they protect the clan together while knowing she was his true mate.

Grant may be injured, but Faye knew him better than almost anyone. Their road may have been rocky, but she couldn't imagine sharing a cottage and living her days with anyone else. Life would never be boring.

Lorna's voice filled the room again and garnered Faye's attention. "So? Are you going to fight for him?"

As Faye studied Grant's cheekbones, square jaw, and close-cropped hair, she knew the answer. But just as she was going to tell her mum the truth, Grant groaned. Faye stood up. "Grant?"

His voice was weak as he said, "Answer your mum."

~~~

Lorna MacKenzie's voice was first to permeate Grant's foggy mind. Once he realized she and Faye were talking about him, he followed their conversation, all while he tried to make his mouth work.

Then Lorna asked Faye if she wanted to fight for him. Grant gave up trying to move and waited to hear Faye's answer.

However, when silence stretched, he decided enough was enough. Grant didn't like waiting around, so he tried to move his head.

Pain shot through his entire body and he couldn't hold back his groan.

"Grant?" Faye asked.

Aware of how easy it was for a moment to pass and never return, especially with the MacKenzies, Grant croaked, "Answer your mum."

"Only if you open your eyes. I need to see how you're doing," Faye replied.

"Faye," Grant growled.

Lorna joined in. "I'll fetch the doctor. However, I'll walk extra slow. You should have two or three minutes. Use them wisely."

Grant slowly opened his eyes, but Lorna was already gone. He finally stared at Faye's face, but said nothing. He wanted an answer.

For a split second, relief flood Faye's gaze. But it was gone the next instant and she narrowed her eyes. "I would castigate you for eavesdropping, but I'll settle for a truthful answer about how you're doing."

"If you want an answer from me, then you answer first."

"Grant, now isn't the—"

"Aye, it is. You and I both had a brush with death over the last year or so. I think we owe it to ourselves and our dragons to be honest. No more beating around the bush."

He half-expected Faye's temper to flare and for her to change the subject. Instead, she placed her hand on his cheek and gently stroked her thumb against his skin.

His dragon spoke up. *Her fingers are warm.*
Everything is warm about Faye MacKenzie.

Faye finally answered, "Aye, I want you, Grant. And not just because you were nearly blown to pieces. You're interesting and I need someone interesting."

"You sure know how to woo a male, don't you, Faye?"

"Hey, I'm just being myself. I could wax on poetically about soul mates and how if we fall in love, it could change the world forever, but I was trying to restrain myself."

The corner of his mouth ticked up. "Just don't try to restrain yourself all the time. I like when you lose control sometimes."

She tilted her head. "Okay, you must be on some heavy medication to say that."

"Faye, let's be serious for a moment, aye? How it is right now, with us teasing one another and being honest, is what I want. Add in your strength and devotion to clan, and there's no one else I'd rather raise a little hellion with."

"What are you talking about? I was the sweetest child. I expect any of mine to be the same." Grant opened his mouth to call out her bullshit—he had grown up with the lass after all—but Faye beat him to it. "Now, I answered your question, so tell me how you're feeling."

Grant wanted to push Faye further on their future, but he didn't want to promise her anything until he knew his own. "My entire body bloody well hurts, which is why I'm staying still."

Faye opened her mouth and promptly closed it. She was hiding something from him.

However, before he could press her, Dr. MacFie waltzed into the room with a smile on her face. "You're awake much sooner than I expected, Grant. Although Aunt Lorna tells me it was her voice that did it. Maybe I should use her for all of my unconscious patients." She winked. "You can thank her later. Let's check you over."

Faye moved away from his bedside, and he wanted to reach out and take her hand. She would give him strength for whatever the doctor would say about his condition.

But since doing so would require moving, he resisted. Grant couldn't risk injuring himself further. If he did, he could never be the strong male that Faye needed.

Dr. MacFie threw back his blanket and squeezed his toe. "Can you feel this?"

"Aye."

She continued poking and squeezing to check for feeling. Grant felt everything.

Once she reached his middle, she slid her hand under his back and gently massaged him. While there was a dull pain, it wasn't anything Grant couldn't handle.

The doctor continued checking and asking questions. However, when she tried to move his head, Grant sucked in a breath.

Dr. MacFie stopped and placed her hands inside the pockets of her lab coat. "When you were thrown by the bomb, you must've hit your back and probably landed at a weird angle with your neck. You having feeling is a good sign, but you need to take it easy for at least a week or two. I don't want any strenuous activity until I say so." She looked between him and Faye. "Understood?"

Grant wanted to tell the doctor he wasn't a randy teenager and could control himself, but he knew she was just doing her job. "Aye."

Faye murmured her assent and the doctor continued, "Right, with the examination out of the way, you can have a few visitors and try to eat something. I'll have a nurse put a neck brace on you and help you sit up. Logan can help feed you, too, or you can enlist someone else's assistance."

Faye jumped in. "I'll do it."

"Good. I'll go fetch a nurse while Finn and Cooper interrogate you."

The doctor left and Faye said, "A neck brace, aye? Will you let me decorate it? I promise not to draw hearts or flowers on it."

"No drawing on the neck brace, or decorating of any kind."

"Not even a smiling dragon?" He grunted and she gave a fake pout. "Aw, you're no fun." He sighed and she winked. "I was just kidding. Now you know there's something worse I can do than help you to eat."

"Why would I put up a fuss about you helping me eat? If I'm lucky, you'll have to lean forward quite a bit and I'll have a nice view." Faye blinked and he chuckled. "Don't look so shocked, Faye. If you can't take my teasing, then you can't do any to me."

Faye rolled her eyes. "I'm wondering if the blast did something to your brain." She moved next to his bed again, but didn't touch his cheek. He was about to dare moving an arm to take her hand when she said, "What happened by the way?"

The door opened and Finn's voice filled the room. "Aye, I want to know that, too. What the bloody hell happened?"

~ ~ ~

Faye loved her cousin and would usually do anything to protect his life.

However, in the present, she wanted nothing more than to kick Finn's arse out of the room and possibly bar him from entering for a week.

Her dragon spoke up. *This way will save time. Once Grant gives his report, we can tell Finn to leave.*

I suppose. But I'm afraid grumpy Grant will return. It's taken him a long time to open up to us. I want more of it.

We can be selfish sometimes, but not now. Whoever placed the bomb could do much worse in the near future.

Grant answered Finn's question. "A bomb went off."

Faye bit her lip to keep from laughing at Finn's frown. Finn replied, "Aye, I'm not an idiot. Did the blast addle your brain?"

Faye jumped in. "He just woke up. Give him a break, cousin."

Grant said, "It's okay, Faye. I just wanted to show Finn that he needs to work on his interrogation skills. I may be injured, but I'm still head Protector and have a duty to improve his faults."

Finn growled. "My faults aren't important right now. I have you and the other Protectors for interrogation. I can bring Brodie in here, but that requires taking him off his current task. He's been quite productive with extracting information from our three Dragon Knight prisoners. Are you sure you want me to waste the time to order him to the surgery?"

"The three prisoners are Dragon Knights?" Grant asked.

Faye nodded. "Brodie found that out fairly quickly. However, they're proving difficult to question when it comes to who gave them the supplies and other resources needed to complete their attack. After all, some of the components we found in the forest were quite expensive."

Grant spoke again. "And the DDA hasn't retrieved the prisoners yet?"

Finn responded, "The DDA has been helping to search the area for other explosives. But stop changing the subject. Tell us exactly what happened in the lead up to the bomb going off. Even the smallest detail could be pertinent."

Faye could tell from the determination in Grant's eyes that he wanted to ask more questions and give his report later. But he finally relaxed on his bed. "There's not much to tell. I'm sure the others told you how we found the sack in the loch, aye?" Finn nodded and Grant continued, "Well, I was merely waiting a few hundred yards from Lochguard's back entrance when it exploded. After that, I don't remember anything until I woke up here. Did you find out anything about why it went off at that moment? I doubt it was a timer since detonating that part of the loch wouldn't have cause any damage but would've alerted us to the new threat."

Finn nodded. "Aye, you're right it wasn't on a timer. The best we can tell, it had a remote trigger. Someone had to be in the area to know when to set it off. We're also trying to determine the communications' range for the device."

Faye put forth her idea. "Or, it might not be a person at all. The architects could have drones watching us and transmitted the command that way."

"Bloody drones," Finn muttered. "The sooner the human parliament creates a law monitoring those devices and implementing stricter restrictions, the better."

"The DDA director says she's fighting for it," Faye answered. "In the meantime, we're thinking of ways to better paralyze the buggers when they draw near the clan. Alistair managed to work with a few other clan members to rig a temporary signal jammer in the outlying areas."

"Wait, since when is Alistair working on projects again?" Grant demanded.

Finn motioned toward Faye. "I'll let her explain it. I have the information I need for now. If I don't get back to Ara, she'll have my head. The amount of nappies we have to change is astounding."

At the love in Finn's voice when he talked about his mate and children, Faye wished to have the same one day. She wondered if Grant would be just as loving and concerned when it came time for them to have a child.

Her dragon spoke up. *That's twice now you've mentioned having a bairn so casually. Could you really modify and change your life around the new responsibility?*

It will be a challenge, but I've never been one to turn down something difficult. Besides, I thought you'd be on board. It means we get to have sex and you can better assess Grant's dragon.

Perhaps. We'll talk more about this later.

Faye waved at Finn. "Go take care of your mate. I can look after Grant."

As soon as Finn left, Faye put all her attention on Grant. "I should fetch Logan so we can put on your bloody neck brace and get some food in your belly. You'll never recover on an empty stomach."

The instant Faye said it, she realized how much she sounded like her mother for a second.

Not wanting to think about that, she took a step away from Grant's bed. But he reached out a hand and caught hers. Looking at his face, she could tell the action took more effort than he would want her to believe.

"Stay," Grant ordered.

She tilted her head. "So you'd rather have me sit by your bed and starve than be without me for a minute or two at most?"

"Faye."

Taking a seat next to Grant's bed, she said, "Okay, I'll stay. Although if you think I'm going to fawn over you for weeks, you'll be sorely disappointed."

"As long as you're there, that's all that matters."

Her beast spoke up. *He keeps winning points.*

Faye didn't answer her dragon. Instead, she reached out her forefinger and traced Grant's lips. They were firm yet soft. She couldn't wait to see what kissing Grant would feel like. Him merely kissing her neck had heated her entire body.

Grant nipped her finger and his pupils flashed. Maybe with a neck brace, they could figure out some kind of arrangement so that she could still kiss him without hurting him. Aye, if he had to merely lay there, it might work.

Her beast spoke up. *His dragon will be as eager to take control as me. Don't kiss him until he's ready.*

You're the last one I'd think would try to stop me.

I want to see what his dragon is capable of. I need him whole.

Grant's voice filled the room. "And if I have any say in the matter, it won't be weeks until I'm out of this bed and back to normal. I want to kiss you properly, Faye MacKenzie, and I can't do that unless I'm well again."

She shivered at the heat in his eyes. It was hard to believe she'd once thought of him as an arsehole. Maturity suited her true mate well. "That will have to wait. My dragon won't hold back, and I don't intend to break you."

He grunted. "I can take it."

Snorting, Faye tapped his chin. "We're supposed to be honest with one another, aye? It's okay to admit a temporary weakness. Someone once told me that."

~~~

Grant remembered all too well saying those words to Faye. It was proving much more difficult to embrace them for himself.

His dragon spoke up. *You had better. The sooner you recover, the sooner we get Faye naked and to ourselves.*

I hope you want more than Faye's naked body. I have a feeling her dragon won't tolerate being an object.

His beast huffed. *She isn't an object. She is simply ours.*

The way his dragon said it so matter-of-factly made Grant smile. Faye asked, "What's your dragon saying now?"

"He's claimed you as ours."

Her pupils flashed to slits and back. "Well, he hasn't earned that right just yet. I can't wait to see how my dragon handles yours."

"That's all the more incentive for me to recover as quickly as possible." Faye's cheeks flushed and a surge of male pride coursed through his body. "I think it's encouragement for you as well."

She leaned over until her breath was hot against his cheek. "Oh, I have a long list of ways to encourage you to get well. But I can't do any of them until you have a neck brace on."

"Care to share a few?"

She smiled slowly. "No."

"Just no?"

"Aye. And none of your demanding or dominance will work on me, Grant, so don't even try. My cousin is clan leader and he can't always control me. You don't stand a chance."

As they stared into one another's eyes, all Grant could think about was pulling Faye on top of him and holding her close. She could help him forget about the pain.

His beast grunted. *No. It might cause damage and we'd take longer to recover.*

And the rational mindset is back. I'm not sure I like that side of you.

Too bad. My priority is claiming our true mate properly. I won't let you delay it. If I have to wrestle away control to allow us to heal, I will.

Stop with the threats. You never follow through.

Faye's voice prevented his beast from replying. "Although there is one thing you can do despite your condition. The doctor should've rung your mum by now. Once she comes, you need to introduce me properly."

"Wait, what? My mum agreed to venture outside her cottage?"

Faye rolled her eyes. "Her eldest son is laid up in a surgery. Of course she's going to come."

With anyone else, Grant would've changed the subject; however, he never wanted to keep secrets from Faye. "How much do you know about my mother?"

She shrugged one shoulder. "Not much, really. Ever since your dad left, she's become a recluse. Although before then, she still was rather shy. One of her cousins is my mum's friend, but no amount of invites could get Gillian McFarland to join in."

"Aye, my mum has always been shy. She preferred staying home to take care of me, my brother, and my father. Us three males were her entire world. I know that might seem strange to you, but she was happy. Then my father left and everything changed."

Faye took his hand in hers. "Tell me."

His parents' history wasn't one he liked to talk about. Drawing on the warmth and softness of her skin against his, he

213

continued, "My parents weren't true mates, but growing up, I never thought much about it. After all, about a third of clan matings don't occur between true mates. My parents cared for each other and suited one another too. When I left to move into my own place and then my brother, Chase, soon followed suit, my mother focused everything on my dad. She had few friends and to be honest, I think my dad loved being the sole focus of her attentions.

"Then my dad decided to leave the clan with the other traitors, and for the first time in her life, my mum was alone."

"But she had you and your brother," Faye said softly.

"Aye, but with me becoming head Protector and my brother finishing up his electrician apprenticeship, neither one of us could stay home as much as she needed. Not even my mum's cousin could make her smile, and she always could do so in the past.

"However, when my mum was just starting to make trips outside of the cottage again, news of my dad's recent capture raced through the clan. According to my brother, when word reached Mum, she locked herself up again."

Grant still felt guilty over not being there enough for his mother. If not for the entire clan's safety being his top priority, he would've found more time for her. Or, so he believed.

His beast chimed in. *You won't say it but I will—she didn't want help. Only when she's ready can we help her.*

Well, maybe with the MacKenzies' influence, we can help her heal. Lorna isn't someone to take lightly.

His dragon sniffed. *Aunt Lorna can't control me.*

Faye prevented Grant from replying to his beast. "Then I hope your offer to lead the Protectors together still stands. You'll have more time to spend with your mother if I take on some of the work."

"Aye, I meant what I said earlier when I asked you to lead with me. Provided I can fly and regain all of my strength, it should work out perfectly. If I can't, then we'll have to rethink the arrangement. There needs to be at least one physically fit Protector in charge of everyone."

Some dragon-shifters would've taken his honesty as a barb, but Faye merely nodded in understanding. "I agree. But we're going to do everything we can to get you back into the skies. Don't even think of trying to push me away, McFarland."

"Why the surname, lass? I have no intention of pushing you away. Since you only call me that when you're scolding me, you should save it for the right circumstances."

Faye raised her brows. "Oh, I'm sure I'll have a few worthy opportunities in the future."

"And you'll be the innocent one until the end of time?" he drawled.

Faye grinned. "I'm glad you understand that now."

Grant chuckled. "Remind me to ask your mum for some true stories of your childhood. While we went to school together, I'm sure there are plenty of tales about you misbehaving that I don't know about."

She stuck out her tongue and said, "Then I'll just have to wheedle stories out of your mother, too."

As they smiled at one another, Grant couldn't remember a time when he'd been so at ease with another person. Between Faye's charm and strength, he was already starting to fall for her.

His beast perked up at that. *How? We haven't even kissed her.*

Sometimes you don't need a kiss to care for someone. Not that I don't want to do much more than kiss Faye MacKenzie.

Before his dragon could reply, there was a knock at the door. Faye shouted, "Come in."

The door opened to reveal Lorna MacKenzie with his mum at her side.

CHAPTER TWENTY

For a split second, Faye had wanted to tell whoever was at the door to bugger off. Time alone with Grant was a rare thing, and she wanted to enjoy it before the next emergency or piece of information came in.

Then it opened to show her mum and Grant's, and her irritation melted away. Gillian's eyes darted around and she looked about ready to bolt.

While it was hard for Faye to understand the female's personality since it was so different from her own, she was going to try her hardest. If there was one thing the MacKenzies had started doing well recently, it was healing individuals and families to make them whole. Faye wanted the same for Grant's mum and brother.

Standing, Faye took a cautious step toward the two older dragonwomen. With a wave, Faye said, "Hello. You must be Mrs. McFarland. I'm Faye."

Grant's mum's voice was low when she replied, "Call me Gillian."

Lorna patted Gillian's arm and gently nudged her inside the room. "I found Gillian near the surgery's entrance. We decided to come check on Grant together."

Gillian's gaze moved to Grant on the bed. After taking a deep breath, she crossed the room to her son. Grant spoke before his mother. "I'm okay, Mum. I won against the bomb."

If it had been Faye's mother, she would've tsked and taken him to task for treating the situation lightly. However, Gillian merely placed a hand on Grant's forehead and whispered, "I'm just glad you're okay."

Lorna motioned toward the door with her head. She wanted to give the pair privacy.

Since being in a strange place with two strangers had to be tasking for Grant's mum, Faye took a step toward her mother. "I'm going to check on the nurse, Grant. We'll be back soon."

Before Grant could say anything, Faye and Lorna stepped into the corridor. As soon as she closed the door, Faye whispered, "I need you to do something for me, Mum. If Grant's to be my mate, we need to get along with his family. It might take some coaxing, but few can resist your dinner invitations."

Lorna didn't bat an eyelash at her casual reference to mating. "Aye, and you want me to invite Gillian? Well, you should know me by now, child. I already did."

Faye blinked. "What?"

"I already knew Grant was going to become part of the family, even when you were being stubborn about it. There are a few more spots at the dinner table. Gillian and Chase McFarland should join us as often as possible. You know how I like a full house."

Her mother was too bloody perceptive. "You do remember how you kept hinting for me to leave, aye? Is Ross boring you already?"

Lorna clicked her tongue. "Ross is bloody perfect. As long as we have our nights alone, the house can be full the rest of the time."

Not wanting to reference her mother's sex life, Faye steered the conversation back to the original subject. "Just make sure Fergus and Fraser behave themselves. A flying dinner roll or being hit with a spoonful of potatoes will probably scare Grant's mum to death. She'll never come back then."

"You have so little faith in me. I already have plans, which include the help of Fergus and Fraser's mates. With my boys grown, those females have better ways of persuading them."

"Mother."

"What? You don't think Ross does some 'persuading' of his own?"

"No, no, no. I don't need to hear about you and Ross."

Lorna shrugged. "You'll be my age one day. At any rate, I'm going to fetch the nurse. Gillian might be able to handle just you at first. You might take after me and be strong-willed, but you're young. She might see you as a daughter and feel less threatened. I have a tendency to overwhelm people."

"You just admitted to being too over the top," Faye drawled.

"Hush, child. I call it being enthusiastic. Now, go and get to know your future in-law."

Faye waited for her mother to take off before she rapped gently on the door.

~ ~ ~

As Grant's mother stroked his forehead, it brought back memories of his childhood. One time in particular he'd fallen severely ill and his mum had stayed by his side night and day until he'd recovered.

Since he knew it'd taken a lot of effort for her to come, he stated, "Thanks for coming, Mum."

"You're worth all the fuss, Grant. I'm just glad you came out mostly unharmed. Are you finally going to give up being a Protector now?"

He sighed. "No, I'm not. And no matter how many times you ask, I'm not going to change my mind. Being head Protector is much more than being in charge of the clan's welfare. It also means I can keep you, Chase, and all of my friends safe."

His mum remained silent a few seconds before asking, "And does that include Faye MacKenzie?"

"Aye," he answered carefully. "Once you get to know the lass, I'm sure you'll see what I see."

"I have nothing against Faye. However, her mother invited us all to dinner and I'm trying to find a way to refuse. That family is exhausting and it's hard to say no to Lorna MacKenzie."

Even just a few weeks ago, Grant would've assured his mother that he would refuse on their behalf. But, he vowed to help his mum heal and did think the MacKenzies could help with it. "Aunt Lorna might be bold, but she has a good heart. She and your cousin Brigid are friends. Maybe you should give Lorna a chance."

Gillian searched his eyes. "You've never tried to change my opinion before. What's going on?"

His beast spoke up. *Just be honest with her.*

I was going to be. Have a little patience.

With a grunt, his dragon fell silent.

"I more than care about Faye, Mum. She's my true mate. Our families need to get along."

She frowned. "Are you sure? You haven't disappeared long enough for any mate-claim frenzy to happen."

"I haven't kissed her yet. Both of us are waiting for the right time. We need to make sure the clan is safe first." He reached out and took his mother's free hand. "Just try going over to their house once. I know you miss Dad. Maybe getting to know the MacKenzies will help with your loneliness."

His mother remained silent for over a minute, and Grant wondered if he'd pushed too far. Then she finally sighed. "There's just so many of them. I will agree to one dinner for your future mate's sake, but I can't promise anything more."

"One meal is a start."

A knock on the door was followed by Faye's muffled voice, "It's me."

Grant looked to his mother and whispered, "You can start with just one MacKenzie to build up your strength. She's the most important one to me." He raised his voice. "Come in."

Faye came in with a huge smile on her face. Shutting the door, she moved to the opposite side of the bed of his mum. "How's everyone doing?"

If Grant wanted his mother to get to know Faye, he wasn't going to allow the polite, fake face to be the one she knew. "I was fine five minutes ago. I assure you I'm not dead."

Faye put a hand on her hip. "I was trying to be nice, but maybe I should stop. Just remember I'm the one who's going to be looking after you. I can make your life enjoyable or make it hell."

"Good. As long as it's the real you, that's all that matters."

Faye opened her mouth and promptly closed it. She moved her gaze to Grant's mother, who was looking from Grant to Faye and back again. Faye cleared her throat. "Sorry, Gillian. Your son is stubborn and strong-willed. I find honesty and calling him out on his crap is the best way to go."

Gillian gave a small smile. "I know, lass. I didn't really have anyone to help me whilst he was growing up."

Faye stood taller. "Well, you do now. Between the two of us, we can strap him down and make him rest, if need be."

"You do realize I'm right here, aye?" Grant murmured.

Faye ignored him and spoke to Gillian. "If you have any tips on how to make him a better patient, I'm all ears."

Gillian hesitated before replying, "There are a few things. He loves hot chocolate with peppermint. If you give him a few mugs, he is more likely to do what you ask."

"Mum," Grant interjected.

His mother met his gaze again. "It's true. If this lass is to be yours, she should know. Otherwise, Faye will be banging her head against a wall when she tries to get you to do anything. I won't get any grandchildren that way."

He glanced to Faye, but he didn't see any uneasiness at the mention of children. He knew neither of them had thought of being parents until recently, but it was a certainty once he kissed her and initiated the mate-claim frenzy. Her expression sent a wave of relief through his body.

His dragon asked, *And why is that?*

You bloody well know why.

His beast huffed. *It'd still be nice to hear you admit it.*

Fine. I look forward to having a child that's part me and part Faye. I can't imagine having a bairn with anyone else.

Faye lowered her face to his and said, "Your dragon is chatty today."

He grunted. "Believe me, I know."

Grant's mother jumped in. "His dragon-half has always been the more rational of the two, although Grant will deny it."

He opened his mouth, but Faye beat him to it. "That's good to know. I can't wait until my dragon can better assess his."

Not wanting his true mate and his mother to discuss the frenzy or sex, he changed the subject. "You two can conspire against me later. If Aunt Lorna has her way, someone will stop by soon to check on me. So how about we just agree now that we all have dinner as soon as I'm released from hospital? I imagine the threat will be contained by then."

His mum frowned. "I hope you're not in here for weeks. You really will drive everyone mad since you hate sitting still."

"I don't need the reminder," Grant mumbled.

Faye bobbed her head. "Aye, I forgot about that. So, be compliant until you're well and I'll smuggle things in for you to do."

"Since you don't like sitting still either, that's not much of a threat," he stated.

Faye raised her brows. "Aye, but I can always leave."

He was saved from replying by a knock on the door. Logan Lamont's voice carried through the door. "I'm here to put on your neck brace, posthaste."

Lorna's muffled voice followed. "There's no need to state it. Just do it."

Faye sighed. "Come in already."

As Logan and Lorna came into the room, the ease between his mother and Faye vanished. Gillian retreated to a corner of the room.

His dragon said, *Give her time. She at least gets along with Faye. That is a start.*

Aye, I'll admit it was good to see her at ease with someone, even if it was to conspire against me.

Logan's voice interrupted his conversation with his beast. "You need to wear this brace as much as possible until Dr. MacFie says otherwise, aye?"

He murmured his assent, but Grant's attention was focused on Lorna talking with his mum. As the two females chatted, Logan placed his neck brace and left. Faye quickly settled in a chair next to him and whispered, "Don't worry. My mum's determined to get in Gillian's good graces. Believe it or not, she's holding back a little."

Grant looked back to Faye's gaze. "She at least seems to like you."

"Of course. I'm extremely lovable."

She winked and he laughed. It caught the attention of everyone in the room. Lorna was the first to speak again, loud enough for all to hear. "It's nice to hear you laugh, Grant. I'm not sure I've heard it since you were a wee lad."

Faye jumped in. "Well, it is me we're talking about. I can make most anyone laugh."

"Faye Cleopatra, stop lying," Lorna ordered.

Faye shrugged. "What? It's true. Ask anyone."

All eyes turned toward Gillian. She murmured, "I believe her."

Lorna clicked her tongue. "Right, then Faye's task is to get everyone at dinner to laugh. That should give you enough time to prepare."

"Mum—"

"Don't 'Mum' me, Faye. You've brought this on yourself."

"It's okay, really. She doesn't need to convince me," Gillian said in a small voice.

"Nonsense," Lorna said with a wave of her hand. "You could do with some laughter yourself, Gillian. As a matter of fact, we all could. Now, how about we get a coffee? We can talk about our children's mating and how we can spoil any ensuing grandchildren."

Faye looked about ready to say something, so Grant reached for her hand and squeezed. She met his eyes and he gave an imperceptible nod. Fighting with Lorna would accomplish nothing.

Lorna looked to the pair of them. "We'll be back to check on you shortly. We might even smuggle back some contraband. You're too thin, Grant, and could do with some meat on your bones."

As Lorna guided Gillian out of the room, Grant kept a hold of Faye's hand. Once they were alone again, she asked, "Why did you want me to keep quiet? Your poor mum is going to be traumatized after a coffee with mine."

"If there's one thing they have in common and can bond over, it's future grandchildren. And speaking of which, I think we need to talk about that. I'm going to be blunt. Before lust clouds your brain, I need to know if you're ready for a child."

"Yes," she answered without hesitation. "But just know you are going to help out as much as me. Although I'm not above using my family to help babysit when there are Protector duties we need to attend to."

The corner of his mouth ticked up. "I suppose having a big family is good for something."

She raised her brows. "They also have my back if you ever try to hurt me."

He growled. "Don't even joke about that, Faye. I'm not my father. I will never intentionally hurt you."

"I never said you were your father. And 'hurt' is a broad term. It could, for example, refer to hurt feelings. If I gain a lot of weight when pregnant and turned into a chubby dragon, you

225

might be blunt and say so. With hormones raging through my body, I won't be above calling my brothers to set you straight."

His dragon growled. *I can take her brothers. As I've said before, they're not soldiers or fighters.*

Maybe not, but they're good at getting in trouble. I'm sure there are ways they could go after us without a physical fight.

His beast sniffed. *Let them try.*

Faye's voice filled the room again. "If any of this is scaring you, then maybe I should rethink the whole kissing and mating you aspect."

"I'm not afraid of your brothers."

"What about Finn? He is clan leader after all."

"If I wasn't laid up, I would pin you against the wall and drive you crazy right now. Maybe that would convince you I'm not giving you up for something as simple as meddling brothers or cousins. You're worth every battle, Faye MacKenzie. And I'm going to do whatever it takes to convince both you and your bloody dragon that you're mine."

~~~

Faye knew she was needling Grant, but she couldn't seem to help herself. It was probably due to so many years dealing with her infernal brothers and their antics. She was a "never say die" type of female.

Her beast spoke up. *He seems confident, but you should tell him it's harder to completely win me over than it is you.*

Can you stop it, dragon? You fancy him just as much as I.

Grant took her hand again and tugged her toward him, garnering her attention. "Are you going to say anything, bloody woman? Talking about feelings isn't one of my strong points."

"Technically, you haven't said anything about feelings," she pointed out.

With a growl, Grant tugged her hard enough for her to fall over his chest. It had to be painful, but he didn't so much as flinch.

He whispered huskily into her ear. "You want feelings? Then I care about you, Faye MacKenzie. No other female can both put me at ease and make my blood boil with irritation. I want you to be mine. Will you bloody agree?"

"That's not exactly the most polite way to ask."

"Faye Cleopatra MacKenzie."

"Well, if you're using my whole name…" She felt a light slap on her arse and she squeaked. "What was that for?"

"Sometimes, you talk too much. Since I can't kiss you just yet, I have to find other ways to catch your attention."

"I really should push you away and storm out."

"Aye, and why aren't you?"

She hated the male smugness in his tone.

Her dragon said, *Be honest. It will make things more fun later on.*

Taking a deep breath, she answered before she could change her mind, "I kind of liked it."

He lightly patted her bum and she wished he'd hold on. She might not be able to have all of Grant just yet, but she wanted all she could get. He said, "Just wait until you're naked and in front of me. This arse will make a nice cushion."

Heat flushed her cheeks at the image of Grant taking her from behind. He might even lightly tug her hair as he did so. "Grant."

"The invincible Faye MacKenzie is embarrassed? I never expected to see the day."

She turned her head to meet his gaze. The desire in his eyes sent a jolt of electricity through her body. "I'm not embarrassed about sex. It's just…different. For so long, I thought I couldn't have you. And now I can, but I still have to wait."

His voice was low as he replied, "Sometimes waiting makes the end result that much more enjoyable."

She searched his eyes. "Someone is being deep today. Are you sure the explosion didn't do something to your brain?"

He wrapped one arm around her waist and placed the hand of his other on her cheek. "My brains, both in my head and in my cock, are just fine. It did help me realize that the only way to woo a MacKenzie was to be more open in all areas."

Faye couldn't resist asking, "Who else were you thinking of wooing? Fraser might be flattered."

"Blasted female," Grant muttered.

She grinned. "Well, you did bring it on yourself."

Rather than reply, Grant's hand traveled from her waist to her arse cheek. As he massaged one cheek, words fled her head as her heart thudded harder. Grant's voice was husky as he said, "What? You're speechless?'

She just managed to formulate a reply in her head when his hand moved further south. When his fingers made contact with her sensitive bundle of nerves, even through the fabric of her trousers, she gasped.

"Aye, I like that sound. I think we need to hear more of it, much more."

As he continued to rub, Faye laid her forehead on his chest. The warmth of his skin combined with his scent and the devilish movements of his fingers made it hard to concentrate. She was so close.

Her beast spoke up. *Let it happen.*

I wanted our first time to be completely naked.

Grant increased the rhythm of his fingers, and Faye lost the battle. Pleasure coursed through her body as she moaned into Grant's chest.

Once her body stopped spasming, she melted into his chest. Grant's chuckle rumbled under her ear before he said, "I think I've found one way to win with you. Your banter is no match for my fingers."

She propped her chin on his pec. "Only because of your injuries am I not giving you payback."

His pupils flashed. "If it involves your hand or mouth, then you can do as much payback as you like. I can lay still."

Well, well, it seemed Grant had a cheeky side. "Seeing as you're injured, you'll just have to wait and see." Grant growled and she smiled. "Actually, consider this your payback." She slowly sat up and tugged off her top. She wasn't wearing a bra and Grant's eyes zeroed in on her breasts.

Aware anyone could walk in soon, Faye didn't hesitate to pinch her nipples and roll them. Grant's eyes never wavered from her actions. And even though pleasure pulsed with each motion of her fingers, Grant's gaze made the feeling almost unbearable. Her breasts ached to have Grant touch her.

Of course, that wouldn't accomplish her task of teasing him. "See? Payback can be a bitch," she stated.

His hand traveled up her back. His rough fingers against her bare skin nearly made her shiver.

When he lightly pressed her down toward him, Faye decided to let it happen. As much as her payback was for Grant, her skin burned to have his hot mouth on her nipples.

Her dragon huffed. *He should wait for that gift.*

Ignoring her beast, she stopped when her nipples were a hairsbreadth from Grant's mouth. The heat of his breath only made them tighter.

Grant never severed his gaze as he drew one into his mouth. As he sucked and nibbled, Faye placed her hands on the bed to either side of his head to support herself. It was almost as if he could read her mind on how she liked being touched.

When he finally released her, his hot breath danced against her wet flesh as he said, "Put your top back on, Faye."

"Pardon?"

The corner of his mouth ticked up. "Well, unless you're wanting to give whoever is coming a free show."

Without lust clouding her senses, Faye heard faint footsteps. The room was only mostly soundproofed. She quickly tugged her shirt over her head.

Once she had it fully on, she just managed to slide from the bed into a chair when there was a knock. Grant whispered, "You might want to smooth your hair, lass, or everyone will know what we've been up to."

If she knew who was on the other side of the door, she would weigh following his order or not. But when a male voice said, "Grant? It's Chase," Faye smoothed her hair and thought of flight routines. She wasn't about to meet with Grant's brother in such a state.

Grant scanned Faye's appearance before replying, "Aye, come in."

A younger version of Grant, albeit with longer blond hair instead of short-cropped brown, walked into the room. When he spotted Faye, he frowned. "Didn't Mum come over? We were supposed to meet here."

"Aye, she did but right now she's having coffee with Lorna MacKenzie." Grant gestured toward Faye. "You'll have to settle for Faye as company."

Faye didn't care that this was the first formal introduction to Chase since getting together with Grant and she replied, "He has to 'settle,' aye? I'll remember that."

Chase spoke up. "Excuse my brother. He's the less charming out of the pair of us."

Chase winked and Faye laughed at Grant's growl. She said, "I haven't seen you since we were children. It seems you're still the lighthearted of the two."

Chase grinned. "Aye, well, I have to be. No one is going to invite me back round to fix their electrical problems if I scare or upset them. Although my good looks help with the females and the males who fancy blokes."

Grant interjected, "Although flirting with the mated lasses should be done at your own peril."

Chase waved a hand. "I'm not going to act on it."

As the two brothers continued to argue, Faye's mobile beeped. She opened the text message. It was from Cooper: *New information. Can you come to central command?*

Grant calling her name garnered her attention. He asked, "What is it?"

"Cooper needs to see me."

Chase jumped in. "I can look after my brother for a bit, aye? From what I hear, you've been here for days. A little fresh air, even if it's just for a short walk, will do you good."

"Chase is right," Grant said. "Protecting the clan is our top priority. Besides, the sooner you find out what's going on, the sooner you can come back and tell me."

Since this would be the first test of their possible partnership, Faye had to trust Grant as much as he would her if the situation were reversed. She stood and looked to Chase. "Just make sure he doesn't try to get out of bed. If you have any doubts, talk to Dr. MacFie or a nurse."

"Faye," Grant started.

"I know you. You'd do the same if it were me injured, don't deny it." Grant's sigh was all the answer she needed. "Aye, well, I'll be back as soon as possible. If anything happens at all, you can text me. Make sure to give Chase the number."

Chase nodded. "I'll make sure he does. He might be older than me, but I don't have to listen to him. We're nearly the same size as adults."

Faye didn't want to point out that Grant had many more pounds of muscles on him than Chase. "Thank you. I'll be back soon."

With one last look at Grant, Faye dashed out the door. Whatever Cooper needed to say, she hoped it would bring them closer to eradicating the threat, at least for a little while. She didn't like leaving Grant's side for long while he was still recovering.

Her dragon said, *Just stop it. He has a clan to look after him. We don't have to do everything.*

Of course there are others who could do it, but it doesn't mean I shouldn't care about him.

Humans and their caring. It wastes a lot of time.

Rather than point out most dragons cared about their true mates from the get-go and hers was just being cranky, Faye picked up her pace to find out what Cooper had to say.

CHAPTER TWENTY-ONE

A week later, Grant watched Faye's face as she slept next to him in the tiny hospital bed.

While he enjoyed her liveliness, he also treasured her still moments. Asleep, Faye's face relaxed and it was hard to believe she was in charge of protecting the clan and not just a young dragonwoman looking for a good time.

Of course, if he could just get out of the bloody surgery, he could take on some of her workload.

His beast spoke up. *We should be cleared to leave today.*

What, you don't like Faye being in charge?

I don't mind her being in charge, but what with all of the planning recently, I don't like how tired she always looks.

Faye was capable, but he agreed with his beast. *The plan for dragon-shifters from other clans to infiltrate the traitors is of utmost importance. Only once it's officially in motion can we slow down and let the others do their work.*

I still say we should find the rogue dragons and fight. They are mostly old and untrained. They will lose.

We don't know how many there are. The Americans could've spread the word. Who knows if dragon-shifters have traveled from other countries to join them. There could be more dragons than we can handle. Even a strong warrior must recognize their limits.

His dragon sniffed. *I suppose.*

Faye's sleepy voice filled the room. "You can stop staring at me."

"Your eyes are closed. You have no way of knowing what I'm doing."

She opened one eyelid. "There. I can see you staring at me. What do you want?"

"What I want is to get out of this bed, get you a coffee, and help take over some of your duties."

Faye snuggled into Grant's side. "But it's warm right here."

"A cup of coffee would get you out of bed before I could blink."

She made a noise in her throat. "Not everyone is a morning person like you."

"I have ways of changing your mind."

"Grant," Faye warned

"What?"

"According to the giant glowing clock on the wall, Dr. MacFie should be by any minute to examine you. No funny business."

He kissed her forehead. "I can restrain myself you know."

"Not if we base it on the last few mornings."

"Aye, well, I like waking you up with an orgasm. It works better than coffee."

"Not today. If you're cleared, then not only can you help me, we can start testing out your flying abilities, too. Nothing strenuous, but a quick jump up into the air would be a good start. Then we can adjust your recovery from there."

"You're forgetting something, Faye."

She took a second to reply, "Crap. Cat and Iris should be back today."

"Aye, and once they do, you have more questioning to do."

THE DRAGON WARRIOR

The exhibition had been a success, except for the final day which had been canceled due to suspicious activity. "We still need to determine if the Glasgow dragon hunters are working with some of the Dragon Knights. The appearance of a sack containing a bomb at the edge of Glasgow, near the event site, is more than a coincidence."

Faye rolled out of bed with a sigh. As she stretched her arms over her head, she said, "At this rate, we're never going to have time for our frenzy."

While they had been creative over the last week, Grant's dragon was impatient to seal the deal. Faye swore her dragon was indifferent, but Faye's increased irritation at the smallest detail proved otherwise. "Stonefire has agreed to help Lochguard whenever we do have time for it. Once your plan regarding the traitors is in motion, we can take a week or so to handle it."

Faye raised her brows. "You don't have to state it so matter-of-factly."

"I know it's your morning mood talking, but be careful or my dragon might try to wrestle away control to kiss you if you give him any encouragement."

His dragon huffed. *I hate waiting. Dragons don't sit back and plan. You should let our instinct take over.*

Too much is at stake.

Faye's voice garnered his attention. "It's more than my mood. I know you're not the most romantic dragonman in the world, but you could at least act as if the frenzy was more than a piece of business. Remember, it'll start a family."

"I know, Faye lass. Put it down to my mood. Being cooped up in this room is slowly driving me crazy."

She sat on the edge of his bed. "A grumpy, unromantic, healthy Grant is better than an injured, happy, charmer."

"It looks as if you're romantic as well," he drawled.

"Oh, stop it. I just want you. That's what I'm trying to say through my morning-fogged brain."

He traced her cheek. "For someone who likes to talk, you have trouble saying what you mean at certain points."

"You don't think—"

"It's one of the things I love about you, Faye." He took one of her hands and kissed the back of it. "Don't ever change."

As she smiled slowly, his dragon said, *Why isn't the doctor here? I want to kiss her, and more. She is ours. Everyone should know it.*

Aye, I know. But we don't have the luxury of being regular clan members with fewer responsibilities. You know that.

It doesn't mean I have to like it. It's getting harder for me to control my lust.

If I have any say in it, Faye will be naked and willing beneath us within a day or two.

As his beast roared at the time frame, Grant's conversation was cut short by a brief double knock and the door opening. Dr. Layla MacFie walked into the room.

Faye smoothed her wild curls, although they popped right back up. "Good morning, Doctor."

Layla held out a small cup of coffee. "Here."

Faye's eyes lit up. "You're so thoughtful."

"More like I want to keep you occupied whilst I examine Grant," Layla said.

Grant tried not to smile, but failed. "Don't put it all on Faye. We're both anxious for today's examination."

"Aye, I know. But whilst you've been recovering well, I don't want to risk your health. Not even your brother trying to sweet talk me is going to change my mind."

"What did Chase do now?"

Layla laughed. "He gave me that coffee. I don't drink the stuff, so I figured a little re-gifting was in order. However, if he brings it a fifth time, I may have to say something."

"I'll have a word with my brother," Grant stated.

Layla smiled. "It's probably nothing. Once you go home, he'll have no reason to keep showing up."

His dragon spoke up. *She doesn't know Chase's persistence.*

I'll have a word. Chase is young and out to impress the lasses.

Twenty-two isn't that young.

Considering Layla is thirty-one, it's young to her and I'd rather he stop wasting her time.

Maybe there's a reason he's persistent.

Bloody hell, I sure hope not.

Layla went to work checking his vital signs, feeling his spine and neck, and asking Grant to move his limbs in certain ways. Once she finished, she placed her hands inside the pockets of her lab coat. That seemed to be a habit of hers. Layla stated, "You are well enough to go home. As for shifting, you need to take it slow. I don't want you flying for more than a few seconds for another week or two."

"Two weeks? That seems overly long," Grant replied.

"We'll revisit my orders at your appointment next week. If I hear of you doing more than merely jumping into the air and flapping your wings a few times, I'll have you brought back here straight away and strapped to a bed. Remember that."

Faye gulped the last of her coffee. "I'll keep an eye on him, Dr. MacFie."

She nodded. "Right, then are there any other questions?"

"What about work?" Grant asked. "Or am I only allowed to sit in front of the telly and let my brain turn to mush."

Layla rolled her eyes. "Male dragons are the worst patients." Before Grant could say anything, she added, "You can work a few hours a day, but no all-night sessions. Make sure to watch him, Faye." As soon as Faye bobbed her assent, Layla added, "Logan will bring round the discharge paperwork and set your next appointment. See you then."

The doctor left and Faye was the first to speak. "Right, then I say we go home to shower, change, and afterward we should be able to attend the video conference with Stonefire. Then we can interrogate Cat and Iris before retiring for the day."

"I like how you said *we* had to shower."

She waggled a finger. "No sex in the shower. At least not yet."

"You just promised me some later. I'll remember that."

Faye opened her mouth, but Logan chose that moment to stride in with a clipboard. For once, Grant was grateful for the distraction of paperwork. Because thinking of Faye's naked body under a stream of hot water wasn't helping his dragon. In fact, the beast was pacing back and forth repeatedly, trying not to think of his lust.

Soon, Grant said to his dragon. *Just wait a few more hours. I'm determined to get it all sorted so we can have her.*

~~~

Faye tapped her finger against the conference table as she stared at a blank screen and willed Bram's face to appear.

Her dragon spoke up. *It's early still.*

I don't care. I want to know if this is finished so I can start planning the next phase of my life.

That's a bit serious considering it's not even noon.

Oh, just shut it. Your fake nonchalance is exhausting.

Before her beast could protest, Faye constructed a complex mental maze and tossed her dragon inside.

Without her dragon nattering on about how much she didn't care if they slept with Grant or not—which was complete bollocks—she was calm enough to stop tapping.

Grant noticed the cessation and whispered into her ear, "Thinking of me again, are you, lass?"

Finn's commanding tone prevented Faye's reply. "Can you two focus for a bit, aye? I don't need Bram teasing me about my randy Protectors for the next ten years."

Bram's voice filled the room. "Now, that sounds like a good idea."

Finn rarely displayed how tired he was, but the circles under his eyes told Faye his nights were anything but peaceful with three newborns. Faye spoke up. "If you annoy Finn right now, that will also annoy Ara. She already has her hands full keeping three children fed and changed. You don't want to make it worse, aye?"

Bram's playful tone was replaced with a worried one. "Is she all right? Tristan and Melanie should be there in the next few days, once all this planning is finished and the area is deemed safe again by the DDA. And even so, shouldn't Finn's family be helping?"

"They are bloody helping," Finn growled. "How about we focus on the reason for this meeting so I can get back to my mate and bairns?"

Faye had observed many video conferences between Finn and Bram. The Stonefire leader rarely gave up so easily, but understanding flashed in his eyes. After all, Bram had a daughter less than a year old. The Stonefire leader's voice filled the room again. "Snowridge is still debating whether they'll help or not. As for Glenlough in Ireland, they have agreed to participate provided we help them in return."

"We as in both of us or we as in Stonefire?"

"Stonefire. I'm going to send Aaron Caruso there in a month or two, while Kai keeps an eye over things here and tries to convince Snowridge to help." Kai was Stonefire's head Protector, and Aaron was his second. "Have you any luck with Northcastle in Northern Ireland?"

Finn sighed. "Not much. They've received word we're inviting Glenlough, too, and that cooled relations right quick."

Faye spoke up. "However, I sensed that Adrian, their second-in-command, might send someone of his own undercover to gather more information. If we can somehow heal the rift between the clans on the isle of Ireland, then we can increase our list of allies."

Bram replied, "Aye, it's on the list of things to do. But it won't help in this instance."

"Let us know what we can do to assist," Finn said. "Since the traitors are originally from here, they won't take any new Lochguard members. It'll also draw suspicion. As much as it pains me to say it, we're counting on Stonefire."

"I like that you'll be owing me a favor, Finn."

"Aye, aye, I know. You can rub it in later. When will you start?" Finn asked.

"In the coming weeks. Aaron has an American cousin who is going to make the crossing and attempt it first. However, I have my best surveillance keeping tabs on the traitors we've found so far. You'll hear the instant any of them move in your direction." Finn nodded and Bram continued, "What about the Dragon Knights? I can't have bombs going off and hurting Ara. She'll always be part of Stonefire, regardless of who her mate is."

Finn didn't rise to the barb. "I'm still waiting for your doctors to identify the mysterious ingredients. Otherwise, the

DDA is keeping as close of a watch on the surroundings as we are. There are a few new techno gadgets around the forest and the clan to alert us to possible dangers."

Faye jumped in. "We're also looking into the incident in Glasgow. It could be that the Knights have cooled off for a bit up here and are focusing on other parts of Scotland, which aren't being as closely watched as Lochguard."

"Still no word on why they placed the bomb in the lake?" Bram asked.

Faye answered, "No. If the DDA hadn't taken away our prisoners, we might've found out more. But they refused to allow them to remain here any longer and it makes me wonder if they know something we don't. Can your mate see if she can find out anything?"

Bram's mate, Evie, was a former DDA inspector. "Ever since the new DDA director has taken office, a few of Evie's old colleagues have returned to their former posts. I'll see what she can find out, although I can't guarantee anything."

"Aye," Finn said. "But it's better than nothing. If things ever bloody calm down, we should request a proper meeting with the DDA director. Maybe then we can sort out a few things."

"Agreed. If there's nothing else, I'll let you get back to Ara," Bram replied.

"You'll hear from me soon enough," Finn said. "And Ara threatened to cut off my balls if I didn't invite you to the dedication and tattoo presentation ceremony in a few weeks."

"I want to be there. We'll see if I can manage it. Say hi to Ara for me."

Once Finn nodded, the screen went blank. Faye's cousin moved his gaze to Faye and Grant. "If you can sort out the questioning of Cat and Iris, I'd greatly appreciate it."

Faye raised her brows. "You being courteous is scaring me."

"Don't start with me, Faye. I haven't slept more than two hours straight in over a week. I also can't drink any coffee because Ara can't have any, per the doctor's orders, and I'm not about to taunt her in front of her face."

Faye smiled. "You are a softie after all."

Grant cut off Finn's reply. "I have a question, Finn. When can I take Faye as my own and claim her?"

Leave it to Grant to just ask out of nowhere if he could sleep with Finn's kin. Finn studied Grant a second and asked, "I've started to approve of you, McFarland, but it's not quite yet the right time. I need you two to find out all that you can from the participants of the exhibition, not just Iris and Cat. But I assure you, as soon as we can breathe a little, you can have your frenzy. Provided Faye wants it of course."

Faye answered for herself. "Of course I do. I've only been asking you every day."

Finn shrugged. "My sleep-deprived brain doesn't remember as much as it used to."

"Bullshit, Finn. Just go home and help Arabella. Grant and I have work to do."

Finn stood, but didn't leave. "I won't keep you waiting forever, Faye. I just need the clan to be safe first. I hope you know that."

She softened her stance. "I know, but not having the male I want above all others is making me cranky."

"Aye, I know how that feels. It took some wooing with Ara, if you remember," Finn said. "Let me know what you find out."

Finn left and Faye turned toward Grant. They were finally alone. "I was wondering if you were going to revert to your verbally challenged self with others in the room."

He grunted and pulled her against his body. "I only speak when needed. With you, it's needed more often."

"Needed, aye?"

"Yes, although words can't always convey what I feel." He nuzzled her cheek and she leaned into his touch with a sigh. "I want you, Faye, and I'll keep asking as many relatives as it takes until I can have you."

She turned her head to meet his gaze again. "Let's avoid asking my mother if you can have sex with me, aye? Or I might have to bring it up to yours."

He slapped her arse. "My mum would turn pink from head to toe."

"Exactly." She kissed his jaw and savored the saltiness of his skin. The small tastes she had of Grant only made her more impatient to have him to herself, but she'd take what she could get. "Now, let's get things in order for Cat and Iris's return. Who knows, Iris may have even brought Max with her."

Grant sighed. "Why would she?"

"Not for enjoyment, but as a witness. He's the one who found the bomb in Glasgow."

"That male has a knack for finding things, both tangible and intangible. He's nothing but trouble."

"But if he can help us solve our case, then we can finally kiss properly."

"Aye, I like the sound of that."

Faye took one last inhalation to commit Grant's spicy scent to memory before she stepped away. If she wasn't careful, she might become addicted and need to start wearing his shirts or jackets to keep him close.

Her beast banged against the mental maze, but it held. She was relying on the mazes more than she liked as of late, but she had to focus or people might die.

That thought sobered her up quickly.

She turned toward the door. "Good. Then let's go to our office and get cracking."

As she strode out of the room and down the hallway of the Protectors' central command building, Faye could feel Grant's eyes on her arse. If things finally turned her way, she'd have much more than his gaze there soon enough.

CHAPTER TWENTY-TWO

A few hours later, Grant followed Faye into one of the conference rooms. Cat and Iris were seated at the table. However, his gaze zeroed in on Max Holbrook fiddling with the flat-screen TV on the wall. "Don't touch that," he barked.

Max didn't stop his actions. "I'm checking to see if there are any recording devices, but I don't see any." He faced Grant. "You should think about adding them. Imagine the wealth of knowledge you could keep for posterity. While I've never asked if dragon clans have official records, there should be some. And given the myriad of ways we can keep them these days, you should embrace as many forms as possible."

Grant debated how to answer the human when Iris simply ordered, "Sit down."

"But—"

"Now," Iris said.

With a sigh, Max slid into one of the empty chairs on the other side of the table. He wondered if the pair had some kind of deal. If Iris had dangled something such as a flight or a visit to a remote location, it could explain Max's behavior.

His dragon spoke up. *That's not important. The sooner we question him, the sooner he can get off our land.*

You're quite hostile today.

He always causes trouble. I don't want any delays or we'll never have Faye as our own.

Regardless, he has information we need.

Faye's voice prevented his beast from replying. "I think it's best we start with Max telling us how he found the bomb in Glasgow."

Max rubbed his hands together. Grant only hoped it wasn't for a long, drawn-out version. "Well, I like to explore my surroundings. Archaeology isn't limited to items from thousands of years ago. Buildings from even a hundred years ago can have interesting finds on or around them. Even the smallest thing can tell us a lot about what happened there." When he paused, Faye waved for Max to continue. "There were some buildings a few streets away, near the river. Did you know that Glasgow was once an important port? I wanted to see what remnants of that time still existed, or to at least try to imagine what it looked like during its heyday. So many former ports have undergone revitalization and it makes it harder to find anything that will help picture times past, especially since it's hard to dig at the fancy new sites."

Grant grunted. "Get to the point."

Max carried on as if Grant hadn't said a word. "Poking around wasn't easy since people were around at that time of day. However, I finally squeezed into an abandoned building that hadn't been used in quite some time. Just as I was starting to find interesting bits laying around, I noticed the rolled-up sack toward the back, where the building faced the water. It looked new and more than a bit suspicious. From experience, I've learned to take dangerous looking things quite seriously, so I rang Lachlan and Iris and that's it. They found it, carted it away, and later told me it was a bomb of some sort."

Grant leaned forward. "My question is why were you wandering around by yourself in the first place?"

Max shrugged. "I'm good at sneaking in and out of places undetected. I like to think I was keeping Iris on her toes."

Iris shook her head. "I was in the loo for a few minutes. Next time, I should just blindfold him and bring him with me."

Faye jumped in again. "Cat, is there anything else you can tell us? Did you notice anyone suspicious at any of the shows or near your accommodations?"

"Not that I can remember, although I'm not the most observant of people unless I'm painting," Cat answered. "Besides, all of the people who'd come to the exhibition previously had been nice enough. The dragon haters had been kept from entering. Security did a good job in my opinion."

Grant looked at Iris. "Did any of the other Protectors find or notice anything?"

Iris answered, "Everyone seemed surprised at the suspicious package. My guess is that it was placed in the building before any of us arrived. The DDA security team had made it quite clear that we couldn't enter any of the nearby buildings to ensure they weren't threats, not even if we were given permission by the owners or residents. We did the best we could from land and air."

Something niggled at Grant's mind about her comment. "Did anyone in particular give that order?"

"Arjun, the head of their security team, never mentioned it. But one of his colleagues did. George Smith."

Faye and Grant exchanged a glance before Grant said, "We need to look into him and also ask Arjun about the order. Iris, can I trust you to question Arjun whilst we look into George Smith?"

Iris nodded. "Of course. I did think it a bit odd, but sometimes the DDA staff don't know what the others are doing. I assumed it was business as usual."

"Aye, and it could be. But I want to be cautious," Grant replied.

Faye spoke up. "The report never mentioned the fact the bomb was at the end of the building facing the water. Between that and the one in the loch, I think the mystery element inside the bomb might have something to do with water."

Iris raised her brows. "Are you sure? None of us would ever set foot in the river in Glasgow. We're all spoiled with clean, untouched lochs or rivers near our respective clans."

Faye tilted her head. "Aye, but the Dragon Knights aren't going to think of such a possibility. To them, we're untrustworthy monsters, and monsters clearly don't care about clean water." She looked to Grant. "We should make sure that Dr. Lewis and Dr. Davies know about the water connection. It might help them narrow down the mystery ingredient."

"Aye, as soon as we're finished here," he answered.

Faye spoke to everyone in the room. "If there are any other details, no matter how small, now is the time to tell us." When all three shook their heads, she tapped the table. "Right, then let's break up and go about our tasks. But if you think or learn of anything, make sure to tell us."

Everyone stood. Cat whispered something in Faye's ear before leaving with a smile. Once they were alone, Grant asked Faye, "What did she tell you?"

Faye raised an eyebrow. "Your super dragon-shifter hearing didn't pick it up?"

"Now is not the time, Faye."

She stuck out her tongue. "A little levity between onerous tasks never killed anyone." When Grant merely raised his brows, she sighed. "Okay. She just wants to meet up for a meal soon and chat. It's called having a friend."

"I know what it is. I have friends."

"Someone is a bit touchy." She searched his eyes. "Is it your dragon?"

His beast jumped in. *Yes, it's me. Taking a shower with Faye was a bad idea. I want her. She should be ours.*

Grant took a deep breath before replying, "Aye, a bit. Let's just focus on getting this all sorted so we can finally let our dragons free."

Faye placed a hand on his chest and his dragon roared. He should push her away, but he wanted to savor the heat of her touch for as long as possible. Her voice was low as she said, "We're nearly there, Grant. We just need to talk with the doctors, reach out to the other clans to check for any suspicious packages near the water, and determine if there's a mole in the DDA's security team. That should be easy peasy."

He snorted. "I have a feeling most others would disagree with you."

She tilted her head. "They might, but you wouldn't. You're my equal, Grant. So if I can deal with it all and handle my grumpy dragon, so can you."

"Isn't yours still in denial?"

"That makes my case worse. Consider yourself lucky yours is so straightforward."

His beast huffed. *I will get the truth from her beast soon enough. She won't be able to resist my charms and stamina.*

Right, because stamina is what a female dragon treasures above everything else.

Many do. You clearly don't understand female dragons.

Faye's voice garnered his attention. "I would ask, but at the exasperation in your eyes, I think I'm better off not knowing."

"Clever lass." He kissed her nose and lingered for a few seconds longer than he should've. Only when his dragon started thrashing did he move away. "That will have to satisfy him for now."

That only made it worse, his beast huffed.

Faye smiled. "Why, you're being romantic again. I like this side of you."

He pulled her tighter against his body. As every curve pressed against him, his dragon growled in warning that it was a bad idea, but Grant ignored him. Her heat and scent only reminded him of what he was fighting for. "Good, because I plan to woo you for the rest of my life, lass."

She grinned. "I do love you, Grant McFarland, quirks and all."

~~~

The words slipped from Faye's mouth before she could stop them. Growing up with so many males in the house, Faye knew they spooked easily if feelings were revealed too early. Had she just bollixed things up? Grant didn't exactly wear feelings on his sleeve like her family did.

Her beast sighed. *Why do you worry so much? If he's not ready, he's not. He's not going to toss you away.*

You are not being helpful.

I'm being honest. In my opinion, that is the best kind of help.

Grant brushed her hair away from her cheek. His touch left a tingling sensation in its wake.

She noticed the corner of his mouth ticked up and Faye tried to focus on his words. "I like how you think I'm the one with quirks."

She raised her brows. "You are. Do you remember my family? If any of us tried to grunt and keep to the edges of the room, warning bells would go off."

"Your family isn't exactly normal."

She narrowed her eyes. She knew he was teasing, but the comment stung. "Don't make fun of my family. Are you trying to piss me off? Because if so, you're doing a pretty good job. Maybe I should retract my earlier statement."

"'Retract my earlier statement,' aye? That's a fancy way of telling me to fuck off."

She gave him the double finger salute. "Just so we're clear."

Grant laughed. "I love when your temper flares."

She blinked. "Wait, what are you talking about?"

He gently took her chin between his fingers and her anger eased a fraction. "I wanted to show you that even with your temper flaring and you cursing me, I still love you, Faye MacKenzie."

She searched his eyes. Could it be true that Grant felt the same about her?

Her dragon sighed. *Stop double-guessing him or yourself. It's strange.*

Rather than respond to her beast, Faye asked Grant, "Are you jesting with me again?"

"No, lass." He moved his head closer to hers. She reveled in the familiarity of his heat as he kissed her jaw. "I love you, Faye. No one else could be my equal and yet my source of ease at the same time. On top of that, few people can make me laugh. You not only do it, but without driving me too crazy beforehand."

Her heart rate kicked up, but she tried not to show it. "I'm trying to decide if that's a compliment."

"Yes, it's a compliment. If I have to survive a hundred dinners with your family to prove to you what I feel, I will. That's how much I love you."

"A hundred, aye? I'm not sure that's enough."

He threaded his other hand through her hair and lightly tugged. "Can't you just accept my words for once, woman? Saying such things isn't easy for me."

She looped her arms round his neck and leaned her chest against his. "Me not giving you a hard time would be odd. Be prepared for a lifetime of it, Grant. Because once you kiss me properly, I have no intention of letting go."

Grant's pupils changed to slits and remained that way for a few seconds. When they finally were round again, Grant released Faye and put distance between them. His voice was strained as he said, "Don't take my distance as a change in heart. I plan to fight for you for the rest of our lives. However, my dragon is getting close to the edge. We'll never be able to protect the clan if I give in too early."

Faye wished she could ease Grant's pain, but life as a Protector was never easy. "Few males would have the strength to resist. And let me assure you that your honesty is another thing I love about you, Grant. Don't ever change that."

"Even if it means I call you a chubby dragon when you're five months pregnant?"

She flipped him off. "Cheeky bastard. Maybe I should make a list for you of which things are okay to tell little white lies."

Some of the strain eased from Grant's face and he grinned. "I like the idea of knowing how to stay out of trouble. That means I can spend more time in our bed."

"Our bed, huh? We haven't even made it into my bed."

Her dragon chimed in. *We'll see if he earns the privilege long term. Still? What else do you want? Him to get on his knees and kiss our feet? You're being bloody ridiculous, dragon.*

No, I'm protecting us. I approve of the human half, but his dragon half is having trouble controlling himself. Maybe he's weaker than me. That won't do.

For the first time, Faye started to understand her beast's reluctance. *I have faith that his dragon is just as alpha as you, if not more. We shall see.*

Grant's voice filled the room. "We'll have to discuss bed and all that it entails in detail, lass. How about we finish our duties so we can hopefully have the frenzy for my dragon's sake."

"Your dragon's sake?"

"Fine, for all of our sakes."

Faye nodded. "That's the right answer. And while we're working, just remember that my mouth is good for more than just talking."

With a wink, she exited the room and she heard Grant groan. It was fun torturing him. He'd be thinking of her hot mouth around his cock for an hour. The tricky part would be in keeping her own fantasies of what Grant would do to her out of her head while they worked.

As they walked down the corridor, Faye couldn't stop smiling. Grant was turning out to be everything she wanted. It was strange to think he'd been in front of her all this time and she'd never noticed.

Her dragon spoke up. *I said before, we weren't ready.*

Faye believed her beast. Grant from two years ago never would've shared clan responsibilities so easily, let alone teased her.

Now all they had to do was ensure they had a long future to live for. The first step was seeing if the DDA's security team had a mole. While the DDA had been cleaned up after the recent arrest of the former director, it seemed there was still some lax security. Maybe one day the DDA and Lochguard could have a better working relationship. Just imagining a future when they didn't have to plead for help made her pick up her pace.

Aye, she would work with Finn and Grant to build better relations. After all, she soon would have a child of her own to look out for.

Faye waited for panic or doubt to set in, but only anticipation flooded her body. Not just for how their child would be created—she looked forward to that bit—but also to raising a wee one to be strong and safe. Faye may not have thought herself mother material until recently, but she wasn't about to be anything but the best at it.

Her dragon sighed. *Why be competitive about this? There are many great parents. I bet even Fraser will make a great one.*

He will, but we'll be better.

Rather than argue, her dragon merely turned her back and laid down. Her beast might be hiding it, but the strain of resisting the frenzy was sapping her energy. She said softly to her beast, *Just a bit longer.*

Grant finally matched her stride and a sense of ease came over her at his solid presence at her side. Together they would tackle any problem that arose and solve it, be it for clan or their own families. If anyone could change Lochguard's spate of bad luck over the last year, it was the two of them.

CHAPTER TWENTY-THREE

Grant sat with Faye inside Finn's office as they waited for their clan leader to arrive. As much as he wanted to drag Faye into his lap and hold her close, they sat in separate chairs about a foot apart.

It was hard to believe they'd both declared their love a few hours ago.

The distance is necessary, his dragon muttered.

Even so, I haven't made any public claim on Faye. I don't want the other males to think they have a chance with her.

Someone is sounding like me, aren't they? But don't worry. Finn is mated with bairns. He's no threat.

I know that. But just walking here was torture with all the males smiling at Faye.

Faye's voice interrupted his conversation. "Maybe we should just head to Finn's house. I'm sure something came up. He's a new dad after all."

Finn's voice carried from behind them. "No to going to my cottage since the triplets have finally fallen asleep. Anyone who wakes them will suffer Ara's wrath."

Grant looked over his shoulder. "If you better soundproof your small home office, video conferences will make your life easier over the next few months."

"Aye, once things calm down, I'll set up a more permanent base at home." Finn moved to behind his desk and sat. "I did manage to get ahold of the DDA director, Rosalind Abbott from my cottage. Bram and I are going to meet with her in the coming months to address some of the holes in their security and staff."

"So Evie's contacts found out something with regards to George Smith?" Faye asked.

Faye and Grant had tried to locate the man, but he'd disappeared. No one had seen him since Glasgow.

"Aye," Finn said. "His National Insurance number turned out to be a fake. A good one, mind you, as it took several hours to determine it belonged to a man who'd gone missing years ago but never officially reported."

"In other words, George Smith wasn't his real name," Grant stated.

Finn nodded. "Exactly. Arjun has assured us that any future events will have a thoroughly vetted security team. Not only has he offered to vet them together, he'll resign if anything like this ever happens again."

Grant liked Arjun's dedication. He'd have to talk with the male in person again soon.

"So the DDA plans to have more exhibitions?" Faye asked.

"It seems so," Finn answered. "Although I told them we need a wee break to get a few things in order here."

Grant grunted in approval. "I agree with that."

There was a knock on the door and Finn said, "Come in."

The tall, dark-haired, and bespectacled form of Dr. Trahern Lewis, the Welsh dragon doctor who currently lived on Stonefire, appeared in the doorway. He said without preamble, "I know what they were planning to do." Finn waved him in. The male shut the door and continued, "They wanted to silence our inner dragons."

Finn raised his brows. "Pardon?"

"The key in identifying the substance and its effects was the water link. Emily and I ran several tests to ensure our results were correct, but when the mystery ingredient is exposed to water it multiplies. It then can penetrate dragon hide and interact with the dragon-shifter hormones in our bodies."

Despite the fact triumph flashed in Trahern's eyes, Grant still wasn't sure what the bloke was talking about. "How about you explain it to us as if we weren't doctors."

Trahern cleared his throat. "In short, it's a type of poison. Once it's released in water, the bacteria grows. Take a swim in the infected water and your inner dragon may never talk to you again."

"You're positive about this?" Finn prompted.

Trahern adjusted his glasses. "I can't be 100 percent positive since I'm not about to ask any dragon-shifter to take a swim in a body of infected water. But all of our tests show a negative interaction with dragon-shifter hormones. To be blunt, most of them are eradicated after a short while."

Faye whistled. "The Dragon Knights have upped their game. It's more than war now—they're willing to use biological weapons on a massive scale. That must violate some sort of world law or agreement. I sure hope you tested the loch to make sure it's clean."

Trahern bobbed his head. "Yes, I did. It appears to be free of the bacteria. However, to ensure it stays that way, I suggest asking the DDA if we can fence off any water near a dragon clan as well as ask for their help to search the area a bit more thoroughly to find if there are any other devices lurking about."

"The fence is only a short-term solution, Doctor." Finn sighed. "But I'll see what I can do. Until then, I'll place a ban on using the loch for now and have the Protectors do another sweep of the surrounding areas."

Grant spoke up. "What about our drinking water?"

Trahern shook his head. "Since it comes from the same source as the local human population, we should be safe. While I need more blood samples from the humans living here to test the effects, my professional opinion is that it can harm humans too if ingested, possibly even kill them, but not if it merely touches the skin. I still need to pinpoint the exact reason, but I believe it's something to do with the chemical makeup of skin versus dragon hide."

"Is there anything else we should know about right this second?" Finn asked.

"Those are the basics. I'll know more after additional testing. I'm sure you can persuade Bram to let us stay a little longer."

"Aye, although shouldn't you be asking me first if you can stay?" Finn drawled.

"Why? You need our help. I know you want us to stay."

Grant resisted smiling at the doctor's matter-of-fact reply.

"Right, then how about you go back to work? Keep us apprised of anything else that comes up." As soon as Trahern left, Finn looked back to Grant and Faye. "Go lock yourselves in a cottage and get shagging whilst you still can."

Grant blinked. "Pardon?"

"You heard me. Right this second, there's nothing you can do to help. Trahern will do the research. Bram and I will talk to the DDA and hopefully notify world governing bodies about the threat of chemical weapons. Iris and Cooper can enforce my new loch ban and anything else that comes up. You've earned a frenzy." He winked. "Enjoy yourselves."

"Finn talking about my sex life is weird, but I'm not going to turn down the offer." Faye stood. "Are you coming, Grant?"

His inner beast roared. *Finally. She can be ours. Claim her. Now.*

Not until we're away from prying eyes. No one else should see her naked body.

Agreed.

Faye's voice cut through his conversation. "Grant? Are you with me? I can tell your dragon is on board from your flashing eyes. Hurry before bombs start dropping from the sky or some other such rubbish and your dragon loses his mind."

His beast growled. *I wouldn't lose my mind.*

Grant gave one last look at Finn. His clan leader made a shooing motion. "You've earned it, lad. Go. We can handle the clan for a week or two. I'll even try to calm down the MacKenzies when they learn their youngest is being defiled."

"Finn," Grant and Faye growled in unison.

Finn chuckled. "I promise to phrase it more delicately." His face sobered. "Go. You two deserve some downtime because we all know it won't last long. Our clan has a penchant for attracting trouble."

His dragon nearly yelled inside his mind. *Stop resisting. You want Faye as much as me. Let's go before another catastrophe needs our attention.*

Grant stood and moved to Faye's side. After taking her hand, he said to Finn, "Thank you."

"Don't go getting all soft on me, McFarland. We had our chat about what would happen if you hurt my cousin. I hope you remember it."

"Finn, mind your own bloody business," Faye growled.

Not wanting to waste any more time, especially since Faye and Finn could go at it for a while once they started an argument, Grant tugged Faye to the door. "We'll let you know when we finish."

Without another word, he took them out of Finn's office and toward the exit of central command. He was overly aware of Faye's warm hand in his. If his heart thudded any harder, he swore it might explode.

Still, despite his dragon's impatience and Grant's instinct urging him to whisk Faye into a corner and take her, there was one choice he wanted to give her, to prove what he meant about working together always. The instant they exited the building, he whispered, "Do you want to go to your place or mine?"

~~~

Faye's heart pounded inside her chest. After so many hours and days of anticipation and wondering, she was finally going to kiss Grant McFarland and initiate the frenzy.

Her dragon was oddly silent on the subject, but Faye now knew why. If Grant's dragon couldn't handle hers, her beast would be miserable. Faye said gently, *It will work out.*

We shall see.

Faye almost didn't catch Grant's question. "Do you want to go to your place or mine?"

Her dragon spoke up. *I like that he asked.*

Faye smiled up at Grant, determined to lighten the situation for the both of them. She didn't want her first memory of being with Grant to be filled with anxiety. "That depends. Can you see the floor in your cottage? Or is it strewn about with clothes, dirty dishes, and bits of food?"

"Not all males live in a tip."

"Are you sure about that? Fraser would live in a rubbish heap if he didn't have someone reminding him to do laundry and wash dishes."

Grant grunted. "I assure you I'm not your brother."

She winked. "And I'm quite happy about that fact."

Some of the tension around Grant's jaw eased. "Can you just make a decision, Faye? There's a fork up here and we live on opposite ends of it."

"Not for long."

"Faye."

While she had never been inside Grant's cottage, she knew where it was. "Mine. It's a bit bigger and we'll need the space eventually."

Faye might be casually mentioning how they'd have a child soon enough, it wasn't driving her to hives the way it once did.

Grant bobbed his head. "Aye, good point. Besides, your place is new and we've been spending our time there already. I like that nearly all of your memories there will be of us together."

"If you're trying to butter me up to get into my pants, there's no need. I'm a sure thing at this point."

"Believe me, when I'm buttering you up, you'll know. I'm merely being honest."

"I do love you, Grant."

He smiled at her. Faye shivered and he murmured, "Good."

"Good? That's all you have to say?"

Amusement danced in his eyes. "Aye. I need to save those three words for the right moment."

She stopped walking. "When is the right moment? If you're only going to dole out your feelings, then I'm rethinking this situation. Your status of 'sure thing' has morphed into 'maybe if you're lucky' at this point."

He stared at her a second and Faye's jaw hurt from clenching it hard. Grant finally burst out laughing and she demanded, "What's so funny?"

"I'm just teasing you, lass. I bet you're not as nervous as before."

She placed a hand on her hip. "No. But now I just want to toss you into the loch and let you take your chances."

"That I can live with." In the blink of an eye, he scooped her up and Faye squeaked. Grant added, "Of course I bloody love you. And you're soon going to find out just how much."

As Grant dashed off in the direction of Faye's cottage, her temper cooled and she leaned against her male. "Sometimes, you're infuriating."

"Aye, well, you'll never be bored. And believe me, I know you hate being bored."

She would try to deny it, but the thought of sitting in a room with nothing to do made her want to run away screaming. "Just remember to take your time because once the frenzy is over, you're going to have dinner with my family. If you don't survive that, you'll never see me naked again."

"Spending time with your family isn't much of a threat any more. Your mum likes me, and I can handle your brothers, especially since Finn seems to be on my side."

She smiled. "Those are going to be famous last words, McFarland."

As he approached her cottage, Grant said, "I'll remember that." He opened the door and entered. After quickly locking the front door, no doubt to keep her family away even though a lock meant nothing to Fraser or Fergus, he raced up the stairs. Once inside her bedroom, he sat her down on the bed.

THE DRAGON WARRIOR

His pupils turned to slits and his voice was husky as he ordered, "Take off your clothes."

CHAPTER TWENTY-FOUR

Grant's dragon snarled and paced inside his mind. *Why waste time taking them off? Just rip them. I've waited long enough. I need her. Now.*

Before Grant could reply, Faye tore off her top and then her trousers. In another second, her undergarments were gone too.

He blinked. "That was fast."

She shrugged, and it took every bit of strength he possessed not to stare at her breasts as they undoubtedly bounced. Just the knowledge she was naked and waiting sent more blood rushing to his cock.

"Clothes can be replaced. Speaking of which…."

Her voice trailed off as she extended a few talons and sliced off Grant's clothes. As the cool air caressed his skin, his body temperature rose a few degrees.

His dragon hummed. *Yes, she knows what to do. Now, claim her. She is waiting.*

Stepping out of his pile of clothes, Grant pushed Faye to the bed and covered her body with his. The heat of her skin against his sent more blood to his cock and made it even harder.

Why are you waiting? His beast growled. *Don't dare make up any excuses.*

I still have my honor.

He stopped his lips a fraction away from hers. "Are you ready, lass?"

Wrapping her arms around him and lightly digging her nails in his back, she answered, "Show me what you have, McFarland."

He crushed his lips against hers and she instantly opened to allow him entry. As his tongue swept inside her hot mouth, he groaned at the same time his beast roared. The need to claim their mate coursed through Grant's body. He spoke to his dragon. *Give me a minute.*

He managed to keep his dragon in check as he explored Faye's mouth. He'd never tasted anything better in his life. Although the sweet honey between her legs was a close second.

His dragon finally broke free and wrestled for control. Grant's strength weakened as his dragon's need to mate increased.

If he hadn't been keeping his beast in check for so long, he could've held out longer. But his control was slipping. If he wanted to be the one to claim Faye first, he'd have to do it quick.

He broke their kiss and moved a hand between her thighs. "Thank fuck you're wet. The foreplay is going to have to wait, lass."

Faye's pupils flashed as she nodded. She was close to losing control as well.

Grant positioned his cock and thrust inside his mate. Faye arched against him as she dug in her nails. "Yes, now move."

At the strain in her voice, he didn't waste time. Grant moved his hips slowly at first, but increased his pace with each thrust. Wanting more of Faye's taste, he kissed her again and never ceased the actions of his lower body.

Just as he started to battle Faye's tongue, she moaned. Judging by the nails in his back, she was close.

He would have to ask her to mark his back later. He wanted her to claim him as completely as he would claim her.

His beast hissed. *Hurry.*

Tightness gathered at the base of his spine, but Grant managed to hold back. Faye should come first.

Changing his angle slightly, Faye groaned and broke the kiss. She clutched and released his cock as she came and Grant finally let go.

As he spent inside his female, Faye screamed louder. His own orgasm sent her into yet another one.

Grant had barely finished giving his last drop when his dragon snarled and finally pushed to the forefront of his mind. Grant was tossed to the back and while he could see and hear everything, he wouldn't have any control over what his dragon would do.

Since Faye's pupils remained slitted, her dragon was in charge too. While their human halves loved each other and wanted the mating, it was time to see how their dragon halves would handle it.

~~~

Faye had barely come down from her orgasmic high when her dragon took over. Her beast snarled. *It's my turn. I need to see what he's made of.*

Her dragon now had complete control of her body and managed to flip Grant onto his back. Placing a talon at his throat, she hissed, "You haven't earned the right to claim me."

Grant's voice wasn't quite his own thanks to his own inner beast being in control. "I'll go easy on you."

She pressed harder until a drop of blood appeared. "Don't even dare. You do that and I will castrate you right now."

Faye said, *Whoa, that's a bit much, aye?*

Her dragon didn't pay any attention. The longer her beast kept Grant pinned, the more Faye worried she might kill him.

Then Grant-slash-dragon smiled slowly. "I like a female with bite."

He roared as he tossed her off the bed. Faye landed on her back, but Grant turned her over so that her breasts crushed into the floor. He also restrained her hands behind her. With his knee also pinning her down, it was going to be difficult to break the hold.

Her beast said inside their mind, *This is Grant. I know him well and can do it.*

She lay still, and Grant's breath soon caressed her ear in his dragon's voice. "And here I thought I might have a worthy opponent."

With a roar, Faye's dragon thrust her head back and it made an audible crack with Grant's nose. Using the split-second advantage, she rolled away and jumped to her feet.

Some males might swear and look at her with hatred, especially as she'd probably broken his nose. However, Grant's eyes held anticipation. "I'm done playing nice. I will win."

"You can try," she hissed. "My human always goes easy on you. I won't."

With a snarl, dragon-possessed Grant charged at her. The move seemed odd since only a novice would make that mistake. However, he changed course and picked up one of the blankets that had made it to the floor. Faye stepped back, but Grant charged and tossed the material over her head. She extended her talons to slice it, but a set of strong arms held her in place.

Grant chuckled. "You're mine."

Faye's dragon hated defeat more than anything in the world. She would get free. She just had to find an opening. There was always an opening.

Grant pushed her forward until her legs hit the side of the bed. Yes. If she pretended to want it, he'd let down his guard.

She allowed him to push her down on the bed. Her front half was on the mattress while she kneeled on the floor.

One second passed and then another. She kept waiting for him to try to take her. That would be her time to act.

She grew impatient. However, a hole was sliced in the top of the blanket and she could see again. Angling her head, she met Grant's eyes. His voice was full of dominance when he said, "Are you ready to yield? I won. You are mine. I earned the right."

Faye spoke inside their mind. *He's worthy. He's proved he can handle you.*

Not yet. I can still get free.

Faye merely sighed and waited to see what the two dragons would do. If nothing else, this was a mating frenzy story for the ages.

Her dragon continued to cut away at the material near their hands. The rustling sound behind them piqued Faye's curiosity. What the bloody hell was Grant doing?

Her beast had almost shredded the material enough to free their hands when a ripping sound filled the room. The next instant, a strong hand pinned her wrists together before slapping cool metal around one and then the other.

Her dragon roared. "That's cheating."

"No. It's called being prepared."

She tried to kick behind her, but Grant's bare feet held her ankles in place against the floor.

She hissed. "I will still win. You are weak. You can never best me."

Grant's breath was hot against her neck. "You're a sore loser."

THE DRAGON WARRIOR

He nipped her and lightly slapped her arse. Her dragon's struggles lessened a fraction and Grant added, "You are my mate and I'm going to claim you. Tell me I've earned the right."

Her dragon tried to break the handcuffs, but they had to be a set strong enough for a dragon-shifter. Grant's feet never budged either.

When Grant gathered her hair and lightly tugged her head back, her dragon hummed inside their mind.

Maybe, just maybe, her dragon was finally ready.

Grant spoke again. "I won't fuck you until you tell me I'm your true mate." He lightly tugged her hair again. "Yield to me."

Faye figuratively held her breath. Her beast was a stubborn one. She might never admit defeat.

"You are not as weak as I thought." She finally wiggled her bottom. "I yield this time."

Rather than think of dragon's use of "this time," Faye cheered. *See? I told you he could handle you.*

Perhaps. Now, shut it.

Grant tore away the rest of the blanket before running his cock up and down her folds. She raised her hips and hissed, "Take me before I change my mind."

Without hesitation, he thrust inside her. "Mine. I'll prove it to you over and over again until you carry my young. No others will have you."

"Stop talking," she growled.

With a grunt, Grant took hold of her hips and moved quickly. As flesh slapped against flesh, both human and dragon hummed at the way he filled her at this angle. And oddly, being restrained and defeated made her dragon purr.

No doubt, that would cause trouble in the future.

Grant moved a hand in front of them and lightly brushed her bundle of nerves. All rational thought left her brain as he continued to rub and move his hips.

Even her dragon moaned aloud.

Pleasure rushed through her body as Grant yelled behind her. His orgasm only made her body spasm harder until she could barely handle the pleasure.

When she finally came down from the high, she slumped against the bed. Her dragon said, *He has earned the right for now. You can handle him for a bit. Otherwise, we'll never conceive his young. If he gets distracted by our beautiful body, I might break one or both of his arms.*

Faye moved to the front of her mind and laughed out loud. Grant's voice, minus the extra dragon huskiness, asked, "What?"

"Unlock me."

Her dragon added, *We still need him. If you don't start fucking him in the next minute, I will try again.*

The handcuffs fell away. Grant stepped back and hoisted her to her feet. When she saw his face, she gasped. His nose was swollen with dried blood at the nostrils. "You should see a doctor."

Grant pulled her against his body. "And risk your dragon's wrath or my own? I think not. You'll just have to put up with my new look."

She snorted. "Wait until I tell the story later."

He growled. "Forget about later. Kiss me now, Faye, or who knows what our dragons will do."

As much as she wanted to tease her mate, Faye wasn't about to test her beast's temper. "Then kiss me, Grant, and show our beasts how fantastic sex can be without violence."

THE DRAGON WARRIOR

He winked before he took her lips. Faye forgot about everything else as the male she loved treasured her mouth and slowly lowered her to the bed once more.

CHAPTER TWENTY-FIVE

Twelve Days Later

Faye peeked over at Grant. "We should've waited to do this."

He tugged her the final distance to Lorna MacKenzie's house. "I consider my wounds love bites, courtesy of your dragon."

She scanned his mostly healed black eye and slightly crooked nose. "Everyone is going to ask what happened. Are you sure your mother can handle it?"

He didn't get a chance to answer because Fraser stood in the doorway and yelled, "It's true. You two have finally emerged from the den of naughtiness."

Faye took a deep breath. She was going to need all the strength she could muster to handle her brothers.

Grant leaned down to her ear. "I'm almost thinking you're not ready for this. Are you too tired?"

She rolled her eyes. "I am days pregnant. Don't start with me or I'll let my dragon handle you."

Her beast huffed. *Stop using me as a threat. What happens between me and Grant's dragon is special. Don't ruin it.*

At least her dragon had changed her mind about Grant. Of course, it had taken them fighting and pinning each other down to do it.

Fraser closed the distance and whistled at Grant's face. "I didn't foresee you losing to a girl."

Faye narrowed her eyes. "I'm not a girl, Fraser. I'm a warrior. Now, shut it before I tell Mum what really happened to her old music box."

Fraser rounded to face her. "Oh, aye? Go ahead. As long as I keep Holly by my side, Mum won't scold me." He nodded solemnly. "Yes, that would be bad for the baby." He lowered his voice and directed his next words at Grant. "You should remember that one."

Not wanting to dignify her brother's words with a response, Faye tugged Grant's hand and they disappeared into the house. After taking two steps inside, Lorna's voice echoed down the hallway. "You'll tell me about Fraser's deeds later. Hurry up and come into the kitchen."

Grant whispered, "How did she hear that?"

Lorna replied, "I hear everything in or near this house."

Faye shrugged. "It's true. Come on before she threatens you with her wooden spoon. And believe me, Mum's threats are always real."

They entered the kitchen to find it jam-packed with her family as well as Grant's.

Finn and Arabella each had a baby, as did Lorna. Holly stood to the side with Kaylee MacDonald, their sister-in-law. Her brother Fergus stood with his mate, Gina, and their bairn. Ross had an arm around her mum's waist. Grant's mother, Gillian, and his brother, Chase, stood toward the back, slightly apart from everyone else. Since Gillian's eyes didn't widen at Grant's face, he must've warned her beforehand.

Faye grinned. "It looks like you're going to need a bigger house soon, Mum."

"Oh, hush. There's always plenty of room. In my day, siblings shared rooms, sometimes three or four to each. Kids today are spoiled. Now, come give your mum a hug."

It took a quick tug to release her hand from Grant's. Faye moved into her mother's arms and her mum whispered, "My wee girl isn't so wee anymore."

Tears prickled Faye's eyes. "Stop it, Mum."

Lorna cleared her throat and released Faye. "I'm going to have more grandchildren than I know what to do with soon enough, but thankfully I still have young Kaylee to mother."

"Aunt Lorna, I'm not that young. I'm an adult," Kaylee answered in her American accent.

She waved a hand. "Young enough. We should have a few years yet before we find you a mate."

Faye rolled her eyes. "Just stop, Mum. Maybe she has dreams that don't include a male. Think about that." Gillian McFarland shuffled her feet and it garnered Faye's attention. "At any rate, I think our guests are feeling left out. Did you even introduce everyone?"

Fergus grunted. "Of course we did."

Gina patted Fergus's arm. "Sorry, he's grumpy and it's my fault."

Fraser spoke up. "You're going to have to let your dragon free at some point, brother. Otherwise, you might go crazy. As much as I'd like to see that, I need you at my back to help protect our family."

"Just to protect the family?" Fergus drawled. "So much for brotherly love."

Fraser flung out his arms. "Does someone need a hug?"

Fergus flipped off his twin. "Sod off, Fraser."

274

Before Lorna could scold the pair of them, Faye explained to Gillian and Chase, "Fergus and Gina are true mates, but they haven't gone through the frenzy yet."

"Gina needed a break from being pregnant," Fergus stated.

Finn chimed in. "Speaking of rest, how about we all sit down? Arabella and I haven't exactly had a lot of sleep."

Lorna clicked her tongue. "Don't speak to me of being tired. I raised all of you on my own."

"But you didn't have three children at once," Finn replied.

Ross rubbed Lorna's back. "And remember, Finn has also had to lead the clan with Arabella's help, love."

Lorna looked at him and sighed. "Aye, you're right. Although don't get used to it."

Ross grinned. "I wouldn't dream of it."

As all of Faye's family herded into the dining room, Faye made a beeline for Gillian and Chase. Chase was the first to speak up. "I've heard rumors of what the MacKenzies were like, and they weren't quite accurate. You're more lively and loving than they say."

Grant crossed his arms over his chest. "Can you try not to insult my mate's family, aye?"

Chase raised his brows. "I was complimenting them. Besides, you still haven't had a mating ceremony, so technically she's not your mate yet."

Faye moved between Grant and Chase. "None of that matters right now." She lowered her voice. "Just know that it's about to get a lot worse. Prepare yourself."

Gillian's voice was soft as she asked, "How much worse?"

Faye shrugged. "Let's just say that from now on, you might want to bring an extra set of clothes with you to dinner."

Lorna's voice boomed from the dining room. "Stop exaggerating, Faye Cleopatra. You of all people shouldn't want the food to get cold."

Faye motioned toward the door with her head. "That's our cue. If you want to leave, just wink at me twice and I'll find a way to extract you."

"Extract?" Grant echoed. "You make it sound like a secret operation."

"It can feel like it at times, you'll see." Faye motioned toward the dining room. "Let's go."

As they all made their way to the door, Faye wasn't sure if she wanted a calm, peaceful dinner or a regular one.

Her dragon huffed. *Just hurry up and eat. I'm hungry.*

Good to see your priorities, dragon.

Faye's stomach rumbled and her dragon sat in smug silence.

Without another word, they all joined her family. She only hoped they didn't send Gillian and Chase running for the hills.

~~~

Grant glanced once more at his mother and resisted the urge to pull her against his side to protect her.

His dragon spoke up. *She will be fine. Mum needs to find her footing with the MacKenzies.*

Only because she asked me on the phone earlier to let her find her way will I do it.

Good. She's trying to be stronger. Let her try. Lorna won't push her too far. She might be strong-willed, but she's also kind.

Aye, I know. I still worry.

They entered the dining room. Out of habit, Grant surveyed the scene.

Everyone sat around a long table. To his surprise, the food lay untouched down the middle.

Then he noticed Lorna standing at the head of the table with Ross at her side and he understood. No one wanted to upset Lorna when it came to her cooking. At her fierce eyes, not even Grant would dare to defy her in this moment.

Faye guided them all to the remaining empty seats. Grant had expected to sit near Lorna and Ross since his mum had some rapport with Lorna. However, they were at the end with Faye's brothers and their mates. Fraser looked at him innocently and then yelped. Fergus whispered, "Behave, Fraser, or I'll do more than stomp on your foot next time."

"Violence is also against the rules, brother. I say that makes us even," Fraser stated.

Fergus growled. "Stop making our guests uncomfortable with your behavior."

Lorna cleared her throat and Fraser shut his mouth.

Grant sat down with Faye on one side and his mother on the other. The second they were all sitting, Lorna said, "Tonight is a special night as we welcome yet another family into our fold. Faye and Grant have fought their destiny for quite a while, but it's good to see they finally had some sense and gave in to it."

"We weren't fighting it," Faye murmured. "We were merely growing up."

"Aye, you were. But sometimes, it just takes the right timing for it all to work out. Still, let's welcome the McFarlands to many years of breaking bread at this table."

"Mum, why are you being so formal?" Fraser asked. "It's a bit odd, aye?"

Lorna frowned. "I'm trying to be nice. Don't ruin it."

Grant jumped in. "How about we eat instead of argue? Faye is hungry."

"Faye is always hungry," Fraser pointed out.

Faye picked up a pea and tossed it at Fraser. It bounced off his cheek and he raised his dark red eyebrows. "That is the best you have? You're slipping in your old age, sister."

With a growl, Faye picked up a roll, but Grant snatched it out of her hand before she could throw it. "You need to eat the food, not throw it."

Faye batted her eyelashes. "What was that, dear?"

Her innocent tone, combined with her hand closed around something he couldn't see, made him suspicious. However, before he could think of what to say without getting into trouble, a glob of mashed potatoes landed on top of his head just as Fraser yelled, "Bingo!"

Lorna clicked her tongue, but Chase plucked up a bite-sized potato and threw it at Fraser. It smacked loudly against his forehead and Fraser grunted. Chase grinned. "Did I forget to mention that I play cricket and can bowl quite well?"

"That's it, this is war," Fraser replied.

However, before Fraser could pick up the nearest plate of mashed turnips, Lorna said, "Stop or you won't eat at all."

All eyes moved to Finn, their clan leader. He shrugged one shoulder as he held a baby against the other. "This is Aunt Lorna's house. It's the one place where everyone listens to her, me included."

Everyone sat in silence. Grant wasn't sure if he was dreaming. He'd never seen the lot of them so quiet.

He glanced over at his mother, unsure of what he'd see. But Gillian sat with a smile on her face, trying not to laugh. Fraser slyly flicked an ice cube at Faye, and his mother did chuckle out loud. Lorna smiled warmly at her. "Aye, they have the manners of wild dogs, but they can make you laugh like no other. And as I always say, laughter is more precious than gold."

"Since when do you say that?" Faye drawled.

"Since now. You lot have always been too busy picking up or tossing food to earn my words of wisdom."

Ross snorted and Lorna glared at her mate. Ross kissed her cheek. "We love you just the way you are, Lorna."

His mother's smile faded and Lorna noticed. "Don't worry, Gillian. Everyone deserves a second chance. We'll find you yours."

Gillian shook her head. "No, I'm fine—"

"Nonsense," Lorna said. "There are several single older males in the clan or in the surrounding human towns. Ross here will help me find one that is worthy of you."

Ross sighed. "Now, Lorna, how about we ask her what she wants, love?"

Faye jumped in. "How about we discuss that later? I'm starving. Since I'm carrying a bairn, you shouldn't keep me waiting. Besides, Holly is probably hungry too."

Holly put up her hands. "I'm staying out of it."

Fraser said, "I'll speak up. I heard her belly rumble. You don't want her to expire right here in the middle of dinner, now, do you, Mum?"

Lorna shook her head. "I'm exhausted from cooking. Just go ahead and eat, but remember that the guests get first pick and then the new or expectant mothers."

Faye snatched four rolls and dumped them on her plate. "Grant, help your mum. I need to load up my plate before Fraser takes all of the best bits of roast, pretending they're for his mate when in actuality they're for him."

Grant expected another row to ensue, but Fraser was busy heaping food onto his mate's plate.

Grant knew that Faye could fend for herself when it came to meals, so he turned toward his mother. "Go on, Mum. I have a feeling that if you don't take something now, you might not eat."

Gillian smiled and said to Lorna, "It looks delicious."

Lorna waved a hand in dismissal. "It's nothing. Next time, we can cook together. I hear you have a gravy recipe to die for."

When Gillian's cheeks flushed, Chase spoke up. "It's true. We've told her many times before that she should offer Sylvia MacAllister some tips. Most of the food at her restaurant is great, but Mum has a few recipes that would drive the customers mad."

"Hush, Chase," Gillian whispered.

"Gillian can share with me in the meantime. Two of us cooking will make things easier when it comes to feeding you lot," Lorna replied. "This house is pretty much a restaurant in its own right, except none of the customers are of the paying kind."

Faye's mouth was half-full as she said, "You wouldn't let us starve. Besides, I tried to get you to teach me to cook, but you always refused."

"That's because you eat most of the ingredients before we start, Faye."

"A cook is always supposed to sample," Faye answered.

"Sample doesn't mean eat everything in sight," Lorna said as she tilted her head.

As Faye and her mother continued to argue, Grant couldn't help but notice the amusement dancing in his own mum's eyes. Between Faye at his side carrying his child and his mother finally enjoying herself for the first time in who knew how long, Grant was content. He may still need to claim Faye as his in front of the entire clan, but he didn't need a ceremony to recognize that she was the best thing to happen not only to him, but to his family as well.

Faye MacKenzie had been exactly what he needed without knowing it.

Epilogue One

One Week Later

Faye tried one last time to tame her wild hair, but every time she smoothed it, the curls just popped up back into place. She hated any sort of product in her hair, so unless she shaved her head, she wasn't going to do any better.

Her dragon sighed. *It doesn't matter. Grant likes our curls and his opinion is the only one that matters.*

So my opinion counts for nothing?

In this case, no.

You're just cranky because Mum made Grant and us sleep apart last night.

I don't see why it was necessary. He is our mate. Nothing changes that.

While Faye was glad her dragon had changed her tune about Grant, the beast constantly wanted to take control and challenge Grant's dragon. *You do realize that in a few months, you're going to have to hold back on your rough and tumble sessions.*

All the reason to cede more time to me in the meantime.

As she tried to think of a response, Lorna knocked and waltzed into the room. "I'm not going to ask if you're ready because I know you are. But I had to see my youngest one last time before she's mated off."

"Mum, it's not like I'm going to Siberia after this. Grant's and my job is to protect the clan. That means we're staying on Lochguard, probably more than other couples over time."

"I know. And while I love all of my children equally, you were the last gift I received from your father. And now I'm having to let you go."

Faye's eyes prickled. "He's here in spirit, Mum. Besides, you always say Fergus takes after him. We'll always have the slightly more serious influence around."

Lorna took Faye's face in her hands. "I'm sure Grant will help as well. Goodness knows that Ross encourages you lot more often than not."

Faye smiled. "He suits you like Grant suits me. We've been lucky, Mum. So let's celebrate instead of cry, aye?"

Lorna kissed her cheek and then nodded. "You're right. Besides, today is a double celebration, and if I start crying for your mating ceremony, then I'll keep going for the tattoo and presentation ceremony for Finn and Ara's bairns."

"You don't always have to be strong, you know."

Lorna stood taller. "What and let Meg Boyd use it against me? No, thank you. I like being the favorite matriarch of the clan, so strong it is."

Faye had tried convincing her mother hundreds of times that she and Meg were friends, not enemies, and that their competitions were ridiculous. However, it had all come to naught, so she merely replied, "I love you, Mum, but the ceremony is about to start and you need to leave."

Lorna wrapped her arms around Faye and she hugged her back. "I love you, Faye Cleopatra."

"I love you, too, Mum."

Lorna pulled back. "Right, then I'm off to ensure your brothers don't cause a ruckus. Come find us afterward, if the clan doesn't mob you first."

Faye smiled. "Even if I have to fight off wild dogs, I'll use Grant as a shield and find you."

Lorna lightly smacked her arm. "Stop being silly. I'm leaving now."

Faye waved at her mother and she was soon alone again.

Even though Faye had never met her father, she wished he could be here.

Her dragon spoke up. *And what about Ross? He makes Mum happy.*

You're right. And considering I never met Dad, it's odd to miss him.

Not necessarily. We wouldn't be here without him.

A sound echoed in the great hall. That was Faye's cue to head out.

Taking a deep breath, she stood tall and exited the small room adjacent to the main hall. The clan's rebuilding efforts weren't quite complete—the great hall had been bombed a little over six months ago—but there was a roof and fires roaring in the fireplaces along the edges. Add in the entire clan's attendance, including a few guests from Stonefire, and it was perfect.

She walked purposefully toward the raised dais at the front, where Grant stood in his kilt-like outfit. He was always handsome to her, but the deep red color only made him more attractive. Of course, it could be that his muscles and tattoo were showing and she had a weakness for them.

Grant's gaze burned in hers as she made her way up the stairs and across the stage to stand next to him. Dragon-shifter mating ceremonies were between two people, and in that moment

Faye didn't register the hundreds of people in the room. The love in Grant's gaze made her smile. "Hey there, stranger."

He quickly winked and took her hand. Grant didn't waste any time. He spoke with a strong, confident voice that echoed inside the hall. "Faye MacKenzie, we've known each other our whole lives. Growing up, we constantly annoyed each other. In the army, we had some more differences and trouble. And yet, last year, something changed. You weren't merely the overly confident and lively female coworker. Aye, you still had those qualities, but a mere touch seared my skin. I think it took us growing up a bit to really recognize what was in front of us. I'm glad we took the chance because I can't imagine anyone else standing by my side through all of life's trials as well as helping me to keep the clan safe. I love you, Faye, and I wish to claim you as my mate. Do you accept the claim?"

Her heart thudded in her chest, but she managed to nod. Grant smiled slowly as he picked up the silver cuff on a stand next to them. It has his name engraved in Mersae, the old dragon language.

As the cool metal slid against the upper bicep of her tattoo-free arm, her dragon hummed in approval.

Faye touched the silver and spoke up. "You're right, we've had our fair share of differences, as most of the clan can attest." A few people chuckled. "But together we make each other better in ways we never could've imagined. You're my perfect fit. Few males would accept a female at their side to protect the clan, let alone know when to take control or cede it. I love you, Grant McFarland, and I want to make you my mate in front of everyone. Do you accept my claim?"

"Aye," he answered solemnly.

She knew he'd done it on purpose, to rile her up, but she didn't fall for it. Faye picked up the larger silver cuff that had her name written in the old dragon language. As soon as she slipped it on Grant's tattoo-free bicep, he hauled her up against his body and whispered, "You're mine forever, Faye. Let's show the clan."

She was going to say he was equally hers, but Grant lowered his head and kissed her. As she opened to allow his tongue, she paid the whistles and catcalls no heed. Faye merely reveled in the taste and feel of her mate. She had more than love, she had an equal. And in Faye's book, that was the most important thing of all.

Epilogue Two

Arabella MacLeod tucked the blanket around each of her babies in the pram. All three of them slept like the dead. They definitely took after Finn in that department.

Her dragon spoke up. *We sleep better these days, too. Being pregnant is uncomfortable.*

Says the beast who made it happen.

Her beast sniffed. *It was instinct. Besides, I think it's efficient to have three at once. We don't have to do it again.*

Finn came up to her and rubbed Arabella's back. "You ready, love?"

She straightened up. "Yes. But tell me, did you find anyone from Seahaven in the hall?"

Clan Seahaven was a tiny clan that had left Lochguard before Finn and Arabella's time, back when human mates were viewed as lesser. Relations were still rocky. "No," Finn sighed. "But baby steps, aye? As much as everyone thinks I can work my magic with anyone, the Seahaven leader is a stubborn bastard."

"Not that you can blame him. The former leader did banish him and the others."

"Aye, I know. But we can talk more about that later." He leaned down over the pram. "How are our three musketeers?"

She sighed. "I wish you'd stop calling them that."

Finn grinned. "I gave you a list of names and that's the one you disliked the least."

"The demon trio doesn't exactly instill confidence when it comes to finding babysitters," Arabella drawled.

"Finn's three amazing offspring is still an option."

"Finn."

"Aye, I know. You're knackered and my teasing isn't helping."

She leaned against his side. "I'm just glad Tristan and Melanie arrived today. They can help us adjust."

The clan had been deemed safe for the time being a few days ago. Finn was still cautious about the lake, but the DDA had finally taken the chemical weapon threat seriously. Between the DDA and the group of Lochguard and Stonefire scientists working on a neutralization cure, Arabella was confident they'd be able to rid the dragons of at least one threat in the near future.

Finn spoke up again. "I still say your brother should've stayed in his own cottage."

She raised her brows. "There's no way Tristan would allow Melanie to stay in a different house for their visit. You know that."

Finn grunted. "Maybe."

She rolled her eyes. "Just forget about my brother. Today should be about Gray, Dec, and Freya."

Arabella stared down at her three babies and smiled. She didn't know how someone could come to love three people so quickly, but she couldn't imagine her life without her three little ones. She might be constantly tired and already had her fill of changing nappies, but she wasn't going to take her children for granted. Her own parents had left Arabella and her brother too early. No matter what it took, Arabella was going to do everything in her power to ensure her babies had their parents for many years to come.

Finn kissed the top of her head. "Don't forget about Faye and Grant. It's their day, too."

"Their ceremony is over. Ours should be about to start."

Bram Moore-Llewellyn, Stonefire's dark-haired clan leader, entered the room designated as the waiting area. Bram was like Arabella's brother, and she smiled at him. "I'm glad you could come, Bram."

"Aye, well, Evie wasn't too happy about staying behind, but it's too dangerous to travel with the kids. Still, I had to come myself to ensure Finn wasn't corrupting the wee ones already."

Finn opened his mouth, but Arabella beat him to it. "He tries, but between me and Aunt Lorna, we should be able to keep it under control."

A devilish look glinted in Finn's eyes. "Speaking of which, Aunt Lorna is anxious to see you again, Bram."

Bram shrugged. "I'm not going to be able to stay for long after the ceremony, so whatever plans you have in the works, you'll just have to be disappointed."

"Which is fine. All that matters is that you're here now," Arabella stated. She paused a second and added, "I hear the music used to quiet the clan for announcements playing so we should get going."

Bram closed the distance and engulfed Arabella in a hug. "I'm happy for you, Ara."

"Thanks, Bram. You played a part in it."

Finn cleared his throat. "As did I."

Bram released her and shook his head. "If you can handle Finn, your children should be a breeze."

Before Finn could say anything, Bram exited the room. Arabella looked up at her mate. "I love you, but stop with the jealousy. Bram is my older brother in all but blood. You are my mate, Finn. I need you by my side for the ceremony or I might start bawling."

He kissed her gently on the lips. "Bawling is allowed. Most mums do it when presented with the future tattoos for their bairns."

"But they aren't mated to the clan leader." The music died down. "Right, then let's see what Dylan and Kevin came up with." She kissed him again. "Thanks for allowing Stonefire's silversmith to help ours."

"Well, Kevin Ogilvie has been backlogged as of late with the recent surge in bairns. It was a practical decision." She gently hit his side and he continued, "Okay, it's more than that. Stonefire is our closest ally. It only seemed fitting that our children receive pieces of history from both."

Arabella nodded and she pushed the pram. Finn helped her as they made their way out and up the stairs of the dais.

Kevin, Lochguard's silversmith, and Dylan Turner, Stonefire's silversmith, stood waiting for them. Three large, wrapped rectangles were propped up behind them.

Once they reached the two dragonmen, Finn faced the clan. "Thank you for coming today, not only to celebrate my cousin's mating ceremony but to also celebrate the arrival of my three children." Cheers went up. Once they died down, Finn continued, "This ceremony is extra special and not just because it's for my three perfect children." He winked and a few people laughed. "Tonight is the first time two silversmiths from different clans have worked together to design tattoos for Lochguard children. I think most of us are already aware of how special our alliance is, but I just wanted to make it extra clear. Only together we can change Britain for the better."

THE DRAGON WARRIOR

The crowd roared and Arabella smiled. Only a few years ago, before Finn had become clan leader, the two clans hadn't even talked with one another.

Her beast spoke up. *That is the past. We need to focus on the future.*

Finn's voice prevented Arabella from replying to her dragon. "Now, without further ado, let's begin."

Kevin and Dylan came forward. One held three small packages wrapped in blankets and the other held the three larger rectangles. Kevin spoke first. "May your children grow and flourish so that they may receive the gifts of our tattoo designs on their sixteenth birthday."

Finn took each small bundle and unwrapped it to reveal framed pictures of the three tattoo designs. Each one was a slightly different combination of edges and curves, taking inspiration from Finn and Arabella's as well as some original twists.

As Finn laid each one at the foot of their children, tears prickled her eyes. She'd just had her babies. She didn't want to think of them being sixteen and receiving tattoos just yet.

Finn lightly squeezed her side before speaking to the crowd again. "Grayson James, Declan George, and Freya Anne Jocelyn will gladly display your artwork to the world when they are of age."

Once Finn finished the ceremonial response, Dylan from Lochguard handed a larger wrapped parcel each to her, Finn, and Kevin. They unwrapped them to reveal much larger versions of the tattoos. They turned them toward the crowd and everyone clapped, whistled, or cheered.

After a minute, Finn shouted, "Welcome to the clan, Grayson, Declan, and Freya!"

The crowd cheered louder. Arabella glanced down at her babies, but they were still asleep. For once, she was glad they took after Finn more than her so far.

Her beast huffed. *I still think they will have our common sense. Otherwise, I may be tempted to toss them into the lake a few times.*

Hush, dragon. You'll do no such thing.

Finn wrapped an arm around her waist and she looked up at her mate. "I love you."

He whispered back, "I love you, too."

As he kissed her, the noise level in the hall rose even further. Arabella had believed her life couldn't get any better than her mating day with Finn. However, as she stood being kissed by her mate with her children in front of her and the entire clan giving their support, Arabella felt like the luckiest female in the world. Her past might've been dark, but her future was brighter than ever.

Dear Reader:

I hope you enjoyed Faye and Grant's story. All of the MacKenzies now have their happy endings, but there are still many more Lochguard stories to tell! I have a list in my office and I'll be writing this series for a while yet.

Also, if you haven't yet read my other dragons series, about the Stonefire Dragons, then what are you waiting for? You can check out the first book, *Sacrificed to the Dragon*, which is available in paperback.

Oh, and if you have a chance, would you leave a review? It would help me out a lot.

Thanks so much for reading! Turn the page for an excerpt from the first book in my science fiction romance series. Even my readers who don't usually like sci-fi are loving *The Conquest*.

With Gratitude,
Jessie Donovan

The Conquest
(Kelderan Runic Warriors #1)

Leader of a human colony planet, Taryn Demara has much more on her plate than maintaining peace or ensuring her people have enough to eat. Due to a virus that affects male embryos in the womb, there is a shortage of men. For decades, her people have enticed ships to their planet and tricked the men into staying. However, a ship hasn't been spotted in eight years. So when the blip finally shows on the radar, Taryn is determined to conquer the newcomers at any cost to ensure her people's survival.

Prince Kason tro de Vallen needs to find a suitable planet for his people to colonize. The Kelderans are running out of options despite the fact one is staring them in the face—Planet Jasvar. Because a group of Kelderan scientists disappeared there a decade ago never to return, his people dismiss the planet as cursed. But Kason doesn't believe in curses and takes on the mission to explore the planet to prove it. As his ship approaches Jasvar, a distress signal chimes in and Kason takes a group down to the planet's surface to explore. What he didn't expect was for a band of females to try and capture him.

As Taryn and Kason measure up and try to outsmart each other, they soon realize they've found their match. The only question is whether they ignore the spark between them and focus on their respective people's survival or can they find a path where they both succeed?

Excerpt from *The Conquest*:

Chapter One

Taryn Demara stared at the faint blip on the decades-old radar. Each pulse of light made her heart race faster. *This is it.* Her people might have a chance to survive.

Using every bit of restraint she had, Taryn prevented her voice from sounding too eager as she asked, "Are you sure it's a spaceship?"

Evaine Benoit, her head of technology, nodded. "Our equipment is outdated, but by the size and movement, it has to be a ship."

Taryn's heart beat double-time as she met her friend's nearly black-eyed gaze. "How long do we have before they reach us?"

"If they maintain their current trajectory, I predict eighteen hours, give or take. It's more than enough time to get the planet ready."

"Right," Taryn said as she stood tall again. "Keep me updated on any changes. If the ship changes course, boost the distress signal."

Evaine raised her brows. "Are you sure? The device is on its last legs. Any boost in power could cause a malfunction. I'm not sure my team or I can fix it again if that happens."

She gripped her friend's shoulder. "After eight years of waiting, I'm willing to risk it. I need that ship to reach Jasvar and send a team down to our planet."

Otherwise, we're doomed was left unsaid.

Without another word, Taryn raced out of the aging technology command center and went in search of her best strategist. There was much to do and little time to do it.

Nodding at some of the other members of her settlement as she raced down the corridors carved into the mountainside, Taryn wondered what alien race was inside the ship on the radar. Over the past few hundred years, the various humanoid additions to the once human-only colony had added extra skin tones, from purple to blue to even a shimmery gold. Some races even had slight telepathic abilities that had been passed down to their offspring.

To be honest, Taryn didn't care what they looked like or what powers they possessed. As long as they were genetically compatible with her people, it meant Taryn and several other women might finally have a chance at a family. The "Jasvar Doom Virus" as they called it, killed off most male embryos in the womb, to the point only one male was born to every five females. Careful genealogical charts had been maintained to keep the gene pool healthy. However, few women were willing to share their partner with others, which meant the male population grew smaller by the year.

It didn't help that Jasvar had been set up as a low-technology colony, which meant they didn't have the tools necessary to perform the procedures in the old tales of women being impregnated without sex. The technique had been called in-something or other. Taryn couldn't remember the exact name from her great-grandmother's stories from her childhood.

Not that it was an option anyway. Jasvar's technology was a hodgepodge of original technology from the starter colonists and a few gadgets from their conquests and alien additions over the years. It was a miracle any of it still functioned.

THE DRAGON WARRIOR

The only way to prevent the extinction of her people was to capture and introduce alien males into their society. Whoever had come up with the idea of luring aliens to the planet's surface and developing the tools necessary to get them to stay had been brilliant. Too bad his or her name had been lost to history.

Regardless of who had come up with the idea, Taryn was damned if she would be the leader to fail the Jasvarian colony. Since the old technology used to put out the distress signals was failing, Taryn had a different sort of plan for the latest alien visitors.

She also wanted their large spaceship and all of its technology.

Of course, her grand plans would be all for nothing if she couldn't entice and trap the latest aliens first. To do that, she needed to confer with Nova Drakven, her head strategist.

Rounding the last corner, Taryn waltzed into Nova's office. The woman's pale blue face met hers. Raising her silver brows, she asked, "Is it true about the ship?"

With a nod, Taryn moved to stand in front of Nova's desk. "Yes. It should be here in about eighteen hours."

Nova reached for a file on her desk. "Good. Then I'll present the plan to the players, and we can wait on standby until we know for sure where the visiting shuttle lands."

Taryn shook her head and started pacing. "I need you to come up with a new plan, Nova."

"Why? I've tweaked what went wrong last time. We shouldn't have any problems."

"It's not that." Taryn stopped pacing and met her friend's gaze. "This time, we need to do more than entice a few males to stay. Our planet was originally slated to be a low-tech colony, but with the problems that arose, that's no longer an option. We need supplies and knowledge, which means negotiating with the mother ship for their people."

"Let me get this straight—you want to convince the vastly technologically advanced aliens that we are superior, their crew's lives are in danger, and that they need to pay a ransom to get them back?"

Taryn grinned. "See, you do understand me."

Nova sighed. "You have always been crazy and a little reckless."

"Not reckless, Nova. Just forward-thinking. You stage the play, think of a few ideas about how to get the ship, and I'll find a way to make it work."

"Always the super leader to the rescue. Although one day, your luck may run out, Taryn."

Nova and Taryn were nearly the same age, both in their early thirties, and had grown up together. Nova was her best friend and one of the few people Taryn was unafraid to speak her fears with. "As long as my luck lasts through this ordeal, I'm okay with that. I can't just sit and watch our people despairing if another year or ten pass before there's new blood. If we had a way to get a message to Earth, it would make everything easier. But, we don't have that capability."

Nova raised her brows. "Finding a way to contact Earth or the Earth Colony Alliance might be an easier goal than taking over a ship."

"The message would take years to get there and who knows if the ECA would even send a rescue ship to such a distant colony." Taryn shook her head. "I can't rely on chance alone. I'll send a message from the alien ship, but I also want the technology to save us in the near future, too. I much prefer being in control."

Nova snorted. "Sometimes a little too much in control, in my opinion."

"A leader letting loose doesn't exactly instill confidence," she drawled.

"Then promise me that once you save the planet, you let me show you some fun. No one should die before riding the sloping Veran waterfalls."

Taryn sighed and sank into the chair in front of Nova's desk. "Fine. But how about we focus on capturing the aliens first?"

Nova removed a sheaf of crude paper made from the purple wood of the local trees and took out an ink pot and golden feather. "I'll come up with a fool-proof capture plan, but I hope you keep me in the loop about what happens next."

"I will when it's time. I need to see who we're dealing with before making concrete plans."

Dipping her feather into the ink pot, Nova scratched a few notes on the purple paper. "Then let me get to work. The staging is mostly done already, but I need to think beyond that. Since we've never tried to capture a large ship before, it's going to take some time. I think someone captured a shuttle in the past, but we'll see if I can find the record."

"You always go on about how you love challenges."

"Don't remind me." She made a shooing motion toward the door. "And this is one of the few times I can tell my settlement leader to get lost and let me work."

Taryn stood. "If you need me, I'll be in the outside garden."

"Fine, fine. Just go. You're making it hard to concentrate." Nova looked up with a smile. "And you're also delaying my next project."

"Do I want to know?"

"It's called Operation Fun Times." Nova pointed her quill. "I sense you're going to land an alien this time. You're a talented individual, except when it comes to flirting. I'm going to help with that."

Shaking her head, Taryn muttered, "Have fun," and left her old-time friend to her own devices. Maybe someday Nova would understand that while Taryn missed the antics of their youth, she enjoyed taking care of her people more.

Still, she'd admit that it would be nice to finally have the chance to get a man of her own. Most of her family was gone, and like many of the women of her age group, Taryn would love the option to start one.

Not now, Demara. You won't have a chance unless you succeed in capturing the visitors.

With the play planning in motion, Taryn had one more important task to set up before she could also pore through the records and look for ideas.

As much as she wished for everything to go smoothly, it could take a turn and end up horribly wrong. In that case, she needed an out. Namely, she needed to erase memories. The trick would be conferring with her head medicine woman to find the balance between erasing memories and rendering the aliens brain-dead. As the early Jasvarians had discovered, the forgetful plant was both a blessing and a curse. Without it, they'd never have survived this long. However, in the wrong dose, it could turn someone into a vegetable and ruin their chances.

Don't worry. Matilda knows what she's doing. Picking up her pace, Taryn exited the mountain into the late-day sun. The faint purple and blue hues of the mountains and trees were an everyday sight to her, but she still found the colors beautiful. Her great-grandmother's tales had been full of green leaves and blue skies back on Earth. A part of Taryn wanted to see another world, but the leader in her would never abandon the people of Jasvar.

Looking to the pinkish sky, she only hoped the visitors fell for her tricks. Otherwise, Taryn might have to admit defeat and prepare her people for the worst.

~ ~ ~

Prince Kason tro el Vallen of the royal line of Vallen stared at his ship's main viewing screen. The blue, pink, and purple hues of the planet hid secrets Kason was determined to discover. After years of fighting his father's wishes and then the ensuing days of travel from Keldera to the unnamed planet, he was anxious to get started.

Aaric, his head pilot, stated, "Ten hours until we pull into orbit, your highness."

Kason disliked the title but had learned over time that to fight it was pointless. "Launch a probe to investigate."

"Yes, your highness."

As Aaric sent the request to the necessary staff, the silver-haired form of Ryven Xanna, Kason's best friend and the head warrior trainer on the ship, walked up to him. "We need to talk."

Kason nodded. Ryven would only ask to talk if it was important. "I can spare a few minutes. Aaric, you have the command."

The pair of them entered Kason's small office off the central command area. The instant the door slid shut, Ryven spoke up again. "Some of the men's markings are tinged yellow. They're nervous. No doubt thanks to the rumors of a monster on the planet's surface."

"There is no monster. There's a logical explanation as to why our team of scientists disappeared on Jasvar ten years ago."

"I agree with you, but logic doesn't always work with the lower-ranked officers and the common soldiers."

Kason clasped his hand behind his back. "You wouldn't ask to talk with me unless you have a solution. Tell me what it is, Ryv."

"I know it's not standard protocol for you to lead the first landing party, but if you go, it will instill courage in the others," Ryven answered.

Kason raised a dark-blue eyebrow. "Tell me you aren't among the nervous."

Ryven shrugged and pointed to one of the markings that peeked above his collar. "The dark blue color tells you all you need to know."

Dark blue signaled that a Kelderan was at peace and free of negative emotions.

"You are better at controlling your emotions than anyone I have ever met. You could be deathly afraid and would somehow keep your markings dark blue."

The corner of Ryven's mouth ticked up. "The trick has worked well for me over the years."

"We don't have time for reminiscing, Ryv. You're one of the few who speaks the truth to me. Don't change now."

"Honestly?" Ryven shrugged. "I'm not any more nervous or worried than any other mission. The unknown enemy just means we need to be cautious more than ever."

"Agreed. I will take the first landing party and leave Thorin in charge. Assemble your best warriors and send me a message when they're ready. I want to talk with them and instill bravery beforehand."

In a rare sign of emotion, Ryven gripped Kason's bicep. "Bravery is all well and fine, but if there is a monster we can't defeat, promise you'll pull back. Earning your father's praise isn't worth your life."

"I'm a little insulted at your implication. I wouldn't be a general in my own right if I lived by foolish displays of machismo."

Ryven studied him a second before adding, "Just because you're a general now doesn't mean you have to talk like one with me."

Kason remembered their childhood days, before they'd both been put on the path of a warrior. Kason and Ryven had pulled pranks on their siblings and had reveled in coming up with stupid competitions, such as who could reach the top of a rock face first in freezing temperatures or who could capture a poisonous shimmer fly with nothing but their fingers.

But neither of them were boys anymore. Displaying emotion changed the color of the rune-like markings on their bodies, which exposed weakness. Warriors couldn't afford to show any weakness. It was one of the reasons higher-ranked officers weren't allowed to take wives, not even if they found one of their potential destined brides; the females would become easy targets.

Not that Kason cared. A wife would do nothing to prove his worth as a soldier to his father, the king. On top of that, being a warrior was all Kason knew. Giving it up would take away his purpose.

Pushing aside thoughts of his father and his future, Kason motioned toward the door. "Go and select the best soldiers to assist with the landing party. I have my own preparations to see to."

"I'll go if you promise one thing."

"What?"

"You allow me to be part of the landing party."

Kason shook his head. "I can't. In the event of my death, I need you here."

"Thorin is your second and will assume command. Give me the honor of protecting you and the others during the mission."

Deep down, in the place where Kason locked up any emotion, a small flicker of indecision flashed. Ryven was more Kason's brother than his real-life brother, Keltor.

Yet to contain Ryven on the ship would be like a slap in the face; the honor of protecting a prince such as Kason was the highest form of trust to one of the Kelderan people.

Locking down his emotions, Kason followed his logical brain. "You may attend. But on-planet, you become a soldier. I can't treat you as my friend."

Ryven put out a hand and Kason shook it to seal their agreement. "I'm aware of protocol. I teach it day in and day out. But I will be the best damned soldier of the group. And if it comes to it, I will push you out of the way to protect your life."

Kason released his friend's hand. "I won't let it come to that."

"Good. When shall we rendezvous?"

Glancing at the small screen projecting an image of the multicolored planet, he answered, "Nine hours. That will give all of us a chance to sleep before performing the prebattle ritual. You can lead the men through their meditation and warm-up maneuvers after that."

Ryven nodded. "I'll see you then."

The trainer exited the room, and Kason turned toward his private viewing screen to study the planet rumored to host the most feared monster in the region. One that had supposedly taken hundreds of men's lives over the years. The story was always the same—a small contingent of men disappeared from any group that landed on the surface. No one remembered how they were captured or if they were even alive. Anytime a second party landed, a few more would be taken.

Over time, the planet had earned a reputation. Even the most adventure-seeking ruffians had stayed away.

However, Kason dismissed it as folklore. Whatever was on that planet, he wouldn't allow it to defeat him or his men. Kason would bring honor to his family with a victory. He also hoped to give his people the gift of a new planet. Keldera was overpopulated, and its resources were stretched beyond the limit. The Kelderans desperately needed a new colony and hadn't been able to locate one that was suitable. The planet on the view screen showed all the signs of being a near-perfect fit.

Even if the fiercest monster in existence resided on that planet, Kason wouldn't retreat from an enemy. Death was an accepted part of being a Kelderan soldier.

Want to read the rest?
The Conquest is available in paperback.

For exclusive content and updates, sign up for my newsletter at:

http://www.jessiedonovan.com

AUTHOR'S NOTE

Thanks for reading Faye and Grant's story. Some of you might've been surprised at Finn and Arabella's side story, but rather than make poor Arabella past her due date, I let her have her babies on time! I hope to have a follow-up novella for Finn and Arabella later and you'll see a bit more of how their life is going. As for Faye and Grant, their baby will come eventually. I didn't end the book with them having their baby because keeping track of the various pregnancies and guessing where the story will be at that time is difficult. Besides, it should be more fun to watch Faye and Grant as she becomes the "chubby dragon" she mentioned in the story, lol. Also, the storyline regarding the dragon-shifter traitors will be picked up in *Aiding the Dragon* (Stonefire Dragons #9).

Oh, and for those wondering, yes, Cat and Lachlan will have a story of their own. :) Alistair Boyd, too, as he's one of the most requested for Lochguard, but his will be a little while yet. The next full-length Lochguard book will be about Chase McFarland (Grant's younger brother) and Dr. Layla MacFie.

As ever, I thank not only my readers but also the people who help make this book a reality:

- Clarissa Yeo of Yocla Designs does all of my covers and is simply amazing.
- Becky Johnson of Hot Tree Editing is fantastic and she really pushed me with Faye and Grant. Their story would've been lacking without her.

- My beta readers, Donna H., Iliana G., and Alyson S. are also vital when it comes to the final product. Not only do they catch any lingering typos, they also point out the minor inconsistencies only a dedicated fan would notice.

Thanks again for reading. All of the MacKenzies now have their happy endings, but there are still many more stories to tell on Lochguard. Until next time, happy reading!

About the Author

Jessie Donovan wrote her first story at age five, and after discovering *The Dragonriders of Pern* series by Anne McCaffrey in junior high, she realized people actually wanted to read stories like those floating around inside her head. From there on out, she was determined to tap into her over-active imagination and write a book someday.

After living abroad for five years and earning degrees in Japanese, Anthropology, and Secondary Education, she buckled down and finally wrote her first full-length book. While that story will never see the light of day, it laid the world-building groundwork of what would become her debut paranormal romance, *Blaze of Secrets*. In late 2014, she officially became a *New York Times* and *USA Today* bestselling author.

Jessie loves to interact with readers, and when not traipsing around some foreign country on a shoestring, can often be found on Facebook. Check out her pages below:

http://www.facebook.com/JessieDonovanAuthor

And don't forget to sign-up for her newsletter to receive sneak peeks and inside information. You can sign-up on her website:

http:///www.jessiedonovan.com

49686569R00191

Made in the USA
San Bernardino, CA
03 June 2017